JET

CONNIE LAFORTUNE

Jet

Sinful Seven series (Book #2)

Connie Lafortune

This book is a work of fiction. Names, characters, and incidents are either products of the author's imagination or are used fictitiously. Any resemblance to actual events or persons, living or dead, is entirely coincidental.

Jet

www.connielafortune.com

Cover Design by https://payhip.com/tinaglasneck

Edited by Peter Gaskin https://reedsy.com/peter-gaskin

Formatting by M. L. Tompsett www.mltompsett.com

To each and every one of you, who realize that abuse, hunger and homelessness is not an option, and does something to make it better.

ACKNOWLEDGMENTS

To my husband, Alan for encouraging me to be the best I can be. Without your support, I'm not sure if I could do what I love every day.

A big shout out to my girls, Sage, Dawn and Tempi who give me the motivation and the encouragement I need to keep on, keeping on. All of you keep me grounded, sane and passionate about doing what I love and because of that I'm forever grateful. Love you bunches.

To my editor, Peter Gaskin for polishing my words to make them shine. You're the star! I'm so thankful we've been together since the beginning and I'm hoping you'll be with me until the end.

To all of my wonderful readers who consistently keep coming back for more, wanting to get lost in my words. And, for all of you newbie readers who will take a chance on me with this book, or the next. Welcome! You all mean the world to me.

To my parents—Jeanne and Roland—who are no longer

of this Earth but are forever in my heart. I love you both to the moon and back, a trillion times ten.

To my Lord and Savior for giving me the gift of words so I can in turn share them with others.

ALSO BY CONNIE LAFORTUNE

Lucas

Private Messages

Bound by Steel

The Claiming of Callan

Because of You

Would you like to know when the next book is available?

Then sign up for my newsletter: **http://www.connielafortune.
com/become-a-fan/**

so you'll never miss another release, cover reveal, or awesome sale
on my books!

INTRODUCTION

Fourteen years ago...

Jet

IT WAS A COLD and dreary night in March when I left my dysfunctional family for the very last time.

My overstuffed backpack weighed me down and left a red welt on my scrawny shoulder. But the pain was so worth it, since I had my old beat-up guitar clutched tightly to my chest. I might have been only thirteen, but I was adamant about anyone taking my music away from me.

Ever again!

During the day, I busked on the streets of New York for petty cash. At night, I'd hide in the alleyways just waiting for the restaurants to throw out their nightly trash. Desperate to fill the ache in my empty belly. Years later, when I met Lucas *Pipes* Knight and *The Sinful Seven* was conceived, I knew walking away a lifetime ago was the best decision I'd ever made. No matter how difficult my life had become, I didn't let anyone take away the only thing I ever loved. Music!

Everyone has the potential to be the best they can be. But daydreams are empty promises that fall by the wayside when words are distorted and truths turn into lies. I learned this at a very early age, which toughened my skin but made me independent and gave me the strength to make it on my own. It wasn't easy, and I wanted to give up.

Then I remembered a quote by Vince Lombardi. *"Winners never quit, and quitters never win."* It forced me to move on even when I wanted to quit.

ENVY

*"**Envy** comes from people's ignorance of, or lack of belief in, their own gifts."*

Jean Vanier

1

_____

JET

WALKING INTO MY APARTMENT after several months on the *Distraction* tour feels irrelevant. Something that should be comforting feels strange. It's as if my favorite pair of jeans are too tight and suffocating. I'm sure that might sound crazy to some, but it's the only way I can describe it. Like I don't belong here anymore.

After tossing my bags on the floor, I walk through every room and throw open the windows. The clean, crisp air assaults my senses, letting me breathe easier. Now it doesn't feel as stifling as it did when I first arrived.

With my hands tucked inside my jeans pockets, I pace around the apartment and take it all in. The colorless walls probably look bare to most—sure, they're drab and in desperate need of a pop of color. For me, they reflect the person I am deep down inside.

Detached, uncaring, and dead.

It's pathetic that this is the only place in this vast

universe that I get to be myself. Not the celebrated rockstar everyone thinks they know, or the bassist for *The Sinful Seven,* or Lucas's best friend for that matter. Just Me, and it scares me shitless because I'm not sure about the man who lives inside of this head anymore.

Too many times to count, I get lost inside of myself and go to an evil place. It's lonely and somewhere I only visit on occasion, but it burrows beneath my skin, festers there, no matter how many years go by. Doesn't matter how long, this hell I make for myself is always waiting to tear me apart. Forcing me to question everything I am or ever thought I could be.

I know it's late, I'm exhausted, and after spending countless nights sleeping on the bus or sharing a stuffy hotel room with Trevor, tonight I do it my way. The only way I truly know how to feel comfortable and safe. Yeah, I might be a grown-ass man, but until you've walked in my shoes, don't judge.

Tossing my sleeping bag and pillows on the floor, I hunker down, clothes and all. This, right here, is where I'll spend the next few days. Once I get my bearings and catch my breath, I'll unpack, shower, rinse and repeat. For me, nothing is in black and white. There's a gray area that lives deep inside of my bones that pulls me under and takes me to a faraway place that only exists in my mind. It's something I've had to learn to live with for a lifetime and I don't foresee it going away soon. I've learned to accept it.

I have no other choice.

Staring up at the ceiling, I try to tick off all of the good things that have transpired over the last few months. Beginning with the audition that started it all, and ending when I walked into this empty tomb. Closing my eyes, I focus on the texture of the hardwood floor beneath me, instead of a soft mattress that a million others before me have slept on. Then, I concentrate on the silence around me, calming me in ways that I haven't experienced in months. Once my breathing slows, I count until I reach one hundred. Only to start over. Again and again.

I allow my thoughts to wander to Lucas and Abby. Lucas is my best friend and the front-man for *The Sinful Seven* and Abby's our business manager. When they first met, he was a sex addict and she was his favorite barista at Java Joe's. To make a long story short, Lucas is only addicted to Abby now.

I truly envy them. They both knew what they wanted, and they went after it. In fact, right about now, they're thousands of miles away on some tropical island soaking up the sun. And each other. I'm happy for them both, it's well deserved after everything they've been through. But I'd be lying if I said it doesn't hurt just knowing that I'll never have that unconditional love with a woman. It wouldn't be fair to give myself to someone when I'm broken. Damaged goods. Well, some might beg to differ, like Lucas, but he's the only one who knows the deepest, darkest parts of my soul. Nothing he could say or do would ever change my mind for that matter.

End of.

Time to move on.

After being on the road surrounded by a ton of people, I'm going to bask in solitude, kick back, and just breathe. Don't get me wrong, the tour's everything I ever dreamed it would be and then some, but I'm so used to being alone that it was all so overwhelming. And now I have Quinn who's like a pit bull with a bone about getting me to do her damn interviews. She's our PR agent and a pain in my ass. I don't know how many times I've refused her requests for an interview but will continue doing so. My fans don't give a damn about my childhood and where I come from, as long as I show up and give them the best performance I can.

And believe me, I do.

Every damn night!

For the next few weeks I plan on relaxing, writing music, and enjoying some *me* time. Lord knows, when it's over it'll be back on the road and balls to the wall once again. Which means more tour buses, airplanes, and hotels. I suppose it's a small price to pay since it's something I desperately wanted my entire life. Still, for someone like me it's a hard pill to swallow. A catch twenty-two because of the demons that take up residence inside of me.

I'm not complaining, but it's been difficult sharing a room with Trevor since my sleeping ritual is off the charts. I'm looking forward to my old habits and routines to give me a sense of peace. Being that I've been on my own since I was thirteen, it's difficult sharing a space with others. It's a good thing that I love Lucas, Willow, and Trevor like family. Otherwise, it would be difficult at best.

* * *

QUINN

BEING ON TOUR THESE last few months has been both exhilarating and exhausting. It might have to do with a certain someone who refuses to acknowledge my existence. Well, that might be harsh—Jet knows I exist, but he refuses to speak to me one-on-one. As the band's PR agent, it's my job to put out the tiny brush fires before they become a full-on blaze. Destroying everything in their path.

Which is the number one reason I want to interview all of them myself. God knows—I've seen how damaging an interview from the media can be, and I despise how they can twist everything around to make someone out to be something they're not. It's the perfect way to end their career before it's even begun. It's so frustrating since Lucas, Willow, and Trevor all agreed to do an interview with me, but Jet flat out refused. I've said and done everything I can think of to convince him otherwise. I did my damnedest trying to convince him that I have his best interest at heart. And the stubborn ass still refuses to give me the time of day. Well, I sure as hell can't force him to do something he doesn't want to do, but I refuse to post only three interviews when there are four band members. That would clearly be out of place.

Truth be told, I know enough about each and every one of them. I could write up an interview, answers and all, but I'd like to get it straight from them. Perhaps I'll call them all in, one-on-one, and do it that way. No pressure, maybe over brunch, asking questions with a few crepes and mimosas to butter them up. Surely, that's the best way, if I know them at all. I should—I find you get to know a lot about someone when you spend every waking moment with them in a crowded tour bus, airplane, or a jam-packed SUV.

So, to say I'm looking forward to some alone time would be an understatement. Don't get me wrong, I love Lucas, Trevor, and Willow like family, but knowing there won't be any testosterone around for miles is liberating. Thank goodness for Willow and Abby who can calm the boys down quicker than a toddler with a lollipop! I just pray that two weeks will be enough time for everyone to gather their thoughts and jump back into the routine.

All the bands I've worked with in the past never took a break in between. They liked to keep the momentum going, and some have been known to last as long as one year! Morris Music, the company I work for, thought it best to give *The Sinful Seven* a short break. Especially since they understand that touring is grueling and a new experience for all of them. It can be overwhelming and very hard on their egos. I'm glad we chose this route. Three months on the road, two weeks off, and back on for three more months. Then they can collaborate as a band, put their heads together, and get ready for their next album. We'll need to toss in a few music videos, too. Their fans loved the YouTube material, so we need to give them more of what they want. That will keep them on the top of the charts until their next album is released and another tour planned.

Since I'm not in town very often, I plan on visiting my parents as much as I can. It's tough on them since I'm their only daughter. Growing up, our house was filled with tons of testosterone. I have five brothers—four older and one younger. I could tell you stories about all the fights, and don't even get me started about them being protective of their little sister. Drew, the baby of our family, just graduated from NYU and decided to travel across the country, staying with each of us a few months before moving permanently to the West Coast. Once he's there, the lot of us will truly be alone since we are scattered all over. Coming together only once in a blue moon to gather for the holidays. So, I can't wait to spend some quality time with them and catch up on all the latest family gossip.

And I can't forget about my girls, Nina, Traci, and Alisa.

I definitely need to make some time to hang out with all of them, too. We always have so much damn fun when we're all together and we've been known to get into a tiny bit of trouble. No worries. All Nina has to do is bat her long dark lashes at some random guy or police officer—yep it's been known to happen—and everything's forgiven. That girl should have been an actress instead of a divorce lawyer. Hmm, come to think of it, those two professions do have a lot in common. Acting comes in very handy when you're in the courtroom fighting for your client. I'll have to mention that to her next time we get together. I bet she'd get a kick out of my analogy. But today is all mine to do whatever I please. Tomorrow's another day, or so they say.

Today I'm going to be soaking up the sun on my back deck while reading a good book. I might even pour myself a glass of wine or two and treat myself to Thai takeout. Why the hell not? After the hell Jet put me through over the last few months, I deserve to cut loose and enjoy all of the little things I've been missing out on. Like peace of mind.

I'm just a simple girl with simple needs, and it's the little things in life that make me happy.

2

JET

IT'S DAY TWO AND I just crawled out of the shower for the first time. Yeah, not one of my proudest moments, but necessary. It took me that long to decompress, and now I'm just waiting on some much-needed sustenance currently being delivered by my favorite greasy joint, the *Hungry Dog Diner*, three blocks from here. I wasn't ready to face the public just yet, so I'd rather give the dude a tip and pay a delivery fee than go get it myself. Maybe in a few days I'll feel the need to wander outside, but there's no rush since in this day and age it's easy to be a recluse with all this online delivery.

When I hear a knock on my door, I slide my shirt over my damp skin. I swear the delivery guy can hear my belly rumble from the other side of the door. Unfortunately, when I pull the door open, there's a woman standing there. Dressed to the nines in her skinny jeans, tank, and heels. Like, what the fuck.

"Well, thank heavens you're not dead. I've called, texted, and almost dialed 911." As you probably already guessed, the person glaring at me right now is not from the diner where I'm desperately waiting for my food. Quinn, the pain in my ass, is standing there with her hands on her hips. No, I do not want to invite her inside, but she takes it upon herself to slide between me and the door jamb!

"Last time I checked I was on hiatus, so I turned off my phone. Oh, and just because you're our PR agent doesn't give you permission to come and go as you please. What the hell are you doing here anyway? Tell me what was so damn important that it couldn't wait for two more weeks?"

She bristles like I slapped her, and damn if it doesn't piss me the fuck off, but if I don't set any boundaries from the get-go she'll try walking all over me. Not a happening thing. Ever.

"If it makes you feel any better, you're the last person I wanted to see. You're not the only one who was looking forward to some downtime. FYI, everyone's on vacation but me. I'm still working to make sure everything is in place and running like clockwork for the next few months." She tosses some papers on the table just when there's another knock on the door. "When you have a minute, I just need your signature and then I won't bother you again."

Ignoring her, I jerk open the door and startle the girl standing there. Great—when her jaw hits the floor at the sight of me, I'm positive she knows who I am. With her hands shaking, she hands me my bag and gets ready to bolt. "Hey pretty girl, don't run off before I pay you." Yeah, I hear a snicker from behind me and maybe it was a dick move, but I kinda did that for Quinn's benefit.

"You're Jet from *The Sinful Seven* and I can't even right now."

I saunter over, my hair still wet from the shower, bend down, and whisper in her ear, "I'd appreciate it if you didn't tell your friends where I live. Ya know, if it got out my apartment might be bombarded with people and that wouldn't be a good thing."

"I swear I won't tell anyone. They wouldn't believe me anyway." I tuck a strand of hair behind her ear and she shudders. I'm going to hell, but then again, after my sordid past it was a given anyway.

"I'll tell ya what. For being such a great fan, I'll hook you up with concert tickets the next time we're in town." Using my thumb, I point over my shoulder at Quinn. "She'll make sure you get four tickets for you and your friends next time around." She practically comes in her yoga pants when I slip her a fifty and tell her to keep the change. Hey, what can I say? I got moves. I just choose not to use them too often.

"I might be your agent, Jet, but I'm not your gopher. You can bring her your own damn tickets. Now please sign these papers so I can get the hell out of here." Touchy.

"I won't sign a damn thing until I read it, and right now I'm eating while my dinner is still hot. So leave them and I'll look it over when it's convenient for me." She huffs as I grab a plate and sit at the island, pushing the papers away so I don't get grease all over them. No way is she going to trick me into doing a damn interview if that's what she's thinking.

"Believe me, if I could have had someone else sign them I would, but Lucas and Abby are in Aruba, Willow is out of town, and Trevor is too. Apparently, everyone's gone except the two of us so I had no other choice. One signature is all I need to represent the band, and that would be you."

What part doesn't she understand? I'm eating first, and if it's band related you can bet your ass I'll be reading it first. I might need to run it by Mr. Miller, too.

A loud rumble interrupts our conversation and I'd laugh, but this time it wasn't me. Looking over my shoulder as I shovel food in my mouth, I capture Quinn's stare. Dammit. Why does this girl torment me so? I push over the other burger and pat the seat next to me. I'm a prick, but after the childhood I've had I would feed an army if I could.

"Take a seat, Quinn. I can't guarantee that I'll sign the papers today, but we've shared plenty of meals together. What's one more?" I continue devouring my food, not paying her any mind, when the chair scrapes against the floor next to me. I watch out of the corner of my eye as she sits down, unwraps the burger, and sinks her pearly whites into the greasy goodness. When a sexy moan escapes, my cock wants to salute the sound.

What the fuck!

"Thanks, I really needed this. All I had was a yogurt and coffee this morning… or was that yesterday? I don't remember, but I owe you big time."

I don't trust myself to speak right now since she has a tiny bit of ketchup on her bottom lip and damn if I don't want to lick it clean.

Quinn is gorgeous, smart, and selfless. Everything I need to stay far away from.

* * *

QUINN

THOSE BABY BLUES HOLD so much sadness, and for the life of me I wish I knew why that was. I'd only be fooling myself to think he'd ever open up to me when his bandmates don't even know the real reason. I'm sure Lucas does, but he's fierce and loyal and I don't blame him for not divulging anything. Truth be told, he's the reason I'm here. Trying to make nice so the rest of the tour won't be so confrontational. Lucas thinks if Jet and I can spend some time together, we might be able to come to some kind of truce. Now I'm not so sure.

"Are you going to finish that burger or just stare at me?" he asks. Crap, I didn't realize his gaze was locked on mine.

"Hell yeah, I'm going to finish. Why? Are you sorry you asked me to sit and break bread with you again?" It's a figure of speech, but he tenses up and I don't know why. No matter what I say or do, he seems to be offended. Coming here was a mistake and I should have just gone with my gut and stayed far away. I'm hoping he doesn't call Willow or Trevor because they're both kicking back at home chilling out. They didn't go anywhere. And I wonder what Jet would do if he knew Lucas was behind this little charade?

Raising my brows, I take a big bite and chew. Challenging him to even try to take it away from me because I will bite. When he chuckles, my skin prickles with goosebumps. He does that so infrequently that it's music to my ears. We finish eating in silence, but not before he slides some fries in my direction and I chow down on them before he changes his mind.

After we've devoured every bite, I get up to clean off the table when he grabs my arm. "I'll take care of that later. Tell me what these papers are all about and why it couldn't wait until everyone was together again."

"It's the itinerary for the rest of the tour, and I need someone to sign off on it." I don't think he's buying it, but he grabs them anyway and starts reading. "If you need me to explain something…"

"I might not have a fancy college education, Quinn, but I can read."

"Why do you take everything I say and do out of context? Contrary to what you might think, I'm trying to do what's right for you and the band. After all, isn't that what I get paid to do? God forbid I try to be your friend, too. You know what, sign the damn papers whenever you're ready and I'll pick them up or mail the damn things for all I care. Thanks for the eats. I'm out of here."

With one twist of the knob, I'm ready to bolt when his heat surrounds me from all angles. And his scent just about brings me to my knees. I need to snap out of this lustful stupor I'm in because he's made it abundantly clear he wants nothing to do with me. His hand appears out of nowhere, slamming the door closed with a finality that has my heart pounding inside of my chest.

Leaning down, he whispers against the shell of my ear, "You're on my turf, Quinn. Which means I don't take orders from you, just the opposite. You'll do what I tell you to do. Now, sit down! I'll read over the papers. If they meet my criteria and I don't need to call our lawyer, I'll sign them so you can get out of my house and hair for the next twelve days. Got it? Good."

It takes everything I have not to turn around and slap his pompous face, but I'm supposed to be here to make peace, not start a war. So, I do what he asks and go sit on the sofa.

As far away from him as humanly possible in this small space. While he's reading over the documents, I scan the room and suddenly realize how impersonal it feels. The walls are a stark white, giving a clinical vibe that isn't the least bit homey and inviting. In my mind, I'm figuring out how to decorate this space when his agitated voice pulls me out of my daydream.

"Are you fucking serious right now? No, I'm not signing this, and if any other member of the band give permission to this, I'll walk away. This is blackmail and I won't be privy to it. I've already told you I won't do an interview and that will never change." Oh, if looks could kill I'd be dead.

"That's part of your contract, and there's going to be plenty of things that are uncomfortable for all of us moving forward. But if you want a career in music, you better get used to it. Your life is an open book and the sooner you come clean, the easier it will be. If you continue dragging your feet like an insolent child, the public will think you have something to hide. That's when it could get ugly, but if you let me do the interview, I'll have your back." My heart breaks when his hands slide down his face, scrubbing away the pain.

"Music is my life, but if I need to walk away because my past is buried and gone, I will. I swear, Quinn. I won't do an interview with you or anyone else. If that means they go digging, let them. They won't find a damn thing. I'm sure you know that since you've done your own investigating." He's right. Every damn word. A twenty-six-year-old Jet Turner doesn't exist. So, who is the real Jet Turner?

"I can't force you to do something you're not comfortable with. If you change your mind, call me and I'll pick them up. Otherwise you can answer to the other three members of your band when they realize you're the one holding up the process. I hope I'll see you when the tour kicks off again, Jet. It would be a shame to get this far and something like this stands in your way. Thanks for the lunch. Catch you later."

I can't stop the tears sliding down my face when I close the door behind me and his screams pierce my eardrums. Angry, hurtful cussing assaults my senses as objects crash against the door, the walls, and anything it comes in contact with. Shaking the frame behind me. God, Jet, what did they do to you?

My hands are shaking by the time my thumb hits the button on my phone. When he answers, he inhales. "Fuck, I guess it didn't go so well, huh?"

"This was such a bad idea, Lucas. He's so upset and I hate leaving him. This is all my damn fault and now he's thinking of quitting the band all because of this damn interview. Call him, please. Promise you will." I'm sniffling so bad that I don't think he can understand a word I'm saying.

"Jet's losing his shit because he hates being cornered. I'm sure he feels like everyone's ganging up on him since he's the only one who's not onboard about the interview. Go home, Quinn. I'll call him to smooth everything over."

3

JET

Pissed doesn't even compare to how I was feeling after my late-night conversation with my BFF. Never did I ever think that Lucas would go behind my back the way he did. The only good that came out of it is I don't need to do the interview, and he now realizes that it's best to keep Quinn as far away from me as possible. If not, I already told him I'd quit the band and they could find another bassist to finish up the tour. I don't give a fuck about breaking a contract when it comes to my privacy. I thought I made it crystal clear all those years ago when I told him straight-up. Well, now he knows after I reminded him about our blood oath, which in my opinion is more binding than a damn piece of paper and a ballpoint pen.

I couldn't sleep a wink after our conversation last night. I'm hurt, exhausted, and in need of a good workout. Reason being I'm heading down to my favorite sweat shop.

Walking into the *Hungry Dog Diner* is the closest to

coming home that a drifter like me can expect. Even with the shiny new faces that greet me as I enter, the aroma settles my nerves. When I get into the kitchen, a head pops up the second I swing open the door and the genuine smile I see tells me all I need to know.

I'm home.

"Look what the hell the cat dragged in." Mack quickly wipes his hands on a dishtowel and rushes over to give me a hug. When he pulls me in and his beefy arms wrap around my tall frame, I choke back the fucking tears that threaten to break me. "I missed you, boy. How long have you been back?"

"Just a few days, but I can see I came just in time. Looks like you need a dishwasher today, huh?" He laughs, his big belly shaking against mine.

"Those damn kids have no work ethic, I swear. Calling in sick and it's not even summertime yet. I'm sure a big rockstar like yourself has better things to do than help out an old man like me."

Pulling away before I cry like a damn pussy, I stare at the kindest man I've ever known. "There's no place else I'd rather be, Mack. Seriously. If you can promise to keep the teeny boppers out of my way, I'm rolling up my sleeves to give you a hand. There's nothing like a hard day of manual labor to get my fix."

"I can't promise they won't recognize a hot shot like you, but I'll keep them as far away as possible. Hey, I almost didn't recognize you with your hair hidden inside that beanie. Oh, and those track pants and long sleeve shirt will surely scare them away." With a wink, he throws an apron at me that has his logo etched across the front. The words *Hungry Dog Diner* stand out in big bold letters.

I don't have time to waste by reminiscing, so I roll up the end of my sleeves and dig right in. There's a shit ton of dishes to catch up on, and it doesn't take me long to find a rhythm just like back in the old days.

The diner is slamming when I swap out my first clean load of dishes for the dirty ones. Of course I get a few curious stares from the rest of the kitchen staff. They think I'm a new guy but I just continue doing what I'm doing and mind my own business.

Mack peeks his head in every now and again to make sure the kitchen's running smoothly and to grab a few orders that are ready to be delivered. He's always helping out which is the reason his business is always booming. He's truly one of the good guys.

After several hours, I'm ready for a break, but I'd never take one without someone to replace me. That's how I roll, and as pissed as I was with Lucas last night I'd never leave the band high and dry. If it came down to me quitting, I'd make sure they had a replacement before walking away. I'd be lying if I didn't say I was glad he let me skip my interview. He promised he'd create a fluff piece that would keep everyone happy. As long as I can read it before it goes public, it's all good.

I can't help smiling when I see people pointing fingers, and hear whispering behind my back like I'm oblivious to the whole thing. Yeah, it makes me uncomfortable as hell since I thrive on anonymity, but it's kind of hard to do now that *The Sinful Seven's* name is on everyone's lips. I know this is what I've been wanting for so long and maybe one day I won't need to look over my shoulder. For now, it makes me uncomfortable. Do they know I'm just a runaway? Or are they whispering because I'm the best bassist around?

If I've learned anything over the years, it's to stop being so damn paranoid. Not every face in the crowd is going to be *his*. Besides, what are the odds I'd randomly come face-to-face with my ruin in an old diner?

Mack enters and takes one look at my grimy apron. "Boy, you need a break." He turns to Harold, one of Mack's oldest and most loyal cooks, and says, "Harold, we need two burgers with the works and spicy fries to go. Jet and I have both worked up a hell of an appetite and since he's volunteering his time, least I can do is feed him." Harold's been here forever so he knows exactly who I am. The rest of the kitchen staff has no clue.

"Coming right up, Boss." He pauses his orders and gets going on ours. I feel a bit guilty but I'll get over it.

"Let's go out back so we can talk. Harold will bring it to us when he's finished, right?" Harold nods in answer and Mack grabs us a few beers out of the fridge before getting ready to head out. It feels like old times and I sure do miss it.

"Hey, I'll meet you out back," I say to Mack. "I just want to switch out these dishes and set myself up for when my break's over. Food should be ready by then. I'll bring it out so Harold won't miss a beat with the orders. It's slamming in here today!"

"You always did put others before your own needs, didn't ya, boy?"

The name "boy" doesn't make me flinch like it did when I was younger. I've learned that it's his term of endearment since he has a hard time voicing how he feels. Well, join the club, Mack. Join the club.

Grabbing a load of piping hot dishes straight out of the dishwasher, I stride into the dining room with my head held low. Imagine my surprise when I come face-to-face with Quinn.

What the ever-loving fuck is she doing here?

* * *

QUINN

THANKFULLY, LUCAS WAS able to wave the olive branch and Jet accepted it. Reluctantly, I might add, and I don't blame him since he thinks we blindsided him. Which we kind of did and I feel horrible for going ahead with Lucas's stupid plan. Being their PR agent, I should have realized it was unethical in so many ways. If Jet wanted to seek revenge, he could easily file a complaint with Morris Music and I could lose my job. I'm hoping it won't come down to that so from now on I really need to abide by his rules and stay far away. No more playing the avenging angel swooping in to save him. Hell, you can't save someone who doesn't want to be saved.

Being alone with him last night would have been perfect if those damn papers didn't come between us. Stupid, I'm so stupid. I should have torn them up and told him the truth. That I was there just to get to know him better when no one else was around. I feel like everyone has opened up to me except him and I just want him to know if the time comes, I'm a good listener.

Dammit, I blew that big time.

What better way to wallow in self-pity than to stuff my face with food. I'm in the mood for another greasy burger he shared with me last night and, lucky for me, I have a photographic memory. So off I go to the *Hungry Dog Diner* to get me some.

The place is jam-packed and there's not a parking spot to be had. I circle the block a few more times before deciding to walk the few blocks. I could use the exercise since I'm sure all of the food I'll be ordering will put me over my calorie limit for the day. Maybe even the week!

Goodness gracious, the scents that waft through the air as I walk inside are addicting. Onions, greasy fries, and the scent of spices is orgasmic. My mouth waters just thinking about my first bite. I read the menu board while standing in line, and everything sounds so delicious. Maybe I should have ordered ahead to save some time, since they're slamming, but I can always take it to go. No biggie.

The line's moving fast so I decide on the double bacon burger and the spicy fries just as I slide up to the counter. I'm just about to place my order when the kitchen doors swing open and blue eyes hold mine.

What the hell's Jet doing here?

We both freeze like deer caught in the headlights. I'm the first to speak when the clerk asks me again for my order.

"Um, sorry. Can I have the number three with the spicy fries and a medium diet cola? Thanks." I hear the bastard snicker when I asked for my diet soda. Yeah, I'm one of those stupid girls who thinks the diet soda balances out all the calories from the nasty food I'm going to devour in a hot second.

I should move over like all the other customers do while waiting for their order, but I'm glued to the spot watching Jet unload dishes before grabbing the dirty ones. If I didn't see it with my own two eyes, I never would have believed it for a second. I mumble something to the clerk about waiting outside since it's too hot in here when he snickers again.

Man, does he think it's because he's all hot, sweaty, and delicious? Holy hell, I didn't just go there, did I? Yes, I did, and I'll be the first to admit that he's sexy as all hell. Big time. But he's off limits and he's made it abundantly clear that he hates my guts and wants nothing to do with me. So, I don't need to be told twice. I storm out the door. The cool breeze feels good against my heated skin, so I wait outside for my food to be ready.

I'm stunned when someone grabs my arm, hauling me into the alley before I have a chance to run. I pity the person since I'm kicking and screaming and trying to claw at his face.

"Quinn, what the fuck!" My heart's beating out of my chest when I realize it's Jet and not some psycho.

"Are you fucking crazy? I could have killed you for fuck's sakes!" His smug look tells me all I need to know. In a nanosecond my gun is pressed against his forehead, and by the stunned look on his face I think it's safe to say he's shocked. I'm a woman who lives alone in New York, of course I have my permit. I'm stupid but I'm not suicidal. He just caught me off guard is all.

"Seriously? You're stalking me but I'm the one with a gun to my head?" Is this guy for real? I have no idea what his deal is. I need to stop this once and for all.

"You forget that I'm not one of your groupies following you around like a puppy in heat. I'm your agent and the best one around. So refrain from talking to me like that or we will have some serious issues. I've been nothing but nice to you, and for some reason you always bite my head off. It stops here and now, you got it? Otherwise, I might need to call

Caleb and let him know I can't work with the band and that would be detrimental to everyone involved. Including you. Now if you'll excuse me, thanks to you, I'm addicted to the damn burgers I had last night. Thank you very much."

I don't bother waiting around for an apology. I march my ass into the diner, grab my food, and get the hell out before Mr. Vicious knows what hit him. I'm so done playing nice. If he thinks I'm such a bitch, he hasn't seen anything yet.

It takes me a few minutes to walk back to my car because there's no stopping a pissed-off Quinn. Ask my five brothers, they know firsthand.

I'm so angry that I don't remember driving home, and that's stupid on my part. But the food more than makes up for the confrontation I had with Jet. I'm slurping the last of my soda when my phone pings with an incoming text.

Lucas: We need to have a meeting when we get back home. If this tour is going to happen, we all need to be on the same page, including you. Jet is a ticking time bomb and it's all my fault. I'm sorry I got you involved.

4

JET

AFTER THE CONFRONTATION I had with Quinn at the diner yesterday, I'm crawling out of my skin. She pulled a damn gun on me! Like what the fuck. Yes, I'm sure I scared her shitless since I practically dragged her into the alley.

What did I expect? That she'd go willingly? Hell, she must have thought I was going to mug her, or worse. I'm such an idiot. This right here is what I'm talking about. Sometimes I see red and that's what happened when I thought she was stalking me.

I was so pissed I called Lucas and ruined his vacation, but hey, it's only fair since he did the same to mine. Going behind my back and sending Quinn to my place to sign those damn papers. What the hell was he thinking? Now we're having a meeting as soon as he gets home to clear the air. The fuck good that's going to do. She's still going to be a damn thorn in my side.

Ah, fuck it. I'm not going to spend the rest of my

downtime worrying about her. She's a big girl and I'm sure she's dealt with more than her fair share of egotistical rock bands and inflated egos. I thought everything was going halfway decent until Lucas stuck his nose in where it didn't belong. Something he's never done before. Ever. Which is the reason this bothers me so damn much. Why did he get involved at all?

Unless payback's a bitch? It's a possibility since I went behind his back to give his dad a ticket to our first concert. In my defense, I knew Lucas would regret it when everything was said and done, since his dad's the reason he got started as a musician. I get why he was pissed, I do. His dad had no right to hold onto a secret for years that could have changed Lucas's life for the better if he'd known. In the end, it all worked out. His father admitted that Arisha was his birth mom and I'd like to think I played a small part in their reconciliation.

This is a prime example of why I never let down my guard. It's the reason why I don't trust people, because no matter how hard I try, they always let me down in one way or another. And maybe I'm reading too much into this Quinn and Lucas thing. I know he's hell bent on all of us getting along, and believe me I'm doing my best. But there's something about Quinn that I just can't put my finger on. I'm so used to people I love hurting me beyond belief that I just wait for it to happen again. I'm my own worst enemy, I suppose. So I need to start building up those walls and keep them strong, resilient, and impenetrable again.

Mack is the exception to the rule. He's the only one who's never let me down. My shelter in the storm and apparently the only one who truly has my back. He knew something happened when I finally joined him for lunch yesterday, but I just brushed it off. He doesn't need to concern himself with my problems. He's got enough of his own and he's already done so much for me.

I owe him my life. Literally.

That's why I'm going back to the diner today and every day that I'm back since his asshole employees are all no-shows. Pieces of shit. He bends over backwards for all of them and they don't even have the decency to treat him with respect.

So I will be spending all of my time working instead of relaxing. It's better than looking at these four walls and thinking the worst, but I will need to figure out what happens after the tour is over. Idle minds and I do not mix. Other than writing more songs for our next album and doing a few music videos, my time will be my own. It's all good, but I really do miss busking on the streets. Not something I can do much of anymore since everyone pretty much recognizes me. Last thing I want to do is create havoc in the streets of Manhattan.

All kinds of memories come rushing back to me as I use the adjacent alley to get to the *Hungry Dog Diner*. I stop, take a breath, and rub the ache that suddenly settles in the center of my chest. I think this might be the first time I've come down here in, what, seven years? Maybe eight? Not much has changed as I see all the cardboard boxes lining the outer fence, while dirty faces peek out to see if I'm friend or foe. Some are too young and shouldn't know what hunger feels like, and some are old enough to remember what it was like to go to bed with a full stomach.

Suddenly, the smell of trash that assaults my senses makes me want to retch when I think that not so long ago that was me. I'm going to be sick. I rush past like I'm watching a horrific scene play out in a movie or some horrible accident where you want to look away but you can't. Peeking through your fingers to see if it's over. Only in this scenario, it never will be. After all these years, it's still not acceptable that there are so many homeless kids on the streets.

I'm panting by the time I slide in the back door and stumble through the kitchen. Mack takes one look at me, doesn't say a word, and escorts me into the back room. I don't know what's worse, being out there or being in here.

"We can't save the world, boy. But we can help wherever we can. For as long as I have breath in this old body, I'll feed as many of them as I can." I should take comfort in his words, but I don't because I know for everyone he feeds there are thousands who go hungry.

I swear I try as hard as I can, but my body's shaking so badly that I just lose my shit. Remembering what I did to survive makes me sick to my stomach, and knowing that some of those little faces might have done the same.

Destroys me!

For the first time in so long, I purge all of the guilt that I've stifled for so many years. My tears are not mine alone but for every girl and boy who is enduring the same fate I did.

Yes, it was my choice to run from my family, but I had my reasons. Unlike others who have that ripped out from underneath them, whether because their parents were divorced, lost their jobs, or just made poor decisions. I don't want anyone's pity, but sometimes a hug will do the trick. I'm a grown-ass man blubbering like a child, but Mack holds me close against his chest. For right now, it's exactly where I need to be.

* * *

QUINN

TODAY, I'M ACTUALLY GOING to take a much-needed day off. After everything that's happened with Jet this week and over the last few months, I need to hang out with my girls and just chill out. I want to forget about *The Sinful Seven*, tours, and testosterone. It might be difficult since they'll want to play twenty questions, but I just might spend the first twenty minutes or so doing a quick recap and after that, nothing. I want to spend the day catching up with their lives and forgetting about mine for a change. Sounds like the perfect way to spend the day.

It doesn't hurt that we're going to our favorite hangout either. The Main Spa. They are the best massage and a mani-pedi place in town, and their delicious fruit smoothies and gourmet dishes are guaranteed to make me relax or I'll die trying.

I'm meeting my friends there in an hour and it's going to be an all-day affair. If we have enough energy at the end of the day, we'll end the evening on the rooftop of the *Loco Tequila* and watch the stars while sipping some luscious margaritas. It doesn't get much better than that.

I'm pulling into the parking garage when my phone chimes. Hell to the no, I'm not answering that ringtone today or any other day. I'm on vacation and Jet can apologize to me when we go back to work. Now that I'm here, I shut off my phone since there's no one I want to talk to but my girls.

"Girl, you look great! You don't need a damn spa day!" Nina air-kisses both of my cheeks when I walk into the lobby.

I chuckle, "When's the last time you had your eyes examined?" An eye roll ensues and we all laugh, reminding me how much I miss my friends. The cons of being on the road for so many months at a time.

"Seriously, working with a hot-as-fuck rock band must agree with you because you're glowing. Spill your guts, baby girl. Which one is giving you those mind-blowing orgasms? We know it can't be Lucas since he's with Abby, so that leaves Trevor or Jet." Ugh, just the mention of that man's name has me fuming. If they only knew the half of it.

"I'm their PR agent and that's all there is to it. It's a professional working relationship. Now, let's go play in the mud since I'm dying to find out what all of you have been up to." When they all start talking at once, I'm grateful that they let it go so quickly. For now.

There's nothing like a full-body massage, followed by a mud bath and a mani-pedi to make a girl forget about her problems. I'm so loosey-goosey that I swear I won't be able to walk when my nails dry. And the strawberry smoothie that I've been sucking on is pure perfection! The girls swear it's full of antioxidants and good for me. I'll take their word for it since it tastes like a milk shake I haven't had since I was a child. Yummy goodness.

"This was the best idea you've had in a long time, Quinn. Although I'm a bit jelly that you were the only one who had a male massage therapist. He was totally hot."

"I swear I didn't plan it. It just happened where he was the next one available, not that I'm complaining. If you girls are up to it, maybe we can go to the rooftop and have a bite and dance the night away."

Traci squeals like a teenager at the mention of dancing. She is such a girlie girl. "Well, it would be a shame to go home alone after we spent all day getting scrubbed and polished, now wouldn't it?" This girl is just too much.

"I agree," Alisa chimes in. "I feel too pretty to waste it on all of you. It would be fun to see how many sharks will circle the water when the four of us walk out onto that dance floor."

"I think it's safe to say it's unanimous. After we finish up here, we go paint the town red. Or green or purple," Nina chuckles and I swear she's so giddy that they must have slipped some alcohol in her smoothie.

"Sounds like a great plan, but should we go home and change first?" I always carry extra clothes in the trunk of my car for last-minute business meetings and such, but I don't think the girls do.

"Will you be mad if we tell you we brought another outfit just in case you didn't want to end the day?" Nina smiles. "Sorry you're the only one who will get stuck wearing what you had on." Oh, she of little faith.

"Wrong. I always carry an overnight bag in the trunk of my car for special occasions."

"Hmm, could it be for all those nights where you do the walk of shame? You can kiss-and-tell and we swear we won't say a word." Yeah, not a happening thing.

"Sorry to disappoint all of you, but it's for business purposes. I never know from one minute to the next if I'm going to have an impromptu meeting. Now, let's finish up, get changed and go grab the perfect spot to dance the night away." This right here is exactly what I need. It's been so damn long since I let my hair down.

An hour later, we're sitting on the rooftop of the *Loco Tequila* sipping our delicious margaritas. We were just in time for happy hour! It just doesn't get any better than this.

Loco Tequila is a rooftop tapas bar that has amazing food, and the Spanish atmosphere just adds to the ambience of the evening. This is by far my favorite place to dine in the city. Small portions are the best way to sample as much food as you can. Several hours come and go and so do the drinks. Men of all shapes and sizes buy us several rounds, dance with us, and try to take us home but we stand firm. We're a bit too tipsy to lower our guard, so we will be drinking water until it's time to leave.

At one in the morning we all get in our cars to head home. It was a good night and I can't remember the last time I felt this contented. I had a great day with my friends and there was no drama, just lots of laughs, great food, and dancing. My feet surely disagree but I just might soak in a hot tub when I get home before heading to bed. After all, I can sleep in tomorrow since I'm still on vacation.

Before getting out of the car, I bend over, take off my shoes, and walk barefoot along the path to my house. I hum a tune absentmindedly until I come face-to-face with someone leaning against my front door.

Jet.

5

JET

QUINN NEVER ANSWERED any of my voicemails or texts. So I decided to go to her place to discuss something that's weighing heavy on my mind. Not a smooth move since she already accused me of stalking her, but if she had answered her phone I'd be sitting at home or sleeping. Now I patiently wait for her to come home. Erasing any doubt that she might be spending the night with her boyfriend or someone else. I don't think I ever asked if she was dating anyone. Not that it matters, but I'll be pissed if I spent the whole night waiting only for her to be a no show.

I'm sipping on a bottle of water when I hear a car approaching, then bright lights blinding me before crunching gravel gets my attention. She's home. I parked my car in the next lot over, so she has no way of knowing I'm here. A dick move, but I like the element of surprise. She can't run and hide that way.

When she slams the car door, I get up from the comfy

swing and stand in front of her door, the porch light illuminating my frame. I don't want to scare her again, it's not my intention. She's humming a tune until she looks up and sees me standing there. I can see the fire in her eyes from this distance. She's not happy I'm here. Too bad. If she had answered me, we'd be relaxing in our own space.

"You've overstepped your boundaries, Jet. You're not welcome here, so I suggest you slither into the night before I call the police. It's late and I'm done with the drama."

"Just hear me out. Then I'll leave and you'll never have to talk to me again. This is important, otherwise I wouldn't have come to your house. Please, Quinn."

Her hands are shaking as she pushes me out of the way to unlock the door. Instinct has me reaching for her arm to stop her. Big mistake. "Let go of me! I swear if you don't turn around and leave, I'll be forced to have you arrested."

After what happened in the alley, you'd think I learned my lesson. But this is too damn important to just walk away. "I promise if you hear me out I'll give you that damn interview, that's how important this is to me. I just had this crazy idea today that if I ran it by you and the band, you'd all be onboard. It would be perfect for our exposure and help so many needy kids. I'm begging you, just to hear me out." She must notice how much pain I'm in because she opens the door and invites me in. Thank fuck!

"You have ten minutes to pitch whatever idea you have and then you're out the door. Oh, and I will take you up on that interview. That's part of letting you in." She drops her keys in a fancy little dish on the sideboard and when I focus on her home instead of her, I'm blown away. "Now you have eight minutes." She tucks her long legs underneath her before sitting on the sofa. Me, I'm too nervous to sit still, so I do what I do best. I pace.

"There's too much backstory to explain it all in eight minutes, so I'm going to get right to the point. It's common knowledge that I ran away at thirteen. I lived on the streets for years and it isn't the kind of life I'd wish on my worst enemy. Today was a wakeup call, an epiphany that I haven't had in a while. Too long and I'm ashamed of it. Anyway, I took a shortcut to the diner. It's an alleyway that's on the side of the one I pulled you into." I stop dead in my tracks when her nostrils flare with the memory. Shit, I shouldn't have gone there.

"Five minutes and counting, Jet."

"I'd forgotten about those faces. Young and old staring at me as I made my way through the filth of that alley. Cardboard boxes where they live—fuck, where I used to live. I have no idea why I never thought of it before, but I want to do a benefit concert for the homeless. Get tons of bands together that are willing to give their profits for one weekend. Kinda like Woodstock was all those years ago. I bet we could raise so much money. Maybe even buy some land, build a village of tiny homes and give the homeless in this city a home." In this moment, I'm so passionate about getting my thoughts across, I don't even realize I'm kneeling in front of her with my hands on her thighs.

"That's very noble of you, but something like this would take months to put together. And did you forget there's still three months left to the tour? When would I have time to organize something of this magnitude? I think it would be tough to gather enough bands who are willing to donate their time."

"What if we run it by Caleb? It would be great exposure

for Morris Music, and I don't recall anyone ever doing anything like this before. It could help NY and so many other cities. All I ask is that you think about it, Quinn. If anyone could pull it off, it would be you." I'm going with the flattery-will-get-you-everywhere routine. Truth be told, I sincerely believe she is the only one who could do this. I might not personally like her, but she's smart and business savvy.

"We can't do anything about it tonight, but I promise I'll make some calls tomorrow. Go home and get some rest. As soon as I find out anything, I'll give you a call. Now, you'll need to excuse me, it's way past my bedtime and my liquor limit."

"You're being more than generous after everything I put you through. Thank you, I really appreciate it."

"Goodnight... or should I say 'Good morning'." She's smiling and I take that as a good sign.

"It will surely be a good morning if the powers that be agree to your proposition. Bye, Quinn." She waves before closing the door, and for a moment I feel a little bit lighter.

Like maybe this could really happen.

QUINN

NEVER IN A MILLION years did I expect to find Jet waiting for me when I came home tonight. Never. Now I'm lying here staring up at the ceiling not able to sleep. My mind is bouncing back and forth with tons of ideas since he left. Some good, some bad, but the majority of them are doable. Lucky for him, I have connections. I've been in the biz for a long time and he's absolutely right. If anyone can achieve this goal, it would be me. I'd need to hire an assistant to help out, though. With the last leg of the tour coming up, I'll need to focus on that to perfection. I suppose a good PA could help me with the charity concert.

Damn, that man has been a thorn in my side since day one. Most would have thrown him out in less time than the ten-minute window I gave him, but the sadness and the determination in his gaze was enough for me to take him seriously. He lived through this. Every tormented minute of his teenage years was spent alone on the streets. Just the thought of him and all those other kids going to bed at night, hungry and alone, just tears me apart. So, yeah, I'm hella onboard with this if we can get the backing to do it.

Grabbing my phone on the nightstand, I swipe to see the time. Five thirty-five is much too early to call Caleb. He'd wring my neck. I need to wait until at least seven which gives me plenty of time to shower and guzzle a pot of coffee. I think I'm going to need it. And I've no doubt Jet will be calling me, desperate for an update. I guess it's time to rise and shine. So much for vacation.

There's nothing like the smell of freshly brewed coffee first thing in the morning, so I decide to make a pot before stepping inside the shower. That way, it will be waiting for me instead of the other way around. I'm surprised I'm thinking this clearly with no sleep. Must be because I'm on a mission for a good cause.

With my second cup of coffee in hand, I press speed dial and wait for Caleb to answer.

"You're on vacation, Quinn. Must be an emergency if you're calling me this early. What's up?"

"Morning, Caleb. No emergency, I just wanted to run

something by you. What are your thoughts on *The Sinful Seven* hosting a benefit concert with a bunch of other bands for the homeless? We could make it a huge weekend event and all the money we raise could be donated to the homeless per Morris Music. Would be great exposure for the label and for all the bands who take part in this monumental event." I fidget for a beat waiting for him to answer.

"First off, I'd say that's very ambitious of you, but then I'd ask if you're having a breakdown. It's a great concept but a huge undertaking. You'd need a bunch of volunteers, and I'm not sure if the board would even sponsor something like this. They want to make money, not dish it out unless it's for a band that's been around for years." I didn't think he'd blow off a great idea like this but I do see his point. "Personally, I like the idea. I'll tell you what, I'll run it by a few of my business colleagues. And even if it's not through Morris Music, we might be able to figure something out. You have a great business sense, and this was a great idea, Quinn. Kudos."

"Well, I can't take the credit for something that wasn't mine. Jet's the one who came up with the idea, I only promised him I'd run it by you first. He really is passionate about this venture and my only hope is that we can make it come true. It would mean the world to him and benefit the homeless as well."

"No promises, but give me a few days to run it by them. I'm sure they will want to chew on it for a bit so don't panic if we haven't heard back by the end of the week. Now, go enjoy the rest of your vacation. If this is a go, you'll have your hands full with the tour and this event."

"Thanks, Caleb. Fingers crossed it works out. I promise I can handle them both. Now I'm just as eager as Jet to see this come to fruition. Take care and have a great week!" We say our goodbyes and I want to wait just a bit longer before calling Jet. Even though I know he's going to be persistent and want everything to move at the speed of light, I can't make him wait any longer.

This is one conversation that I can't have via text. After last night, I'm certain he needs to hear the reassurance in my voice if I want him to understand the importance of patience. He picks up on the first ring.

"What's the verdict? Did Caleb love the idea or shoot it down? I've been pacing ever since I came home last night." I can just picture him running his fingers through his hair while pacing. See, this is exactly the reason I called instead of texted.

"Just the opposite. He really liked the idea, Jet, but it might take a few days before we have an answer. We both need to be understanding, and give them the time to make their decision." Yeah, I can hear the loud puff of air that he's been holding in.

"I guess that's a good thing, right? If he didn't think he could make it happen he'd have said no from the get-go. Thanks for believing in my cause and proposing the idea to him."

"You're welcome, but we need to be prepared for both outcomes. He told me upfront that he didn't think the board for Morris Music would go for it, but he has contacts he's going to get in touch with. We might not hear back until next week, but no news is good news, right?"

"I suppose. But we could get ahead of the game and start planning just in case. It couldn't hurt and we are on vacation so it's perfect timing." My heart squeezes when I hear the hope in his voice. I'm not sure if I've ever heard that from this melancholy guy before and it breaks my heart. Yes, we have the time, but I think it would destroy him if we start something and then it doesn't happen.

"Stupid idea, I know," he adds after a beat. "We could go through all the BS and then he pulls the rug out from underneath us. I'm sure you have better things to do with your time off than plot and plan with an asshole like me."

There are a few things on God's green earth that just slay me. One is hopelessness and the other is abandonment. But I have a gut feeling that Jet Turner is going to destroy me before all of this is over. Being the empath that I am, I say, "Sure, it couldn't hurt to get the ball rolling."

SLOTH

*"That destructive siren, **Sloth**, is ever to be avoided."*

Horace

6

JET

I'M ASHAMED OF MYSELF for judging Quinn the way I did when we first met. Don't get me wrong, I still don't like her and damn if I can put my finger on why. But she pulled through and for that I'm grateful.

I jumped at the chance when Quin invited me over to brainstorm. For hours we jotted things down and came up with a great plan. We figured out some of the bands we'd like to invite. The ones we thought would jump at the chance for exposure and because they thought it was a great cause. Unfortunately, I should have known there was a hidden agenda. There always is.

"Let's take a break," she says. "We both could use something to eat. I don't know about you but when I stare at the computer screen for too long everything becomes blurred. I have greasy leftover pizza. Are you game?"

"Sounds perfect. Thanks." I wander into the kitchen with her, only because I need to stretch my legs. Sitting in the same position isn't good for my arthritis. Yep, one of the many gifts I have from sleeping on the ground. "Need me to help with anything?"

I've been around her long enough to know it's not a good sign when she bites her bottom lip. "Nah, it's all good, but this might be a good time to start on that interview that you owe me." Yep, and now I've lost my appetite.

"You're persistent, I'll give you that, but I'm afraid you're going to be very disappointed. My personal life is my own, so be forewarned that I'm only going to share what the public already knows. I'll take my secrets to the grave with me." I'm not even aware that my hands are running through my hair. A sign that I'm as uncomfortable as it gets.

"Fair enough, but can I ask you something that I swear will never go further than this kitchen?" Now I'm curious.

"You can ask, but I can't promise you that I'll answer."

"Okay, but I'm asking anyway. Why were you doing dishes at the *Hungry Dog Diner*, which, by the way, is the coolest freaking name I've ever heard."

"Just helping out an old friend, is all." Truth right here.

She's quiet as she busies herself with plates, forks, and something for us to drink. Both beers. I like her style. "By saying 'old friend' are you referring to their age or someone you've known for a long time?"

"That's for me to know and you to find out." With her tenacity, I'm sure she would, too.

With the pizza heated, we sit down to eat. I lied, I'm starving, and I think I could evade these questions for the rest of my life—even if I'm uncomfortable.

"Your turn," she smiles. "Ask me anything, and no it's not an interview." I'm taken aback because, truthfully, I'm not used to this laid-back Quinn. The one I know is all brash and business. With that said, I still don't trust her. Hmm, maybe that's what's bothering me so much. Friends close and enemies closer.

"Any brothers and sisters?" I ask. I'm not afraid if she asks me this one since my answer would be no.

"No sisters, but I do have four older brothers and one younger one. Yes, it was hell growing up. Still is. The lot of them are very protective of their only sister."

Holy shit, I might feel a little bit of sympathy for her right now. Just a little. "Wow, that's crazy, but I bet the holidays are fun."

"They used to be, but it's difficult getting together now that they're all married with children living all over the country. I might be the only one who goes home, since I'm the single one." She looks sad and I'm not sure if it's because she's single or something else. I shouldn't give a shit but I do.

"You're too young to settle down. Especially with all the traveling you do. Not many men could handle an independent woman such as yourself."

"Thanks, but I'm actually older than you, and my biological clock's ticking like a time bomb. Although, I don't know if I'll ever be ready to settle down and have kids. Maybe one day I'll adopt a bunch of them when I'm too old to tolerate the narcissistic rockstars that I've been dealing with over the years."

"Ouch, I think that might have been directed at me." She almost chokes on a bite of pizza and I'm ready to smack her on the back when she vigorously shakes her head.

"In the beginning, I might have thought that about you, but not anymore. You come off as being standoffish, but you're just the opposite. I'm slowly learning that you're caring, sincere, and enthusiastic about what you believe in. All amazing qualities."

Is she trying to pacify me? As soon as I let my guard down, is she going to pounce like a tigress ready to rip out my entrails for a feast? Maybe, but I'm not sticking around to find out. "Hey, thanks for the grub but I got to head out. I'm second shift dishwasher at the *Hungry Dog Diner* again tonight." Quinn looks disappointed, but I can't stick around. I just can't.

"Okay, well I think we covered a lot of ground today so we'll be ready when Caleb gives us a thumbs up. Don't work too hard." She walks me to the door and it makes me uncomfortable. Feels too familiar. Like a date or something, and my mind is suddenly unsettled.

I need to get the fuck out.

The doors barely open when I bolt with a thanks on my whispered breath. This is the reason I don't get too close to people. I really don't know how to connect and fully interact with anyone.

I peel out of the driveway like a man possessed. I bet Quinn takes back everything good she ever said about me after that little episode. I wouldn't blame her. Somedays, I can't even stand the sight of myself.

Sadly, it's just another day in the life of Jet Turner.

QUINN

I'M STUNNED SPEECHLESS as I watch him squeal out of the drive. Was it something I said? It's apparent he doesn't know how to accept a compliment. Even after all these years he's fighting his demons. Understandable, since he's been on his own for so long. I need to remind myself that Jet is a work in progress. I suppose I would be too if I lived the life he did. Standing on the outside looking in, it's so easy to think the life of a rockstar is all glitz and glamor. Little do the fans know that it's not all that and a bag of chips.

I close the door before the dust has a chance to rush in. Everything was going so well and I thought he was opening up to me. Dammit, Jet! Here we go again. I feel like we take one step forward and three steps back. I'm getting dizzy from all this back and forth, but it would all be worth it if we were on the same page when we go back on tour. It would make all of our lives so much easier and cohesive.

It's too late now to do anything, so I load the dishes and opt for reading a book I started a long time ago. Hoping it will keep my mind occupied and far away from *The Sinful Seven*. My life hasn't been the same since I've taken them on, and, truthfully, I don't know if it's for the better. Time will tell, but I still have a long road ahead of me before I can make that call.

Grabbing my book, I head out to my screened-in porch. It's my little getaway from the hustle and bustle of the world around me. It overlooks my small fenced yard with all its colorful shrubs and perennials. I'm gone so much that it basically takes care of itself. Exactly what I needed when I bought this place a few years back. It's perfect for me.

Sitting on the chaise, I open my book and get lost inside the pages. Dreaming of perfect men with Adonis bodies and the happily-ever-afters of a romance novel. Unfortunately, it doesn't last long when I start feeling guilty about the way Jet stormed out of here. Should I send him a text? I hate that I'm the one worrying about what happened when he's the one who left the way he did. Still, I'm unsettled so it can't hurt to send him one and let him make the next move.

> **Me:** Let's get together the same time tomorrow and brainstorm some more. K?

I wait, but nothing comes. I foolishly stare at my phone, and when nothing happens I go back to reading. But my mind is a million miles away now. All I can think about is a thirteen-year-old child roaming the streets of New York. Alone. I shudder to think what could have happened to him.

Now I'm restless, so I grab my phone and google "homeless kids". What pops up is too much for me to comprehend.

Tons of articles on missing and exploited children, endangered runaways, and a master list of missing children. The list goes on and on. Some articles are more promising than others when I see that there are houses and shelters where they can go for a place to sleep, but I'm sure there's not enough room for everyone. God, how scared are these kids? Wandering the streets, never knowing where they're going to place their head at night for some much-needed rest. Not even mentioning how safe they will be when they do.

After an hour of searching for his name, yes I did go there, I find nothing. Did his family not care or is the case too old for them to give a shit? How can I ever look into his startlingly light-colored eyes again and not see the faces that will forever haunt me after today? I'm angry! So angry that we live in the twenty-first century and shit like this still happens. Now I'm more determined than ever to make this damn concert happen.

I'm itching to call Willow and Trevor so I can run things

by them, but I hate to interrupt their vacation. Besides, I've yet to get confirmation from Caleb that it's a go. Now I know how Jet feels since I'm desperate to get started. But I can't just sit around and wait for it to happen.

Grabbing my purse and slipping on my shoes, I stumble to the door when my phone pings. Yes, a text. I'm a little disappointed when I check to see who it's from. Willow.

She must have read my mind. Swiping, I open up her text.

Willow: I hate to bother you on vacation, but I thought maybe we could have a girl's day out?? I'm missing you and Abby and I'm kinda bored.

Me: I know how ya feel. I couldn't wait for this damn vacation and now I'm restless. When do you want to get together?

Willow: Now?? LOL, if you're not busy.

Me: Nah, I was just going for a drive. I'll pick you up in thirty minutes.

Willow: Cool.

Two heads are better than one, and maybe—just maybe —we can figure out how to heal Jet in the process.

When I arrive, Willow slides in and buckles up. "Glad you called since I was going stir crazy. Pick your poison. What do you want to do?" I ask.

"Let's grab a few drinks and just chat. There's been something I wanted to talk to you about, but not with everyone around." Okay, so now she's piqued my curiosity. Not sure if that's good or bad.

She's quiet, almost nervous since it looks like she's playing with her keys while waiting for the waitress.

"I find the best thing is to just get it off your chest. So, what did you want to talk about, Willow?"

"He likes you. Like a lot. And I know he has a weird way of showing it, but he does." Okay, who are we talking about here?

"You need to give me a hint of some kind because I have no idea who we're talking about."

"Jet! He's crazy about you. I know what you're thinking, but just hear me out. Remember when we were in elementary school and the boys would constantly pick on us? That's what he's doing with you."

"Well, we're not in school anymore and I think you couldn't be more wrong. He tolerates me, but that's okay since I'm not interested in getting involved with him or anyone else for that matter."

7

JET

I'M COUNTING DOWN the days until Lucas and Abby get home. Two more to go. Maybe once we're all together again, things will fall into place. For now, I work. Hard labor seems to be the only thing that's getting me through. Both Quinn and Willow have been texting and trying to call but I've been avoiding them. Not sure why, but I have a feeling they're trying to gang up on me. It could be my paranoia, but it's weird it came out of the blue after I stormed out of Quinn's the other day.

The only problem I have when going to work is Amelia. She's the pretty girl who delivered my burgers, and ever since I promised her concert tickets, well, I guess she thinks we're best friends. It's cute and so is she. For now, I just let it go since she's been keeping my secret. Honestly, that's epic for someone who's only seventeen. Most chicks would be gossiping to all their besties that Jet from *The Sinful*

Seven is washing dishes at the *Hungry Dog Diner*. Right? Of course they would.

"Hey Mack, I'm taking my break." He nods in acknowledgement as he helps Harold flip burgers. Dishes are caught up, so best time for me to head out back for fresh air.

Kicking back, I lean against the building and slide down until my butt is on the little patch of grass out back. Popping the tab on the can of cold soda, I take a huge gulp. I usually don't indulge in this sugary goodness, but for some reason I needed it today. I almost choke when a shadow brushes by, kicking my boot. "What the fuck!"

"Dude, chill. I'm sorry but I was trying to go around, and your long legs got in my way." Amelia, wonderful.

"Since when do you come in by the back door and not the front?" She's coming back from a delivery and I don't like the thought of her being in the back alley.

"It's kinda rush hour and there's no place to park. It was easier this way. Mind if I join you?" She doesn't give me a chance to answer before she pops a squat next to me. Great.

"Mind if I ask you a question?" Oh, here we go. I knew it was just a matter of time.

"You can ask away, but it don't mean I'll answer you."

"Yeah, I kinda figured that but I'm asking anyway. You have a girlfriend?" Okay, so picture me taking a swig, swallowing, and choking all at the same time. Yep, you got it. By the time I can breathe again, it's time for me to go back to work while she smacks my back. "Sorry, I shouldn't have done that to an old man like you. You could have died."

"You just don't know when to quit, do you? I gotta get back."

"Hey, before you do I just want to ask something for a friend. Um, say someone writes songs and they're pretty good, how would they go about getting someone to listen to them?" Asking for a friend? If I had a buck for every time someone said this, I would be a very rich man.

"I'd tell them to start their own YouTube channel. With a ton of practice and the right following, they could kill it. We did that when we first started out." I stretch out my hand after standing. Her smile is contagious when she reaches for my hand and I pull her to her feet. I'm a little scared of that starry gaze she's giving off. Damn, I hope she's not crushing on me.

"Dude, get over yourself." With a chuckle she walks off. Damn, is she a mind reader?

"Amelia! Orders up! Where the hell ya been?" Mack bellows as she rushes to grab her orders. Stuffing them inside her delivery bag.

"Sorry, boss. Just popping a squat, but I'm going now." This kid is gonna be the death of him, but I know by that smirk on his face, he's taken with this young spitfire.

After she leaves, I rib the old man. "She's got you wrapped around her little finger. Admit it."

He's quiet for a beat before his eyes meet mine. "Just like you did all those years ago, boy." What? Is he insinuating that she's a stray like me? That's how he refers to all the homeless kids. He refused to mention the word homeless for fear if someone was listening, it would be detrimental to all involved. Damn. Amelia?

I work the rest of my shift in silence. Just lost in my head after what Mack told me. I still can't wrap my head around the fact that Amelia is on the streets. Fuck! Another wake-up call for me to get these damn concerts in the bag.

"Catch ya tomorrow, boy. Now get the hell outta here and don't look back. Nothing you can do." Yeah, he knows it's eating a hole right through me but there's something I can do and I'm tired of waiting. "You could let her have my old room. It's time."

He shrugs as he points in my direction. "I offered, and she refused. Too damn independent for her own good, that one. Maybe you could convince her. She might listen to a famous rockstar instead of an old relic like me."

"Can't hurt to try. Is she still here?"

"Think so. Her shift ends in fifteen, so you might be able to catch her." He smacks my back when I walk out the door in search of my new co-worker. And, wouldn't you know she crashes right into me as I round the corner. The obscenities begin immediately as I grab her arms so she doesn't hit the floor.

"Dammit that hurt like hell! Now I know what it feels like to have a head-on collision." Oh, she's a funny one all right.

"We need to talk. Come with me." She doesn't fight me as I drag her down the hallway and into my old room, but she starts to protest when I close the door behind me.

QUINN

MAYBE I OPENED UP a can of worms by mentioning to Willow what Jet wants to do, but the vison of all those kids on the street is just too much for me to bear.

"Truthfully, I don't know why it took him this long to mention it to you, since he's been talking about this for years. Did you know that every cent he has, he donates to the shelters? He does it anonymously since he doesn't want the recognition."

"I was under the impression he didn't have a ton to begin with. Where would he get the money to do that?" Seriously, as far as I know, none of them have held a job other than working the clubs on the weekends.

"If you could see his apartment, it's bare bones. He's not materialistic like so many others, just the bare necessities. Whatever is left over after he pays bills, he donates. I swear he still goes days without eating so he can give to others. Jet is selfless and needs very little to survive. He's truly amazing." If I didn't know any better, I'd say she has a crush on him and mum's the word. I'm not telling her I've already been to his apartment, because that would just lead to more questions.

"Maybe I should just shut my mouth, but I trust you so I'm gonna lay it all out. Jet and I hook up now and again. We trust each other and somehow it works. No strings, no commitments. Just friends with benefits." Wow, hell, I didn't see that coming. But what do I expect from a bunch of musicians? This is tame compared to what I've seen and heard in the past.

"You won't get any judgement from me, Willow. Trust is something that can bond a person for life. I say if it works, go for it."

"Go for what? Did I miss something?" Our mouths hang open when we both look up to see Jet sliding in the seat across from us. How the hell? "Don't let me interrupt. Keep on keeping on." His little smirk makes me believe that he heard the last part of our conversation.

Kill me now.

"How the hell did you know we were here?" I can't help questioning him because I find this very unnerving.

"Trevor told me you guys were coming here for dinner, so I had to crash your party. Thanks for the invite." Sarcasm doesn't look good on him.

"It's a girl's night out, and last time I checked you were not a girl." Willow winks at Jet and for the life of me, I feel jealous. Jealous that she knows this mercurial man on an intimate level. A man who keeps everyone at arm's length. I don't like when the green-eyed monster rears her ugly head. This is so not me. Where is the confident Quinn who existed before I met *The Sinful Seven*? Scrap that. Met Jet Turner, the sexy bassist who brings me to my knees.

"Quinn, are you okay? You look a bit pale." Great, now he's a freaking comedian!

"I'm fine, thanks for asking. I thought you were working?" Let's change the subject back to him and see how he likes it.

"Working?" Willow's head spins around so fast, I have nightmares of the Exorcist happening right here and now.

Jet is none too happy I spilled the beans, but hell if I care. He's the one who's here uninvited, so there's that.

"I've been helping out at the diner, no biggie." Apparently Willow is privy to this information since she just shrugs it off. Color me stupid with these two. No, I won't go there.

"Congrats on finally deciding to put your vision in motion. Quinn mentioned that you're waiting for the thumbs up to do a benefit concert for the homeless. I'm one-hundred percent onboard and I'm sure the guys will be, too. We've known this has been another dream of yours for so long now, so how cool is it going to be when this happens?"

Just let it be known, if I don't make it out of here alive it's because the looks that Jet are giving me are killing me. Truth is, I'd be dead in a heartbeat. Maybe sooner.

"Yeah, we're waiting on Caleb to call," he says. "Speaking of, has he been in touch with you yet?" I'm starting to realize after these few months that his raised eyebrow is his signature move. Much like Elvis had his lip thing.

"No, not yet. I'm sure it will take time for him to call a meeting together and have a decision made. We just need to be patient."

Leaning back so his chair is teetering on only two legs, he quips, "Why don't you call him? I'm getting sick and tired of waiting." Ah, come again? Did he just demand me to call? Hell to the fucking no.

"Forcing Caleb to move any faster than he already is would be a sure-fire way for him to drop this whole idea. I'm not going to do that. Oh, and just an FYI, just because it's been your vision, I call the shots, not you. Excuse me." I'm so angry that I need a trip to the ladies room to calm down. Why does he insist on pushing my buttons the way he does? Just when I warm up to him, he does something like this to piss me off.

I didn't need to use the restroom, so I just stand in front of the mirror and scrutinize myself. Is it just me, or did I age ten years since dealing with Jet for the last several months?

Gripping the sink to the point where my knuckles turn white, I just breathe. Desperately trying to figure out why he treats me the way he does. He's not a man of many words to begin with, but when he interacts with the band, a light shines in his eyes. With me, not so much. I'm sure it comes down to trust and knowing them for so long, but I do have the best of intentions.

Taking a deep breath, I let go of the sink and my anxiety. With my head held high I walk back into the restaurant. Just to deflate when I see Willow sitting at the table, alone.

Jet's gone and I'm not sure if that should make me angry or grateful.

8

JET

IT'S ONLY BEEN TWO days since Quinn called Caleb, but it feels like weeks. I understand that she got in touch with him on a Friday and most labels have the weekends off. But I'm not a very patient man and as much as I'd like to call him, I'll refrain. Time is not on my side since we'll be leaving for Connecticut in less than a week. I was hoping we'd have time to figure it all out before travelling for another three months. If we get the green light, it's going to be so damned hard waiting until we get home. My only consolation is that Quinn and I did have a chance to start scheming and dreaming. For now, I just need to be thankful we had that time to hash it all out. I'll be the good little boy and do whatever I'm told since Quinn claims she calls all the shots. Once this tour is over, I'll do whatever I damn well please.

Lacing up my shoes, I get ready to go for a run. It's been ages and I feel like I need the exercise. Grabbing my phone, keys, and earbuds, I get ready to leave when my phone vibrates. Any other time, I'd ignore it, but it's from Willow so I swipe and read the message.

> **Willow:** Trevor and I are getting rusty, wanna come over and practice or just mess around?

Messing around sounds amazing, but I'm sure she didn't mean sexually, since her cousin would be under the same roof. Most likely his mom, Mrs. C would be there, too. So much for going for a run since I don't want to be all sweaty and sticky when I walk in the door. Hell, tomorrow is another day and I'd be lying if I didn't say my fingers are begging for a little bit of string action. Old habits die hard, and it's been days since I picked up my guitar.

> **Me:** Sounds great. I'll be there in twenty.
> **Willow:** Can't wait!

Thank goodness we have a set of instruments at Trevor's house, since our gear is still on the equipment truck far away from here. Come to think of it, I hope they are guarding that damn thing, because there's a ton of money tied up there. Before leaving, I shoot a text to Carl, our equipment manager.

> **Me:** Please tell me that our equipment is all safe and sound because I'm seriously thinking of getting on a damn plane to go check.
> **Carl:** No worries. All the trucks and tour buses are in an old airplane hangar onsite, and guards are there twenty-four seven. Relax, that's what you pay us for. Enjoy.

Me: Thanks, appreciate it.

While driving to Trevor's I flip on the radio, which is something I haven't done in ages. I'm freaking when *Distraction* blares from the speakers on station WBCS. Hell yeah, this never gets old. Hearing our songs on the radio is old school but so damn cool I can't stand it. I kind of want to drive longer just to see if they play more of our songs, but I decide to just pull into his driveway.

I'm still wearing my shorts and running shoes when I walk in the door. Trevor appears from around the corner and takes one look at me. "Bro, were you going for a run? How long has it been since you've pounded the pavement?"

"Too damn long, and I'm starting to feel like I'm getting thick in the middle."

"You're as sexy as ever, Jet," Willow says. "Do you want me screaming your name like all of the girls at the concerts?" I think Willow would tell me that even if I was an old man sitting in a rocking chair.

"You think so, baby?" I pull her in for a hug and plant a wet one on the top of her head.

"You're here to jam, not bang my cousin. Now get your asses downstairs and let's do this. Now, I'm the one who needs the exercise since my arms are hitting me in the face every time I wave." Fucking Trevor. We're bent over laughing when I hear a voice that shouldn't be here.

"What's so funny?"

Willow hurries downstairs as Trevor smacks my arm and follows her.

Pussy!

"Quinn, fancy meeting you here." I've no doubt Willow

left out the fact that she invited her too, since she knows I would have gone for my run instead.

"I hope you don't mind, but Willow invited me and I jumped at the chance. I can't wait to see where you guys jammed all these years." Oh, I bet she would.

Willow avoids me at all costs as I grab my guitar, slip it over my shoulder, and check the tuning. Not that it needs it, but it gives me something to do with my hands. God knows I want to choke the little shit for not mentioning that Quinn would be here.

"This is spectacular. Seriously, Trevor, you guys could have recorded your own albums down here with this setup." No one dares mention that Lucas was opposed to the idea. He had his reasons.

"A little less conversation. Let's practice." Yep, I'm an asshole, but I didn't come here to play catch up. I want to jam and hopefully get rid of this toxic tension that has been hanging in the air since Quinn invaded our private sanctuary.

Just because I'm feeling rebellious, I break out with, *Another One Bites the Dust*, by *Queen*. Quinn's eyes are as round as saucers as Trevor joins in and Willow sings. Yeah, we got some mad skills and can play cover songs probably just as good as the originals. And I don't think there's a person on the face of the earth that isn't familiar with this song, so there's that too.

After I'm done fucking around, we start with our playlist from our last concert. Love these guys because we do all of this without speaking. It's just our nature since we've been doing it for so damn long.

We keep at it for hours and I'm now covered in sweat. Without thinking, I reach over my shoulder and pull my shirt over my head. It hits the sofa, right on the side of Quinn.

Oops, my bad. Damn, I should have wiped myself down before tossing it. I can feel Quinn's stare burning a hole in my chest. I'm guessing she likes my ink and she's trying to decipher it from far away.

Not going to happen.

In fact, I can guarantee you that she'll never get close enough.

* * *

QUINN

I REACH FOR THE water bottle on the table beside me and take a long drink. Trying to quench the fire burning inside of me ever since Jet took off his shirt. Oh my stars, the ink on this man is insane. In a very good way.

I'm hankering to walk over there and read the script that covers every inch of his body. Only to spin him around and see the written word on his back. I'm afraid if I do, I'd drool. No lie. He's tall, lean, and so damn delicious that I just want to reach out and touch him.

Damn, that was so unprofessional.

Maybe I find him alluring because he's so quiet and mysterious. And we all know what they say about the quiet ones, right? I bet he'd be great in bed. Yes, I just went there. In all honesty, I haven't been laid in six months and this man lights my fuse.

It's not the first time I've seen him without his shirt on, but for some reason his tats seem more pronounced when he's playing guitar and it's really hot! Okay, I'll stop now but if you could see what I do, you'd be drooling. I swear.

"We've been at this for hours," Willow says. "I don't

know about all of you, but I'm a starving Marvin." Willow is so damn perfect and cute. I just love her to pieces.

"Let's break and go raid the fridge," Trevor answers. "I'm sure Mom has tons of leftovers just waiting for us."

"I'm down for it. I can't remember the last time I had a decent meal." Everyone goes silent after Jet makes this announcement. He senses it, so he quickly recovers the mood.

"Guys, did you forget I'm working at the diner? I was fucking joking, but I want real food instead of burgers and fries. Don't tell Mack but Mrs. C's cooking is out of this world."

I've yet to meet the mysterious Mrs. C, but I've heard so many good things about her. It's so sad that such a good woman spends her day going through chemo and radiation treatments. It's always the good ones who have so much to bear.

Trevor's the first one up the stairs and Willow follows. I hold back but am shocked when Jet places his hand against the small of my back and allows me to go in front of him. Is he checking out my ass? I highly doubt it because it's a known fact he doesn't like me very much.

Laughter hits us as we open the door and watch Trevor pull a massive amount of food out of the fridge while Willow dots kisses all over this tiny woman in the center of the kitchen. The elusive Mrs. C, I presume.

"Mom this is Quinn, our PR agent and the glue that keeps us together. Quinn, this is my mom, and the best cook in the world." Trevor's introduction leaves little to the imagination.

"It's wonderful to finally meet you, Mrs. Collins. I lost count how many times they wanted to hire you to go on the road as our personal chef." Truth, the food at some of the venues was atrocious.

"It's nice to finally meet you, Quinn. Please, all of my friends call me Mrs. C. Thank you for taking care of my brood while they're on the road. I'm sure it wasn't an easy feat keeping everyone in line, especially my Lucas." She slowly walks over, takes my hands, and kisses my cheek. She's so sweet and frail, standing around five feet.

"Did I hear someone mention my name?" Lucas, in all his magnificent glory, swoops in and sweeps Mrs. C off her feet. She's laughing and crying since her 'brood' is together again. It melts my heart. A smiling Abby is close behind.

"I thought you were on vacation for ten days," Mrs. C says to Abby. "What happened to change your mind?" I'm blinded when Abby holds up her hand and she's sporting a dazzling engagement ring.

"We're engaged, and I couldn't wait to get home to show all of you!" Everyone's talking all at once and it's difficult to hear over the buzz.

Jet's the first one to congratulate the bride by picking up Abby, swinging her around and planting a kiss right on her lips. With a roar, Lucas separates the two and laughter ensues. I'm standing off to the sidelines feeling like the fifth wheel when Lucas realizes I'm here, struts over and picks me up, and swings me around too. "Congratulations. Now put me down, you idiot." He grabs his chest like he's offended.

I fight my way through the bodies so I can properly congratulate Abby. She's smiling from ear to ear as she holds out her hand to show me. "Girl, he did good! It's beautiful and huge!" I pull her in for a hug and she holds me tight. Abby is *The Sinful Seven's* business manager, but just a few months back she was a barista at Java Joe's. When the coffee joint was sold by her asshole brother, Lucas swooped in and saved the day.

"I want to hear all about Aruba, and how he proposed," Mrs. C says. "I can't believe you guys cut your vacation short to come back home." If I was in paradise, I don't think I'd ever want to come home.

"Lucas wanted to clear the air with Jet after what happened. It's been eating away at him for days, so I'm the one who suggested we leave. Besides, I couldn't wait to show everyone my ring. I might be a bit biased but I think it's gorgeous." All the girls gather around Abby and we all ooh and ah over the brilliant bauble. He really did good this time around.

"We were just getting ready to chow. I'll grab more chairs and plates. Hope you guys are hungry after the plane ride." Trevor takes it upon himself to play host and I jump right in to help him. I'd rather stay busy and out of everyone's way.

Once the table is set, we all sit down to have a celebratory meal together. I'm thankful that Willow invited me here today, otherwise I would have missed out on this happy occasion. A part of me realizes that I shouldn't be here, but another part of me feels like I belong. Not sure why, but I'm going to cherish this moment since I know it's fleeting. In a little over thirteen weeks, I'll most likely be heading somewhere else. Working with a new band and getting to know everyone all over again. So, for now, I'm going to enjoy every moment until it disappears.

9

JET

WHO WAS THAT guy who wanted his solitude a week ago? Yeah, that would be me. I never thought I'd be the one to admit it's great to have the gang together again. Working at the diner and brainstorming with Quinn was the highlight of my vacation, but now that everyone's back, we can jam.

One of the first things we did after eating last night was clear the air. Lucas explained his reasoning behind setting me up with Quinn, and I get it, I do. But I also reminded him that I don't warm up to people the way he does. It takes me longer, if ever, to feel comfortable with someone. We made each other a promise to stay out of each other's business from now on, and I'm thinking he agreed readily since I had tons to say about his engagement. Too soon is what I wanted to preach, but I know he doesn't want to hear it. Besides, it's not my place. Whether friend or foe, no one's going to change his mind on this one.

Don't get me wrong, I like Abby. And I'm thankful she

chose him since he's had his share of women in the past. If anyone can tame him, she can.

Last night we stayed at Trevor's just like in the old days. Funny, it does seem like years ago when in truth it was only a few months ago. Quinn left after the engagement festivities and I was relieved when no one asked her to stay. Yeah, I'm an asshole, but even after all these months I don't feel comfortable when she's around. Maybe it's because she's constantly staring at me. I feel like she can see right through me and read me better than any book out there, and it makes me uncomfortable. Always has and always will.

So, for today, we're going to kick back and chill and just play catch up.

Lucas and Abby are stretched out on the leather sofa, while the rest of us are sitting on the floor in a semi-circle. Listening to all the funny shit that went down in Aruba with these two. All you need to do is visualize high tide, hot sand, and rough seas while they're naked. Yep, spells disaster. They're damn lucky they didn't drown.

"I swear Abby's still finding sand in all her girlie—" Lucas stops short as a quick smack lands across his shoulder from Abby and we have a good laugh. "On a more serious note, Jet, fill us in about this benefit concert you and Quinn are trying to put together."

"We've been brainstorming a ton of ideas, and I think we have it all figured out. As soon as we get the greenlight from Caleb, we'll contact as many bands as possible to join. Then, if every band sets up a campaign page and sells online tickets, they can reach tons of their fans and die-hard concert goers. We could also sell T-shirts with a special logo on it for the benefit. I'm sure one of us can come up with a cool slogan and add the band names with dates. I don't know, but

I have a million thoughts running through my brain to the point where I can't shut it off."

Abby's so excited, she sits up and leans her elbows on her knees. "With careful planning, this has the potential to be an amazing fundraiser for a very worthy cause. I'm sure we'd have tons of bands wanting to donate their time."

"Exactly," I respond, "and I don't care if they're big or small, if they're willing to give up their time, I'm more than happy to let them join. Hey, we all had to start somewhere. This could be the big break they need to be seen and heard."

Questions are coming in left and right, and it's hard for me to keep up with all of them. "Okay, Quinn and I don't have all the answers. One of the biggies is what venue would be able to pull this off. Another thing for us to figure out is how long can we keep this gig going. A day, a weekend? How would that play out?"

All of a sudden Trevor gets an epiphany. "Hey, speaking of Quinn, why isn't she here today?"

"Right? I'll call her and see if she's busy. If not I'll ask her to come on over."

I quickly stop Willow from making that call. "I'd rather you didn't. It's our vacation and all we have is a few more days before going back on tour. Seriously, Quinn is just an organizer and I'd like to keep it real just for a little longer."

"Bro," Lucas says, "it's time we had another chat. Alone. Follow me." Is he fucking serious? Lucas stands over me, and for a split second I feel like I'm back in that trailer and it's hard to breathe. "Jet, it's me. Lucas."

When my vision clears and I notice him squatting down in front of me, I feel unhinged. Shaking it off, I push him away and stand of my own accord. On wobbly legs, I rush out the front door. My long legs carry me forward as Lucas calls out my name.

"Jet, I'm sorry. Wait up, please. I wasn't thinking." Damn straight he wasn't.

Bending over, with my hands plastered against my thighs, I try to shake off the fog from my brain. I haven't had a flashback like that in years. Lucas knows not to touch me, so he just stands in my peripheral with his hands in his pockets.

"Do you want me to grab a pint or a bottle of Jack? Tell me what you need."

"For everyone to leave me the fuck alone! I'm so damn tired of everyone pushing Quinn down my throat. I can't tell you why she rubs me the wrong way. I wish I could, but the last thing I need is for my friends to play matchmaker. Or to force me to do something I'm not comfortable doing. Yes, we collaborated and I stopped over at her house and she stopped over at mine, but it was because I fucked up big time and I'm not going into that right now. Please, I just can't right now." I storm off in the opposite direction and I'm well aware that my car is parked in Trevor's driveway. Right now, I really don't care.

He doesn't try to stop me and that's a good thing since I don't want to be stopped. I'm feeling like I'll lose my mind at any minute, and if I do, I don't want my friends to witness me falling apart.

So, I keep on walking. And walking. Until a familiar sight greets me.

My solace, my home.

My sanctuary.

* * *

QUINN

SINCE I HAVEN'T HEARD from Caleb yet, I decided to go for a walk to burn off some pent-up energy. My mind wanted to visit a plush green park with children playing, laughing, and having fun with their families. Sadly, my feet had a mind of their own when I found myself walking down the alley beside the diner. The exact one that Jet mentioned that night. Now, I can't erase the tragedy that unfolded before me. Children of all ages hiding in cardboard boxes, wearing tattered clothing. Innocent faces that bartered for money, doing anything that would get them a hot meal to fill their empty bellies. I spent every last dime I had on me, granting them what they begged me for. I wanted to take them home to bathe them and let them sleep in a warm house so they felt safe. Even if it was for a few hours. Someplace where they wouldn't need to hustle or try to steal for themselves.

Deep down inside, I'd known this was happening. But, like everyone else, I guess I turned a blind eye. Always thinking that someone would take care of them. I was so damn wrong. Most of the people passing by that alley avoided looking down there at all costs. Pretending it doesn't exist. All of these kids are falling through the cracks. As adults, it should be our mission to make sure that they're being taken care of. I can't and I won't just look the other way or forget that I've seen this any longer.

As soon as I got home, I did the unthinkable. I called Caleb. "Since your first call wasn't an emergency, is it safe to assume this one could be?" he asked.

"I took a walk down the alley between Fifth and Ninth on Main. Homeless children line the walls, living in cardboard boxes, begging for food, selling their bodies, Caleb. Anything so they can eat—"

"Quinn, I'm well aware of that spot and it's not happening just in the city of New York. It's worldwide, and unfortunately one concert isn't going to fix the problem."

I'm sobbing like a baby because my gut's telling me that he's already made up his mind. I can't even right now. "Caleb, I'm begging you."

"Contrary to what you think, I'm on your side. I want to help but I've already spoken to a few of my colleagues and they think it's a waste of time and money. The best advice I'm going to give you is don't ever go there again. You can't save everyone; it will just drive you mad. Quinn, I promise I'll get back to you sometime tomorrow with an answer."

I'm devastated when the line goes dead. Really, what did I expect? That he'd rush right over here, open his wallet, and feed everyone?

Desolation hits me right in the center of my chest. What do those poor children do when they're feeling this way? How can they find comfort when there's none? I can always call family or friends, but what would they do? I don't know how to turn all of this around and I feel so small and helpless. All of the planning that Jet and I did seems so trivial compared to how monumental something of this magnitude truly is. One insignificant concert such as this would be like putting a Band-Aid on a festering wound. It just wouldn't be enough. Will anything ever be enough?

There's so much anxiety building inside of me that I feel volatile, like I'm going to blow at a moment's notice. I need to do something. What, exactly, I have no idea. But *something*.

I don't waste my time getting inside my car, because,

truthfully, I don't want to be confined inside of a small space. Right now I need the vastness and the open air, so I walk. I've no idea where I'm going, but I just put one foot in front of the other and keep going. When I'm tired and can't go any further, I'll stop. Call an Uber and then go home. Until then, I'm on the move.

I pass the *Hungry Dog Diner* and contemplate stopping in for a burger, but decide against it. It's best if I keep on walking just in case Jet's working. He's sure to accuse me of stalking him again if I do. I walk by several quaint shops and bars and enter a side of town that looks familiar. This is the street where Trevor lives. Do I stop in, or keep on walking? I should cross the street or go back the same way I came. I don't want any of them to think I'm so desperate that I want to hang out with them while I'm on vacation. *Vacation.* What a joke.

Crossing the street, I head back and stop short when someone calls out my name. "Quinn? Quinn, wait up." I turn to find Willow running towards me. Damn, I wasn't quick enough. "Do you need a ride? Hey, where's your car?"

"Hey, Willow. Funny thing, I was taking a walk and didn't realize I had walked this far out. I'm heading back now."

"I was just leaving Trevor's house, let me give you a ride." I know if I tell her no, she'll insist.

"That would be great, I'd really appreciate it." We both head over to where she's parked and I slide in when she unlocks the door. "Is the gang still hanging out?"

We buckle up before she answers. "Nah, Jet was the first to leave and then Lucas and Abby left soon after. I wanted to help Trevor and Mrs. C clean up before I left. There's always so many dishes when we're there."

"Mrs. C is the sweetest woman I've ever met. She really loves all of you guys so much."

"You know she's my aunt, right?" When I nod, she continues. "When my dad went to prison, my mom and I moved in with Trevor and his mom for a few years. One of the reasons Trevor and I are so close. He's more like my brother than my cousin. Sorry, I'm rambling. I'm sure you know all of this already." She gets quiet and for some reason I think something else is bothering her.

"Is everything okay, Willow? I only ask because sometimes I feel like whenever I'm around it's uncomfortable for all of you. Am I right?"

She fidgets a little in her seat and with her body language I don't need her to answer. For whatever reason, she's uncomfortable.

"We all love you, Quinn. We all think of you as our sister more than our boss." Oh, I sense a "but" coming. She doesn't continue until she pulls into my driveway. Shutting off the car, she turns towards me, resting her leg on the seat. "It's just that Jet gets upset whenever we mention your name."

GLUTTONY

*"**Gluttony** is an emotional escape, a sign something is eating us."*

Peter De Vries

JET

MEMORIES OF A FUCKED-UP kind have been coming back to me like a vengeance ever since my meltdown yesterday. If there was a way for me to cut open my brain and cleanse it until it was pure, white, and clean, I would. Unfortunately, there's no cure for what plagues me. Just a constant misery that reminds me of where I came from and what I've done.

I startle when there's a knock on the door, but there's only one person it could be. I call out, "Come in."

The door opens, and my savior's standing there holding a tray filled with everything breakfast and a pot of coffee. "Thanks for letting me crash here last night, Mack."

"No reason to thank me, boy. This will always be your room whenever you need it." Placing the tray on the table beside me, he turns to leave.

"Mack, will this feeling ever go away?" His heavy sigh speaks volumes, more than his words ever could.

"The only one who can answer that question is you. Not

me. No one would be happier to see you set your demons free, but you need help. Someone you can talk to who can forgive you for what you've done to survive. God knows you can't forgive yourself. Hell, start with everyone in the band. You'd be surprised how freeing it could be to confide in your friends who love you regardless or in spite of your past. No one carries your burden quite like you do, boy. Only you can torture yourself so harshly."

I know he's right. Lucas told me the exact same thing. But, cutting myself open and confiding in Trevor and Willow just seems impossible. Besides, not even a shrink, priest, or whoever I decide to tell won't heal my soul. And I truly think that's what hurts more than my psyche ever did. I've been broken for so long now that I don't know how to truly live.

"After I eat and clean up, I'll be out there to help you," I say. "I'll be leaving at the end of the week again and I won't be back for several months. So I'm going to help you out as much as I can between now and then."

"Suit yourself. I never refuse good help. You know you're spoiling me for all the idiots who will come after you." When he stands in front of me, he grabs my nape and says, "They say blood is thicker than water, but I call bullshit. You ain't my blood but you're my son, boy. Never forget it." Letting go, he turns and walks out the door.

It takes everything I am to hold back my emotions that are swirling around like a storm inside of me. This is the first time he's ever called me his son and it overrides all the fake "I love you's" that have been force-fed to me over the years.

What a heavy discussion this has been first thing in the morning. Now I need to get my ass up and prove to the man that I'm worthy of that title.

There's something I find therapeutic about taking dirty dishes from the dining room, loading them up in the industrial dishwasher, and restocking them in neat stacks. If only my life could be run through that dishwasher and come out clean.

The day flies by and I decide to go back to my place once my shift is over. I can't hide in my old room forever, and just knowing that it's still there after all these years is comforting.

I'm hot, sweaty, and in desperate need of a shower. Kicking off my shoes, I start stripping the second I walk through the door. Tearing off my damp shirt, I send it flying across the living room. Next come my pants as I trip and stumble while hopping on one leg. It would have been so much easier if I had sat down to pull them off, but my mind is focused on the cool water sluicing down my overheated skin.

Turning on the water, I set it on the coldest setting and pull the knob before stepping in. The rush of cold hitting my chest causes me to suck in a breath. I'm gasping for air as I duck my head under the showerhead. It's ten times worse than the brain freeze you get when eating ice cream too fast. With a pounding heart, and clenched fists, I stay there for as long as I can stand it before adding the hot water to the mix. Trembling takes over and I hold on to the wall in front of me for support.

Once my body adjusts to the temperature, I grab my body wash and shower off all the sweat and grime of the last few days. Never taking for granted what it feels like to go weeks without bathing when I lived on the streets. It's a feeling I'll never forget, as long as I live.

After closing the water, I towel dry and throw on an old

beat-up concert Tee and a pair of track shorts. There's no closet full of suits, fancy clothes, and expensive footwear in this apartment. Clean clothes are all I need to feel grounded.

Grabbing my guitar, notebook, and pen, I sit down to put my thoughts to paper. Being vulnerable and raw is the best time for me to write some more music. Lucas would like our second album to be a collaboration of songs by all of us, so no time like the present.

> *I lived my life as if I'm silent*
> *Buried in the darkness of my soul*
> *Like a child without a voice*
> *Screaming on deaf ears*
> *Why isn't anyone listening?*
> *Can't you hear my cries?*
> *Or do you look away*
> *My pain too much to bear*

QUINN

"Jet gets upset whenever we mention your name."

I'M NOT SURE WHY this sentence has stripped me of all resolve, but it sure as hell did. It's devastating to know that he feels this way when all I've tried to do is be his friend. I know I shouldn't let it bother me, but it does. Why the hell do I care if one arrogant musician doesn't like me? I've worked with hundreds of them over the years.

Unfortunately, this knowledge sets the tone for the rest of

the tour. It won't be easy pretending like I don't know about this revelation, making our working relationship unbearable. After helping Jet with the nuts and bolts of the charity concert, I really hoped he'd realize I was on his side. That we were both working together for a grand venture and a wonderful cause.

I could tell the minute Willow spilled the beans she regretted it, but it was too late to take back. She tried covering for him by mentioning he'd had a bad childhood. Nothing I haven't heard before, but I'm beginning to think excuses are like assholes. Everyone has one.

Besides, I've known a lot of people who have had a hard life but they don't act like idiots like he does. Ugh, it's so damn frustrating just knowing in a few days we're going to be stuffed together like a bunch of sardines again. I don't have a choice and I'm not a quitter, so I'll finish what I started. When it's time to walk away, I will. No looking back.

When my phone rings, I'm tempted to ignore it. I'm in no mood to talk to anyone, until I notice it's Caleb's number. With trembling hands, I swipe. "Hi Caleb, I'd like to apologize for calling you yesterday."

"Well, I apologize for hanging up on you, so now we're even. Look, I'm not going to pull any punches. I have good news and bad news. What would you like first?"

Is he kidding me? "Give me the bad news first. Save the best for last."

"I just knew you'd want the worst first. Okay, so the whole idea of a huge benefit concert is out of the question. The backers want a new album as soon as possible to keep the momentum going. You know the deal, that leads to another tour and the circle is complete. That's the bad news, but the good news is if *The Sinful Seven* agree to do one more month on the road, all the proceeds will go to the homeless, in the city they're performing in. And the backers will find the bands to perform in each city. Which takes some of the pressure off of you and the band. You can all concentrate on the venue and the concert. Is this satisfactory?"

"If it were just me, I'd say go for it, but I really need to run it by the band. It's a great plan, but it's not exactly Jet's vision. Give me until the end of the day and I'll give you their answer. Thanks for everything, Caleb. It's more than I expected, really."

"Good, I'm glad we could come up with something solid so all parties could benefit. Once I have your answer, we can get the ball rolling if they agree." We say our goodbyes and before I get ready to run out the door, I contemplate calling a meeting. Since it entails the band, I need to have them all in the same room and not one-on-one.

As much as I hate to contact Jet directly, I feel the need to reach out since this started with his vision. Taking a deep breath, I start a text, delete, and start again.

Me: I just received a call from Caleb. Since this concerns the band, is there somewhere we can meet?

I stare at my phone waiting for his answer. When it doesn't come immediately, I'm ready to text Lucas. No need —just as I finish that thought, the phone rings in my sweaty palm. I should have known he'd want to talk.

"Why do we need a meeting? The band already agreed, so what's this all about?" He's agitated and I knew he would be. Now I want to talk face-to-face instead of on the phone.

"It's complicated. We should get together and talk about it, is all."

"Is the answer a yes or no, Quinn? It really doesn't get any easier than that. Seriously." An unintelligible swear comes through the phone. Now I'm getting angry.

"Out of courtesy, I texted you first since it was your idea, but I'm seconds away from texting Lucas so he can reign your ass in. I'm tired of your attitude and your ungratefulness. So, I'm going to pick the place. Meet me in an hour at *The Golden Palace*. Be there or not, I don't really care." I press "End" and immediately call Willow. After briefly filling her in, she agrees to call Lucas and to tell Trevor. They'll meet me there in an hour.

I'm the first to arrive at *The Golden Palace* since it's only three blocks from my house. I'm nervous since the band is coming and I want privacy. "I have some very important people meeting me here today and privacy is of the utmost. Is there a room or a corner of the restaurant where we could be secluded? I know it's last minute and all."

"How big is your party?" When I let the hostess know there's only six of us, she ushers me into a small room off the kitchen. It's perfect, with just a large table in the center that seats eight. It looks more like a makeshift office or conference room.

"This is perfect. Thank you so much. One more favor. Is it possible to let them in by the kitchen?" Her brows hit her hairline and I feel like I need to explain. "They're musicians, *The Sinful Seven*, in fact, and we wouldn't want to create chaos in your lovely restaurant."

"Discretion is necessary. I'll make sure they are escorted to the kitchen entrance. Will they be arriving all together?"

Crap, no. I need to text them all to come in on the side instead of walking through the front door.

"No, they will arrive separately. I'll make sure to tell them to arrive by the side door. Thank you so much."

I quickly shoot a group message to let everyone know.

Me: Park away from the front if possible and someone will escort you around the building.

Everyone shoots me a thumbs up response except Jet. Well, screw him. I'm done playing nice.

11

JET

I'VE NO IDEA WHY she's being so secretive, but it's pissing me off. I have a sinking feeling in my gut that whatever her answer is, I'm not going to like it much. I don't bother answering her text, it's a moot point. I'm not a child and I can read, so why waste the time?

I'm pulling into the restaurant right behind Lucas and Abby, so I follow them to the corner of the parking lot. Willow is already waiting, and as soon as we get out of our cars a blonde with legs for miles rushes over. No doubt she wants pics and autographs.

"Hi, my name's Cindy and I'll be escorting all of you inside. We're going to use the employee entrance by the kitchen so we don't cause a scene. Please follow me." I'd like to say "Gladly", but that's the old me. The new me couldn't care less.

Cindy hurries us through the side door, and we walk through a small break room with a fridge and microwave.

We then head down a long hallway before she leads us through a wooden door where Quinn's waiting for us.

"Thanks, Cindy, you're a lifesaver." Long Legs excuses herself and says something about bringing us drinks, but I'm too focused on someone else to pay any attention.

"Just get to the point, Quinn. Did Caleb say yes or no? Is that too much to ask for? Why didn't he call me instead?" Lucas gives me a look to shut up and sit down, but I don't take orders from him or anyone else for that matter.

In three short strides, my knuckles are hitting the edge of the table, and Quinn and I are eye-to-eye. "Yes or no?"

A hand lands on my shoulder and I want to punch the fucker who dared touch me, but when I glance over, it's Abby. My heart races at the thought of almost hurting her.

"Jet, please sit down so Quinn can tell us the answer. Intimidating her isn't helping anything. Please." Oh, she's smart, this girl. She knew I'd crumble.

Yanking off my beanie, I rake my hands through my messy hair and pull up a damn seat. I'm tired of waiting. I just want to know the fucking answer. Is that too much to ask?

Quinn stands and begins pacing around the room, which does nothing for the nerves bouncing around inside of me. Fuck, this isn't good.

"Caleb called to let me know the board decided against the charity concert." She holds up her hand when everyone starts complaining. "Hang on, guys. Let me finish. He had another idea and I'm sure we can make it work. Hear me out." A knock on the door has her backtracking so she can open it. Enter Long Legs and her entourage.

We all shut our mouths as they bring in trays of food and drinks. Once they've placed the last tray on the table, the three sneak a peek or two. Hey, I'm used to it, no biggie. Before leaving, Long Legs puts some kind of buzzer on the table. "If you need anything else, just press this and I'll pop in. Otherwise, your privacy is our main concern."

"Thank you, Cindy," Quinn says. "You've been a lifesaver. I think we're good for now." With a nod, she walks out, but not before I wonder if she's a screamer or not. Sorry, I'm human after all.

"As I was going to say. His new plan seems fair, and I think once I explain everything you'll all be onboard. I took the liberty of ordering appetizers and drinks, so help yourself and I'll explain everything." Everyone's too upset to eat, but we go ahead and grab some beers and a couple rounds of shots. I have a feeling we're going to need them.

"Caleb suggested we add another month onto the backend of the tour." Trevor grouses as he should, since he's left his mom alone throughout the tour. Well, technically, she's not alone since she has a nurse twenty-four seven, but he wants to be there since he's family. "I know it's not ideal, but if we agree, then Caleb will book the venues, the bands, and he can do all of the PR stuff. Basically he'd be doing my job so I can focus on the rest of the tour. Everything— tickets, merchandise, all of it—will be taken care of. All the money will go to the homeless in each of the cities we play in."

I slam my hand down on the table so hard, everyone jumps. "I wanted all the money to go to NYC since that's where we live. I've been donating a ton of money to homeless people everywhere, but I wanted to focus on here." I really don't know why I'm feeling like this, but everything is suddenly out of my control.

"Jet, come on man," Lucas says. "This is an amazing

opportunity. If we pass it up, we'll never get another chance again." Yeah, it's easy for Lucas to say since it wasn't his vision, it's mine! "Think about it, we can just concentrate on the tour while Caleb and his minions do all the hard work. It's a win, win."

Why is everyone looking at me like I'm the only one who doesn't think this is the best thing since peanut butter and jelly? "Since you've already made up your minds I guess majority rules, right?"

Willow shakes her head. "No, not at all. If this proposal doesn't sit well with you, then we won't do it. But before you give us your final decision, just think about how many lives will benefit because of this. Jet, we can cram a ton of concerts in one month and that would be bank for a wonderful cause." When she stands, walks over, and hugs me from behind, I thaw. She's right, this is so much bigger than me.

Opening my eyes, I'm met with a fiery gaze. Quinn doesn't look happy that Willow and I are touching. Does she know we've slept together? Is she jealous? I highly doubt it, but I do love torturing her for no apparent reason.

Grabbing one of Willow's hands, I pull her around until she's sitting in my lap. No, I'm not a big fan of PDA, but if not for this girl right here, I'd have stormed out of this room. "I'm glad to know that I have one person who has my back," I say. "Tell Caleb it's a go, but I want to be in the loop since it's my baby. Got it?"

Quinn hates it when she's not in control, but she relents. "Loud and clear."

* * *

QUINN

WILLOW AND JET LEFT hand-in-hand right after they agreed to Caleb's conditions. I can't figure out if I'm pissed because they were together or because he said to keep him in the loop since it was his baby and had the balls to walk out the door! It didn't seem to bother anyone else, but I'm sure it's because they're used to it. Me, not so much, but it's none of my business so I pretended like it was no big deal.

The four of us stayed and ate a ton of food while putting our heads together to do some plotting and planning. Now I'm emailing Caleb with all the details. We'll see if he agrees to our suggestions. I've no doubt he will, since PR is what I do best. Besides, he's always trusted my judgment in the past.

I'm still fuming that the two of them left. It's not like I didn't know they slept together since Willow mentioned it to me before. But it was all the proof I needed that he's no more interested in me than I am in him. I guess knowing and practically seeing it are two different things. I know they have an open relationship, I've seen them all take off with groupies a time or two after a show. Don't get me wrong, I'm not complaining. I'm used to the whole sex, drugs, and rock and roll stigma. But, I must admit, *The Sinful Seven* is certainly different than any other rock band I've ever worked with in the past. Other than Jet's dreadful attitude, they're a breath of fresh air.

After my last relationship failed, I made a vow to never get involved with another rockstar. Everyone warned me that Zander Stone was too much for me to handle and I didn't listen. Too blinded by love to see the truth when it was right there in front of me. Did he ever love me?

Maybe, but if he did it was short-lived and fleeting. The sexy front man for *Rebel Riot* left a hole in my heart that will never heal. Unfortunately, I learned the hard way that mixing business with pleasure was a fiasco in the making. It lasted for a year and once the tour was over, so was my marriage. Now all I have to show for it is a broken heart and divorce papers to match. Yeah, we were stupid and eloped on a whim and that's when things started falling apart.

Wow, how did that happen? One minute I'm stewing about Willow and Jet and the next I'm comparing them to my failed relationship. As far as I know, they're just friends with benefits. I suppose that's not a bad thing considering they trust each other completely.

Since we'll be leaving on Sunday, which is only four days away, I need to concentrate on the rest of the tour. I've been so preoccupied with the benefit concerts that I've put everything else on the back burner. No more, time is ticking and there's a ton of things I need to do and one of them is going to my parents tonight for dinner. It will be the last time we're together for, well, too long since adding that extra month on the tour will be four months in total. I'm tired just thinking about it, but I'd be lying if I didn't say I was excited.

After stuffing myself earlier today, the last thing I want is to eat a big meal. I'd be happy with a few glasses of wine paired with a charcuterie board. Which is the reason I texted my mom to let her know. This is how that went.

Me: Had a meeting today and I pigged out. I hope you're not making a ton of food.

Mom: Dad's cooking steaks on the grill and we're

having baked potatoes with a side salad. Eat whatever
you can and take the rest home with you?
Me: I'm leaving in a few days but I suppose that would
work. Okay, see you in a bit.

What she's not saying in so many words is he cooked
enough to feed an army, which he always does. If that's the
case, they'll be eating leftovers for the rest of the week. My
brother is a bottomless pit, but he's not a big fan of reheating
food so there's that.

Before leaving, I send over the confirmation email for
the band's photoshoot tomorrow. I had everything set to go
when Jet and I first discussed the benefit concerts. Once
Caleb gave me the go ahead, I called to let them know we're
ready. Lucky for us, they had a cancellation for tomorrow.
This works out perfectly since we'll be leaving soon. Now, if
Jet and Lucas can behave, we'll get through it. Sometimes
they can butt heads, but at the end of the day, it all
works out.

I love how my mom always meets me outside whenever
I come over. It's a tradition that we've been following ever
since I graduated from college. She claims it's the only time
we get a chance to chat since my dad monopolizes the
conversation. Not true, but I indulge her because she's the
best mother in the whole world.

"Hey mom. I can smell that steak all the way out here.
Delish." She reaches out with her arms extended as if she
hasn't seen me in years. I fall right into them and I'm
immediately engulfed in love and warmth. Then it hits me
like a ton of bricks. Jet doesn't have anyone to hold him like
this and my tears threaten to fall.

"If you start crying, sweet girl, then I'm going to follow.

What's wrong?" I refuse to discuss anything personal about my clients with my family so I shrug it off.

"I'm going to miss having Thanksgiving and Christmas with you guys this year." I pulled that off the top of my head but now I'm really sad just thinking about it.

"Do you like your job, Quinn? If you answered yes, then that makes all your sacrifices worthwhile. You're a smart girl, and Dad and I are proud of the career you've built for yourself. Holidays are all about family. We can get together when you come home. All we want is for you to be happy. It's all we want for any of our children."

"I do love my job, Mom. Working with a bunch of egotistical rockstars isn't the easiest, but I have a good bunch this time around. Promise."

"I know you like to keep your professional life private, I understand, but after what happened last time, well, I worry about you. I don't want to see you getting hurt again." Ah, she's referring to Zander but refuses to speak his name.

I'm saved by my dad when he yells, "Dinner's ready, stop meddling!"

12

JET

THE CROWD IS WILD, and my heart's beating to the rhythm of the mob. Security is crazy as we exit the limo, the scene tight and cramped. Not even a piece of paper would fit between us. With our heads down and the fans screaming, we do the best we can to rush the short distance between the car and the entrance. The screaming is relentless, but when someone shouts, "Jethro," it stops me mid-stride. Impossible. There's no way I could have picked out a random name from this screaming frenzy. I continue my way forward, and just when I'm about to walk through the double doors, I hear it again. "Jethro!"

One glance from Lucas and I think maybe, just maybe he heard it too. We don't have time to investigate so we keep on walking. I've no doubt I'm as white as a ghost. That's to be expected when you hear a voice that's been haunting you for over thirteen years.

My legs feel like they weigh a hundred pounds as we

make our way backstage. This was not my idea, but the illustrious Quinn wanted us to do a photoshoot for the benefit concerts, so here we are. I have no idea how the press found out about it. Apparently there's a snitch somewhere in this building.

We're led into a room with four chairs and makeup artists ready to go to town. Great, I love looking like a clown.

"Can I get you something to drink?" Now that's a loaded question.

"A bottle of Jack would be great," Lucas snickers. We both laugh like a bunch of teenagers. Wasn't meant to be funny, but sure as hell came off that way.

"I can offer you coffee, tea, soda or water but that's all we have." We all decline since we want to get the hell outta here as soon as possible.

One long and boring hour later, we're positioned in front of a blue screen. Apparently they can stick a pic in the background of any city they want. Which will happen when we play in that city. It was Quinn's idea, one of her better ones.

They take a zillion pictures of the whole band, then individual ones. Then some of just me and Lucas, the list goes on and on. Four grueling hours later we're being escorted out the door. All I want is a cold beer and to wash this shit off my face.

As we rush back to our limo, I'm dead last. The crowd has thinned out and security is grateful. I'm halfway to the limo when someone screams loud enough to be heard over the crowd. "Jethro, it's been too long." I bump right into Lucas as he scans the crowd. This time, I know he heard it too.

Turning around, he gets in my face. "Get in the fucking limo. Now!" I don't have a chance to tell him he has a better chance of seeing god.

Security's not happy when I break the line and stalk towards the crowd. Funny how they're screaming in their little walkie-talkies as I scan the crowd. I'm oblivious to what's going on around me as I look from left to right. I'm focused on one thing and one thing only.

Him. If he's here, I want to see the fucker.

"Jet, get in the limo, now." Oh, now Quinn, my boss, wants to take control again. She makes the biggest mistake she can when she grabs my arm. I lose my fucking shit.

I'm ready to jump over the damn barrier when I see him. How I can pick him out of a crowd this size is beyond me, but I do. The years haven't been good to him, but when you're a filthy sinner, they never are.

Instead of getting lost in the crowd, he slowly walks over to where I'm standing. No fear and no shame. The only difference is now I'm not a child but a man. Doesn't mean my heart isn't erratic and my palms sweating, but I've been waiting for this day for forever.

It's impossible for us to see each other eye-to-eye since he's six inches shorter than me. I like the idea that he's the one who needs to look up to me after all these years.

He's a predator, molester, and the bane of my existence. My ruin.

"Jethro, how's it going?" He's goading me because I know nothing would please him more than if I hit him with a bunch of witnesses present, so he could sue me. Not happening. I suddenly decide that it is best to ignore this piece of shit and move on.

"My name's Jet Turner, you must have me mixed up with

someone else." I turn to walk away and everything in me wants to kill the motherfucker. Instead, I concentrate on the faces of my bandmates and make a decision that I'll have to live with for the rest of my life.

Joseph P. Lawless doesn't define me.

"See ya around, Jethro." I've no doubt he will because after all these years, I finally have something he's always wanted. My music.

My whole body's trembling as I crawl into the limo. No matter how hard I try to stop it, I can't. "Here, drink this." I'm grateful when Lucas hands me a glass of whiskey. I don't even care where it came from. I down two fingers in one gulp. The burn brings tears to my eyes, but my body quiets almost instantly.

"Did you know that guy?" Trevor asks. He has no clue just how well I know that asshole, but I'm not going there. Ever.

Lucas covers for me in a flash. "Nah, just another looney tunes looking for something that ain't there."

Everyone starts talking about the shoot and about leaving tomorrow for the second leg of the tour. Me, I just stare out the window, too lost in my own thoughts. Wondering how long it will be before the other ball drops. I should have known that something unexpected was going to drop since things were going too well.

"Is there anything I can do, Jet?" Quinn's Spidey senses are in overdrive and I hate it. Everyone's forgotten about the incident but her. Last time I checked, she wasn't a shrink, a priest, or a friend for that matter. So, I do what I do best.

"Yeah, you can mind your own damn business." Well, that shut her up.

* * *

QUINN

CLEARLY HE'S UPSET, which leads me to believe he lied. He knew that man. Why else would they be staring each other down with so much malice and unresolved hatred? And the fact that Lucas handed him a drink and then squashed Trevor's question immediately. That was all the proof I needed. For today, I'll let his flippant remark slide off my back. But before we leave tomorrow, Jet Turner will learn to respect me or I'll be taking the next flight home. I'm done giving him my all, when he gives me nothing in return.

As soon as the limo pulls into the parking lot, Jet opens his door and storms towards his car. Lucas and Abby are right behind him. Abby loves keeping the peace, so she invites everyone to her place. Trying to cover for the scene that plays out not twenty feet away. Lucas and Jet are in a heated discussion which isn't meant for all of us to hear.

I've never interfered with anyone else's personal life, but if I let this continue, either one of them will start the tour with a black eye. Something needs to be done and I've appointed myself the mediator of the group. So the hell with it.

Slamming the door, I stomp over and place myself in the middle of them both. I know better than to touch Jet, so I give Lucas a push with the palms of my hands. "Knock it off, you guys. You're causing a commotion which will have security here in a flash if you don't."

I spin around to confront Jet with my arms crossed so he knows I won't touch him. His eyes are wild and manic.

Whoever this man was in the crowd, it has him frazzled beyond belief. "Jet, you're upset. Let me drive you home."

"I don't need anyone to fucking drive me, I'm fine!"

"Bro, you had a glass of whiskey," Lucas says. "If you get pulled over you're fucking screwed and so is the tour. Now either I drive you home or Quinn will."

He stares off into space and I can see his fortitude crumbling. I'm afraid if he stays here any longer, he's going to fold. "Have Willow drive me home."

"No can do. Everyone drank except me and Quinn. Look, if you come home with me and Abby, I promise I won't bust your balls. Sound like a plan?"

"I don't want to go anywhere with you. Quinn will take me home." Well, it's a start, but now I'm worried he'll lose control before I get him home.

I use the key fob to unlock my door and sigh in relief when Jet slides in. The slamming of the car door is proof he's not too happy. Best he's unhappy in the cab of my car than behind bars for fighting in the street. With his best friend. Before I get in, I turn to Lucas and say, "I'm sure he'll be fine once he's calmed down. I'll text you after I drop him off."

"Thanks, but I don't think you driving him home is going to help. He needs to release some of the tension and anger he's holding back. I wish he would have just hit me to get it all out."

"Very noble of you, Lucas. Unfortunately, I don't want any fighting amongst anyone. Talk later."

I'm silent as I slide in, buckle up, and start the car. I don't want to play twenty questions, and with our track record I'm truly surprised he wanted me to drive him. Or that he listened and let me.

The drive doesn't take more than thirty minutes and we've been quiet the whole way, other than the music erupting through the sound system. Pulling up to the curb, I park the car and wait. I really don't know what to say to him. Sometimes it's best not to say anything since I've no idea what transpired between the two. I'm surprised when he's in no rush to leave, so I wait.

He's staring straight ahead when he says, "Can I ask you a question?"

"Of course, anything." I do mean that.

"What would you do if there was someone who wanted to take away the very thing that made you feel alive?" I'm sure he had no idea that I'm an expert on that matter.

"I wouldn't let them. I'd leave, fight, or do whatever I needed to do." After what happened today, I add, "Within the law, of course."

He nods, doesn't speak as if he's mulling everything over. I know he's not drunk, but Lucas was right by not wanting him to drive. Being as upset and angry as he is could have ended in disaster.

"Thanks, I just needed someone to solidify that I'd done the right thing." Okay, and what the hell is that supposed to mean?

"I know we've had our differences and all, but if you ever want to talk, I'll listen. I'm pretty good at it, just ask my friend Nina." He turns slightly, but not enough for me to see those sad blues.

"Good to know, but there's no reason to wake the dead. Nina's lucky, I bet you're a great friend." When he opens his door to leave, I reach over and touch his arm. Then realize what I did. Shit.

I'm surprised when he doesn't flinch or pull away. When

he's halfway out the door, he says, "Thanks for the ride. I apologize for being such an asshole. See ya tomorrow."

My throat is tight and dry and I find it hard to swallow. Closing my eyes, I rest my head against the steering wheel. All I can envision are those homeless kids in that damn alley and Jet being one of them. I'm startled when the passenger door opens and Jet sticks his head inside.

"You okay, Quinn?" I want to be honest and tell him no, but then again I'd need to explain.

"I started with a migraine and I left my medicine at home. I should be fine in a minute or two." That's a lie. Sometimes they are debilitating and I need to lie down.

I'm nauseous when my door opens and Jet reaches inside. "What are you doing?" I slap at his hands as he unbuckles my seatbelt.

"You need me, so I'm driving you home so you can take your medicine. I'm fine, Quinn. Really." He sighs and it sounds so damn loud. "Lucas didn't want me to have my car because he was afraid I'd try to find that man at the shoot. End of." I'm in too much pain to fight him, so when he slides his arm under and lifts me, I lean against him. Then everything turns to black.

JET

AFTER SHE PASSED OUT, I buckled her in and drove her home. I made sure to unlock her door and then came back to carry her into her bedroom. Once she was on the bed, I closed all the shades so it was dark as night. I placed a cool cloth over her eyes, went to the fridge and grabbed water and her pills. Now, I'm waiting for her to wake.

Under different circumstances, I'd be freaking out, but my mom used to have terrible migraines and I took care of her. So, it's not my first rodeo. It's one of the reasons I wanted to bring her home. I didn't want her driving and I'm really fine.

Quinn's not my mother.

I'm confused, pissed, and anxious. I wanted to kill that fucker where he stood and I might have if it hadn't been for my bandmates. The problem with men like him is they're as lethal as cancer. They might lay dormant for years and when you least expect it they come back with a fucking vengeance. I'd bet my life that it's only the calm before the storm.

She stirs when I take off her shoes. Damn, I wanted her to rest.

She's not my mother.

Pulling off the cloth, she tries opening her eyes. "Hey, leave it on. I've got your meds and some water. Can you sit up a little?"

"Jet, I think s-so." I grab the pill that I placed on the table and open the water bottle. Her attempt at sitting up is a fail.

"Here, let me help." Very gently I slide my hand behind her back, lifting her enough to take a drink of water. Then I place the pill in her hand. "It's your Imitrex that was on the kitchen counter." With a shaky hand, she places it in her mouth, then takes a sip of water. Slowly, I rest her head back on the pillow, which I know feels hard as a rock. With a sigh, she falls back to sleep.

No way am I leaving until she's capable of being on her own. Migraines are debilitating. It might be days before she feels like herself again.

She's not my mother.

This is the first migraine she's had since I've known her. I'm feeling guilty since I know for a fact that stress can trigger them. I've been the number one cause of her stress for quite some time now. That's got to end right here and now. She doesn't deserve my wrath when she's been nothing but nice. Which is the problem. Quinn is everything I'm not. Knowledgeable, authentic, and decisive. I have an eighth-grade education and I've been hiding and lying my whole life.

When her cloth slips from her forehead, I grab it and walk into the bathroom. Running it under the cold water, I squeeze the excess water and then return to the bedroom. A part of me wants to relive the days on Palmer Street while I'm doing this, but I won't let it. I'm not in Connecticut anymore. I live in New York and I'm a member of *The Sinful Seven*. I repeat this mantra as I once again place it on her forehead.

Not my mother.

There's a comfortable chair in the corner of the room, so I sit down and pull out my phone. I see a few messages from Lucas and I ignore them. I hate that I'm pissed at myself for doing the right thing. But then another part of me is angry because what if it had been the only opportunity I ever had to kill that motherfucker. After what he's done, he should be dead. By my hand.

"Jet—" In three long strides I'm sitting on the edge of Quinn's bed.

Not my mother.

"How ya feeling?" With the cloth still in place, she reaches out to me.

"A little better. Thirsty." I reach over and hand her the bottle. I'm not sure if she needs help when she leans on a trembling elbow, spilling some as her cloth falls off.

"Here, let me help." Standing up, I slip my arm behind her back and let her lean against me. A few more sips and she's ready to lie down again. She's really weak and that bothers me.

Not my mother!

Once she's back on the pillow, I go into the bathroom to grab a dry towel. When I return she's sleeping again. Dammit. I don't want her to stay in wet clothes. Should I risk undressing her, or leave her like that?

Quinn decides for me when she suddenly sits up and

vomits all over herself and the bedding. Now I have no choice.

"Oh no." When she tries getting out of bed I make a decision.

"Quinn. Don't move. Let me carry you into the bathroom." She's crying and shaking her head, but it's the only way I can think of to keep it contained. Gross, but true.

"Abby—"

"She can't carry you. I promise it will be okay." I don't waste my breath explaining I've done this before.

Not my mother. . .

We make it into the bathroom without incident. Breathing through my mouth is something I learned a long time ago. Can't smell a damn thing like that. I kneel with her still in my arms and place her inside the tub. Now she's fighting me. "I can undress myself, please. Wait outside."

"Not happening, Quinn. You can struggle with your clothes if that's what you want, but you're not steady on your feet so you won't be bathing alone." A moan like a wounded animal leaves her throat, and I know it's because she's so independent and doesn't want to ask for help.

Too bad, 'cause I'm not going anywhere.

QUINN

I CAN'T BELIEVE THIS is happening right now. If I had just paid attention to my body, I would have realized a migraine was just under the surface waiting to strike. My medication is usually on me at all times, but I'd forgotten it on the kitchen counter, exactly where Jet found it. Dammit, I'm angry at myself for being so stupid. Now, he's standing over me like I'm a sick child. His determination just slays me.

"Jet, please. I can do it." When he folds his arms over his chest and shakes his head, I give in. I'm not strong enough to fight him so I unbutton my blouse with trembling fingers. He's right, I'm so weak and I'm not sure if I could stand if my life depended on it.

One by one, I peel the clothes from my body. Thankfully there wasn't anything in my stomach. I'm sitting in the tub when he takes my blouse and rinses it under the faucet in cold water. I want to die. This man who's been a thorn in my side for, well, forever, is cleaning my puke. After he's rinsed my skirt, he glances over his shoulder. "Bra and panties are next, Quinn. Then I can throw everything in the washing machine if you have one." Oh kill me now.

"It's a piggyback kind in the kitchen closet, but you can leave it until tomorrow." Another shake of his head and a finger twirl to let me know he's waiting. Now more than ever I wish Lucas had taken him home. But, if he did, I might still be sitting in my car in the parking lot. Or worse, dead on the side of the road. I shudder at the thought.

"Now, Quinn. You're shivering and we need to get you inside of a hot shower. Pronto." Swallowing the lump in my throat, I pull down my panties, shift my leg, and then lean forward to unhook my bra. I suck in a breath when he reaches out his hand. So, this very humiliated girl gives him what he's asking for. Not funny.

My arms cover my chest and I lean back against the cold tub. It feels good but then it doesn't. I'm so fucked, I know I am. He's going to stalk in here and take control and I hate feeling so weak and out of control. Everyone knows I detest depending on anyone.

My heart's hammering inside my chest when I hear him enter a few minutes later. I'm so afraid to open my eyes as I hear the rustling of clothes. No way, I can't see this man naked. I just can't. Sexy rockstars are my downfall, just ask my ex.

I jump when his breath skitters across my face. Just a hint of whiskey lingers, making me wonder if his lips taste the same. I'm so screwed. Imagine what would happen if I wasn't feeling so out of sorts.

"Put your arms around my neck, boss. Shh, don't cry. I promise this is our little secret. No one needs to know." I do what he asks, and the next thing I know his naked chest is pressed to mine. How is it possible that I'm hot and cold at the same time?

Jet's so gentle as he holds me up while trying to set the water. I'd help but I'm really not capable at this time. So, I let him do his thing and a few seconds later, he turns us around so the water is striking him first. Testing it to make sure it's not too hot. Jet Turner really is a good guy after all.

Once he adjusts the temp, we spin around and now I'm under the gentle pulse of the showerhead. The water is perfect and so is he! I haven't opened my eyes, for fear of what I'll find staring back at me. If it weren't for him still wearing his boxer briefs, we'd be skin on skin. It's evident that he finds me attractive, even in my condition. Under any other circumstances, I'd slip my hand inside those briefs, but this is not the time.

"Hold on tight, baby. I'm going to wash you up now." And he does, every square inch of my body. I should have protested when his fingers glided between my legs, but it felt too damn good and I had no words. Just gasps and moans as

I almost orgasmed over his fingertips. Maybe I did, I don't remember.

The water is turned off way too soon, in my opinion. My arms are wrapped around his waist and my eyes have been opened for a few minutes. How can I not look at his gorgeous body since it might be the last time?

I try to look away when his fingertips trace the contours of my face and he tilts my head to meet his steely gaze. His blues to my brown. Wow, just wow. I could drown in those stormy eyes. "Feeling better?" I nod because I still can't find my voice. If someone had told me this morning that I'd be in the shower with Jet today, I'd have pinched myself to see if it were a dream. And I'm not sick enough to forget he called me baby. Yeah, I got it bad and that's so fucking dangerous.

For a second, I think he's going to kiss me, and then he reaches over and grabs one of my fluffy white towels, wraps it around me, and carries me bridal-style into the bedroom. I'm confused when I notice the bed has been stripped.

"I was going to make the bed but didn't know where you kept your extra sheets." I'm overwhelmed with emotion. Tears threaten to fall but I won't let them. While I was in the tub, he did all of this and even thought to put clean clothes on the chair for me, too.

He rushes over and drops to his knees when my tears spill free. I can't contain them any longer as they tumble down my flushed cheeks. I need to ask. I just do. "Why?" He looks confused. "Why did you insist on helping me today?" I sweep my arm across the room and the towel slips, exposing my breasts to hungry eyes. It lasts a split second, until he hangs his head.

"My mom used to get terrible migraines, and when she did I would take care of her." A snippet of his past and I cling to it tightly. This is the first time in all these months that he's opened up to me. The last thing I want is to scare him away with too many questions. "She died of a brain tumor when she was thirty-two." I can't even right now. "Please don't say you're sorry. It was a lifetime ago. Sheets, where are the sheets?"

Emotions are swirling around inside of me. I need to buy some time to reign them in since he clearly doesn't want any sympathy. "Sheets are in the hall closet on the top shelf."

14

JET

WITHOUT REALIZING IT, I wrap my arms around her and she does the same to me. We cling to one another and I find comfort in her touch. It's odd, but it feels good at the same time. It's something I've only ever felt with one other person, my mom.

"The only person who knows about my mother is Lucas."

"You're secret is safe with me. I'd never betray your trust, just like I know you're not the kind of guy who would gloat about what happened to me here today." She's right. I might be a dick, but I'd never intentionally humiliate someone just for a laugh. Not my style.

"Let's get you dressed and back in bed. How's the headache?" Trying to pretend she doesn't have an effect on me is impossible. My cock's straining through the wet fabric of my briefs as I peel the towel from her damp skin. She's dressing herself with just a little guidance from me when she stands up to put on her yoga pants.

"It's still there but in the background. The shower was a lifesaver, thank you." I'd love to respond with, "My pleasure," since I was able to touch her in places I only dreamed about. This girl is drop-dead gorgeous and so out of my league it isn't funny. I'm desperate to keep busy since I want to strip her down and worship every inch of her body. Fuck, I haven't craved anyone like this in so damn long.

I take my time switching over the clothes then grab what I need. As I begin making the bed, I watch her struggle to stand. She's so damn stubborn and independent that she hates someone doing something for her. "I swear if you try walking over here I'm going to spank you." Her mouth forms a circle and she sputters something unintelligible. Might be for the best. I'd love nothing more than to mark her tight ass with my hand.

After I've finished, I pick her up and carry her to the bed. Placing her gently on the nice clean sheets. It's all worth it when a satisfied groan leaves her lips. "Thank you. I'm sure I'll sleep the rest of the night. You can take my car and go home, we can swap out tomorrow."

"Nope, not going anywhere. Can I get you some tea, crackers, or something to eat?" I'm asking her and it's not my house so I haven't a fucking clue what's in her kitchen.

"Crackers sound good, but I have no tea. Everything is in the pantry. Grab whatever you want. I'm sure you're starving." I hadn't thought about it but I really am.

"Coming right up. Not only am I a phenomenal dishwasher, but I can whip up a mean snack. Just wait and see." There, a tiny smile proves she's starting to feel better. I can't help wondering if we'll be back to butting heads tomorrow.

Her kitchen is every cook's wet dream. State-of-the-art everything. This townhouse doesn't look too old so that might be why. I thought my apartment was nice but after seeing this, I'm jealous. No lie, but for the amount of time I spend there it serves its purpose. Especially now that we've been on tour.

I grab a fancy tray and cut up cheese and salami, and add some crackers and fruit from a bowl on the table. The salami is for me, Quinn won't be able to digest something so greasy. After grabbing a few bottles of water, I walk back to the bedroom and find her fast asleep. I knew she was fighting it, but she needs to rest. I sit down on my favorite chair and nibble at the snacks I brought. It's just enough to sate my hunger, for food, but not for her.

I'm mesmerized by her beauty, and everything about her. Willow was correct in her assumption that I had a crush on Quinn from the very first day. It was one of the reasons I treated her with disdain. I knew she'd be the type of woman I'd fall hard and fast over, but I refuse to go there. I have absolutely nothing to offer her.

Sometimes loving someone just isn't enough.

A part of me wants to run, the other wants to stay close by her side. Every damn day and twice on Sundays. Something my mom used to say. I never understood why, but it stuck. She was my world and I would have gladly died in her place if I could have. She was a light too bright to be snuffed out so soon. I, on the other hand, only had my music. Even to this day, that's all I'll ever have.

I'm still stunned that I confided in Quinn about my mother's death. Now the three of us know and I kinda like the fact that someone else knows. It's almost as if I don't have to carry the weight of the world anymore. Stupid, I know, since Quinn never met my mom, but if she did, I'm sure they would have loved each other. Maybe that's why I'm drawn to Quinn. She has a radiance about her, too.

Placing the tray on the table, I stride over to the bed and sit on the edge. She's sleeping so soundly, I hate to disturb her. I can't stop wondering how she'd feel if she found me gone when she woke. Relieved, most likely. Yeah, I sense she's attracted to me even though she works closely with other bands. Which is all the more reason to leave, but I've never been good at doing the right thing. So I curl up behind her and pull her close. Her back to my front. We're spooning and it's unlike anything I've ever experienced before.

Just for tonight, I don't need to sleep on the floor. I'm going to sleep beside a woman who accepts me for who I am. The good, the bad, and the ugly. Even if she doesn't know my truth, I have a feeling she wouldn't judge me or treat me any differently. It's going to be a long time before I tell anyone about my past, if ever. I just pray that Joseph P. Lawless doesn't take that choice away from me. Otherwise, I might be on the run just like I was over thirteen years ago.

* * *

Quinn

I'M CONTENT WHEN I wake up to a warm body wrapped around me. It's been so long that I'd forgotten what it felt like to be all tangled up with someone first thing in the morning. Knowing it's Jet just makes it all the better. I thought he'd take me up on my offer and cut and run, but he stayed. Maybe Willow was right. He does like me after all. Which makes me giddy. Forget what I said earlier about being involved with another rockstar. Clearly they're not all the same. And I know Jet's demons don't even compare to anyone else's.

As much as I'd love to stay here longer, my bladder is protesting. The moment I try to escape, his arms grow tighter. "Mm, stay. I'm not ready to get up yet."

Did he forget where he is? He must have because he wouldn't want to snuggle with me in the morning. Morning? No, no, no, I have a meeting at eight. "Jet, I need to go, it's—"

"It's five in the morning. You have plenty of time so just stay here for a few more minutes. Please." I want to ask, "What did you do with Jet?"

"Okay, but only for a little longer. I'm not sure how steady I'll be after yesterday." His eyelids flutter open and I'm greeted with the windows to his soul. Bright, amused, and lustful. I'd like to stay but I got to go. "I need to go to the little girl's room." A big sigh and then he opens his arms wide.

"Hurry back." Um, if I did then I have a feeling we'd both be naked and I'd be riding his morning wood. Yep, how the hell do I unfeel that pressing against my back? I can't and if I'm being honest, I don't want to!

I feel his eyes on my back as I slowly make my way to the bathroom. I'm feeling better, just a bit unsteady. I do my business and when I bend over to brush my teeth, I feel his warmth against my back. Okay, why is he in here with me?

"Not everyone has extra toothbrushes hanging around so I'm just going to put a little on my finger. No biggie." Okay, I admit, I like the fact he's checking up on me. It's nice and refreshing. Opening the top drawer, I grab a pack and hand it to him.

"Thanks. Is this a hint that you have a lot of overnight guests?" I almost choke on my toothpaste.

"No. When they're on sale, I stock up. Not that it's any of your business."

"Touché! How are you feeling?" Without thinking, I cup his cheek. I don't pull away when I realize how intimate this feels, it would be too obvious. I do love the feel of his five o'clock shadow. So soft, you wouldn't think.

"Better. Today, I'll remember to take my meds with me. I have a meeting at eight and then the band has a press conference, remember?" This feels surreal. That's he's in my house and we're talking about the band.

"I remember. I'll need you to drop me off to grab my car, if you're up to it." He looks hopeful and this is huge for me.

"Absolutely, I'll make us some coffee. Take your time." This is where we would kiss if we were dating, but we're not. Does anyone use the word "dating" anymore? Nah, maybe exclusive, hooking up or whatever.

I'm just pouring the coffee into two huge mugs when he joins me. Come to think of it, I don't think I've ever seen him drink coffee. Not like Lucas who's addicted to the stuff. "I'm not sure how you take it, if at all." Oh, that smirk on his face could be interpreted as devious and dark.

"I don't drink it too often, but when I do it's black. Thanks, hits the spot." I join him at the island and we sip in silence. How do you thank someone for coming to your rescue? I shudder to think what would have happened if he didn't.

"Thanks a bunch for doing everything you did yesterday. You went above and beyond and I'm forever grateful that you insisted on staying. You could have easily walked away."

"I'd never walk away from someone who needs me. Well, maybe one person, but that's another story for a different day. You're good people, Quinn. I gave you a lot of shit and I'm sorry, but being on the street has taught me a few things. Who to trust and who not to. You've earned my trust and then some." Well, last time was a kissing moment and this feels like a hug moment. Do they go hand in hand? They sure could, and if it did we wouldn't leave this house. I feel his magnetism down to the tips of my toes.

I need to clear my throat since I don't trust my voice. In less than twenty-four hours, we went from enemies to friends. This is one of those moments that will be forever etched in my soul. Weakly, I manage to say, "Thanks, I hope you know I'd do the same for you."

Staring into the darkness of his coffee, he nods. "Appreciate it more than you'll ever know."

This is getting intense so I need to go. "Grab some breakfast, I'm going to get ready." I practically run into the bathroom. My skin's flushed at the thought that he's seen me naked. And his wet briefs left nothing to the imagination. God, that man is addictive.

I take my sweet-ass time in the shower and I swear I can still feel his fingers sliding through my slick folds. Kneading my breasts while his hot breath scorches my skin. I do believe I did come on his talented fingers last night. Sweet Jesus. How can I go to work with him every day and not fantasize about him? Once the water becomes tepid, I step out and towel off. I need to get a grip, otherwise I won't be able to get any work done today.

I'm floored when I step out and he's folding the laundry

he did yesterday. I could get used to this very easily. "We need to get our stories straight before you drop me off," he says. "I hate lying to everyone but I don't know what else to do."

"I know, and everything I've come up with sounds wrong. I'm not opposed to telling them the truth. As long as we skip the part about the puking and you sleeping with me. We could tell them you slept on the sofa in case I needed you."

"Hey, I'm down for anything. We'll tell them you had a migraine, I drove you home, and I stayed the night with you. On the couch. Perfect. Okay, you almost ready? It's seven and you have a drive ahead of you."

"Let me grab my briefcase and keys and then we'll get going." Jet's already waiting outside when I lock up. He's leaning on the car door with his face lifted towards the sky.

Silent and moody.

When I press the lock, he slips inside and it's back to business as usual.

15

JET

SOMETHING INSIDE OF ME snapped in place after Quinn dropped me off. I have no explanation for the sudden shift, other than spending time taking care of her. It's the reason I went straight home to shower and change instead of meeting everyone at Trevor's for breakfast. I hate to blow them off, but I needed to gather my thoughts and figure this one out. Is it possible I'm starting to care about her, or is everything that's happening related to my mom? Damned if I know, but I promised myself a long time ago I'd never get seriously involved with a woman after what's happened in my past.

I can't comprehend how this woman can be my friend and foe at the same time. We're like two rams butting heads when we're doing band business, and yet when we're alone, there's an attraction that's indescribable. Part of it is physical, there's no denying that, because let's face it, she's beyond beautiful. It's the other connection that's confusing the shit out of me. Maybe it's because she believes in me, in us as a band, that I find so damn appealing. I don't know, and the longer I think about it the more confused I become. Maybe I'm just analyzing it way too much.

It doesn't help that Lucas has been blowing up my phone with tons of messages about yesterday. Not about what went down with Quinn, he has no clue. He's worried about me running into that piece of shit I met the other day! He's afraid if I'm left alone, I'll go after him. I'm not that stupid, especially now that I have so much at stake. No use texting him back since I'll be seeing him in a few hours for the stupid press conference. I'd have to admit that this is the worst thing about being a musician. I get that my life is supposed to be an open book, hence the reason Lucas created that mock interview about me for Quinn. The fans were none the wiser and that's exactly what I wanted. It was a win for both Quinn and me.

Now we can put those damn interviews behind us and move on since *The Sinful Seven* was featured in this month's *Music Report*, with said interviews. They were thrilled they had an exclusive and we can tick off another thing that was on our bucket list. I'm loving the fact that over the last few months we've been able to do just that. It feels great and it's only the beginning.

Since I wasted too much time already, I decide to go for a drive before meeting everyone at the press conference. I mentioned to Mack I'd be late getting to work, and he told me to take the day off. Not sure about that but we'll see how things go after the press conference.

With an hour to kill, I take the Palisades Parkway, kick on cruise control and enjoy the scenic drive. I have a lot of fond memories on this road since it's the route Mack took me on when he first taught me how to drive. And the same route where I almost killed the both of us when I didn't use the brakes rounding a curve. I can't help chuckling when I think about the look on his face once I got the car under control. I swear he peed his pants. I almost shit mine but he didn't yell at me. In fact, he thanked me for not killing him since he had no clue how I pulled out of it. Looking back, I think I had an angel sitting on my shoulder whispering in my ear, "It's not your time. You can do it." Yeah, I feel her presence with me ever since I left the asshole in Connecticut. My mom's been my guardian angel through it all. Every step of the way. It's not like a warm hug and a soft kiss on my cheek, but it's as comforting as it can be until we meet again. Love you, Mom.

Before I get too sentimental, I turn the car around and head back into the city. I'll only have minutes to spare if the traffic is light and I don't want my sexy PR agent getting her panties in a bunch if I'm late. Not going to lie, thinking of her panties in a bunch or in a heap on the floor makes my cock throb. Yeah, I saw her fucking naked and it took every ounce of willpower I possess not to touch her the way I wanted. She was sick, but I'm only human and my cock didn't know any better. Quinn is perfection and I'm just the opposite. I need to stay away before my darkness rubs off on her.

I'm relieved to see Lucas's car when I pull into the parking lot for the conference. It's not that I need someone to hold my hand, but there's strength in numbers. Especially since I hate the media with a passion. It wouldn't be so bad if they told the truth, but I know how they love twisting everything around to sell a story. I've seen it so many times that I lost count. One of the reasons I want to stay under the radar. The second you grab their attention they swoop in like vultures and rip you apart.

Lucas raps on the window before I come to a complete stop. Great way to get hit by a car. "You good?"

I slide out and slam the door behind me. "Yeah, no worries. I told you I'm not going to do something stupid."

"I'd like to think you won't but I can't imagine what was going through your mind when he called you out. Just knowing his fucking MO made me want to clock the fucker. Abby had to hold me back and she doesn't know the half of it."

"And let's keep it that way, too, Lucas. I know she's your woman and everything but it doesn't give you the right to tell someone else's story."

"Bro, I wouldn't do that and you know it." Yeah, I do, but I needed to throw it out there. I just bump his shoulder as we all walk inside. Oh joy, we're here.

Filing into that room is daunting since all eyes are on us. I'm not stupid. I hear some of them snickering and whispering as I pass by. Oh gee, I wonder why? I'd much rather be playing on stage in front of a thousand adoring fans than under the media's scrutiny. They've all been warned ahead of time: no pictures before and during the conference. I know their fingers are itching to get a few in and I'm surprised they're actually listening.

We all take a seat, and by the time Quinn walks into the room twenty minutes later I'm ready to walk out the fucking door.

* * *

QUINN

I'M HYPERVENTILATING AFTER Caleb handed me the list he compiled with all of the bands who have agreed to do the benefit concert for the homeless. I'm humbled that so many would come forward and give their time for such a worthy cause. Some are big-name bands that have been around for years. One of them being *Rebel Riot*, which is the reason I can't catch my breath. My ex-husband's band. It's suspicious that they would bother with something of this nature, unless he found out that I'm *The Sinful Seven's* PR agent. Which he very well could have since it's public knowledge. Hell, all anyone needs to do is pop my name in a search engine and it would be linked with theirs.

"You're white as a ghost, is everything all right?" Caleb would have to point that out. Now all eyes are on me and I need to cover my tracks.

"Couldn't be better. I'm just overwhelmed that so many bands are kind enough to help us out. Then again, I knew that the American Organization of Musicians would pull through. They always do."

"Absolutely, and they also know that if the time ever came we would reciprocate. It's how this community comes together. When someone has a call to action, they answer that call. Now, let's get ready for the press conference, shall we?"

Folding up the list he gave me, I tuck it into my briefcase. I'm sure the band will be ecstatic when they see it, especially Jet. I won't begrudge them their reactions either, it is a very good thing. I'll just need to leave my feelings at the door and get through that night as best I can. Thankfully it's going to be one of the last concerts for the event. Ending the tour in LA will give us plenty of time to get home and for me to recoup. If luck is on my side, I won't have too much interaction with Zander Stone.

I paint a smile on as I walk into the conference room. The band is already sitting in wait of what's to come and by the look on Jet's face, he's not happy. Well, it's part of the job so he needs to take the bad with the good. Since there's only one seat available and it's next to him, I take it. The press has been warned, no pictures before the conference begins, and it looks like they're adhering to the venue's policy. Good. Leaning over, I say, "Everyone ready? We're about to start."

One by one they acknowledge me, except Jet. Okay, so is he still acting like we don't get along? I don't know, but now's not the place to get into it. As soon as the wall clock strikes ten, the reporters' hands go up and their cameras flash.

The first person I choose, a reporter with WMBC, asks, "Jet, I was there yesterday when there was a confrontation between you and a man in the crowd. Care to explain?" Damn, is this the topic everyone is going to focus on?

"No confrontation, just a case of mistaken identity. Next question." I'm stunned, so proud that he kept a level head and squashed the question.

"Is it true that Jet had the idea to start the benefit concerts after the scheduled tour?" We agreed last week that I would take all the PR questions.

"*The Sinful Seven* is a team effort, and when there's a disparity they always go with majority rules. Next question?"

The press conference lasts an hour and other than the very first question, all goes smoothly. All of these band members are professionals and I couldn't be prouder of them. They deserve a celebration and then I can go over the list of bands that are on board. So far, twenty signed up and that's amazing.

"Let's go celebrate," I say with a smile. "I have something I want to share with all of you." Jet seems to be in a better mood, joking around with Lucas just like they used to do. Makes me happy that whatever differences they had, they were able to work them out. "You guys can pick the place since this is all about you. We need to let our hair down before we leave for the tour day after tomorrow."

They eventually agree on the *Hungry Dog Diner*. It was Trevor's idea and once again Jet looks uncomfortable. Crap! I quickly try and recover the situation. "I'm sorry to be a Debbie Downer, but I'm not feeling a greasy burger. I'm in the mood for Italian, anyone else?" Abby's like a little kid and soon Willow joins the crazy train. Before you know it, Lucas likes the idea. So, *Al Forno* it is.

Since we all came separately, we decide to meet each other there. Jet lingers longer than the others. Only the two of us remain in the parking lot when he saunters over like a tiger stalks his prey and pins me against the car door. "This is the second day in a row that you've saved me. If I didn't know any better, I'd swear you like me."

He would be absolutely correct in his thinking. "I'm just helping out a friend, that's all. And for my own selfish reasons." The way he's staring at my lips is making my heart palpitate. I'd love to fist his shirt, pull him close, and crush my lips with his.

He's a breath away when he responds, "What selfish reasons, Quinn?" I lose all train of thought when he captures my response and his lips possess mine.

"We should get going," I whisper against his lips because his kisses tease and tantalize, making me weak and vulnerable.

He groans and I can't stop the grin spreading across my face. "Going to dinner is the last thing I want to do, but I'll meet you there."

LUST

*"The **Lust** for comfort murders the passions of the soul."*

Kahlil Gibran

16

JET

MAKING SMALL TALK TONIGHT while Quinn sits across from me is absolutely insane! Especially when she keeps touching her lips. Yeah, they look a bit bruised because I kissed the hell out of her before coming here. She still feels me on her lips, and I bet she can taste me, too. My cock has been hard since I left her this morning. No easy feat to hide since I've been busy all day. I'd rather be eating her out than sitting in this damn restaurant with a raging hard-on.

Once we finish eating and the waitress has cleared off the table, Quin reaches in her bag and pulls out a sheet of paper. "Okay, so what I have in my hand here is the reason we're celebrating. Caleb gave this to me when we had our meeting before the conference. It's a list of all the bands who've signed up for the benefit. You should all be very proud of yourselves, there are some big names on here. I'll pass it around."

Willow's reading the names out loud and I barely hear a

word she's saying, I'm too busy watching Quinn biting her bottom lip. She only does that when something's really bothering her, so I can't wait to get my hands on that list. She was fine until she pulled it out of her bag. She senses me staring, so she musters up a reassuring smile. Fake, but I'll give her an A for trying.

Everyone's excited by the time I get my hand on the damn thing, and when I scan the page, I'm disappointed nothing pops at me. Yeah, there are big names here, like *Rebel Riot*, *Wicked Immortal*, and *Unbroken* to name a few, but nothing that she should be upset about. Unless she's worked with a few of these bands and didn't get along with them. Now that's a thought. I'll need to do some investigating and see what I can come up with. My very own private detective shit.

Folding it up, I reach across the table to hand it to her. When her fingers brush against mine, I'm instantly hard. Yeah, she's going to be the death of me because after tasting her, I want more. How much I'm willing to sacrifice is to be determined, but I'll have her underneath me before we leave. And that's in less than thirty-six hours. I'm not making any commitments, but we have four months left to this tour. I'll need to shake things up a bit. My days of sharing a room with Trevor are officially over.

"You okay?" I had to ask her because she's too damn quiet. I worry another migraine is coming on.

"I'm fine, thanks. Just tired from the lack of sleep last night." I should have known our conversation wasn't private.

"Oh, do tell why you didn't sleep last night." This coming from the quiet one of the bunch. Willow.

Personally, I didn't mention a word about last night but

I'm not sure if Quinn did or not. So, I wait for her to make the next move.

"My plans to take Jet to his home last night drastically changed." All eyes are on me, like I'm the bad guy. Questions abound. "No, no, no. Stop. He's the one who came to my rescue. I suffer from terrible migraines and it happened right before I was going to drive him home. I passed out in the driver's seat so Jet drove me home and carried me into the house. He ended up spending the night on the couch just in case I needed someone during the night. I'm so grateful he was there."

Abby reaches over and grabs Quinn's hand. "Oh my god, that's so scary. Thank goodness Jet was there to help. I can't even imagine what could have happened if you guys were on the road."

"We could have been killed," I say. "That's what could have happened. Now that we all know about Quinn's migraines, we'll be more aware."

Quinn nods. "I have a prescription medication for my headaches and I'd forgotten it on the kitchen counter. Believe me, it was scary. I'll never forget to throw them in my purse ever again."

Lucas claps me on the back. "Glad you guys are okay. Could have taken a turn for the worse. Sounds like someone's watching out for you." It's not the first time he's made a reference to my mom. He has no idea how she died, I never told him, but he knows she's gone. I didn't feel the need to be specific.

We finish up our dinner by having a few drinks at the bar. It's been a hectic day, and after last night Quinn and I decided to stick to seltzer water. There's too much to do in the next few days to get buzzed, and I wanted to be one hundred percent sober when I go home with her. We all say goodnight in the parking lot and go our separate ways. Except me. I follow Quinn home. Like the stalker I accused her of being.

She doesn't seem a bit surprised when I pull in and park right behind her, but she does appear hesitant to get out. This might make or break our very fragile friendship, but I need to try or it will constantly eat away at me.

I open her car door and reach out. I'd never force her into doing anything she doesn't want to do, but I wouldn't be here if I didn't think the feeling was mutual. Chills dot along my spine when she takes my hand and steps out. "Jet, what are we doing?"

"I can only speak for myself, but I'd like to think it's two consenting adults who want to act out on this attraction between them. Do you feel it?" When she nods, I slam the door closed and press my body against hers while resting my hands on the roof of the car. Caging her in.

"This is such a bad idea—" I don't give her a chance to finish, I lean in and steal a long, deep, intoxicating kiss. I fucking love the way she moans against my mouth as my tongue parts her lips and I dive in for a taste. Sweet with a hint of lime.

My fingers itch to flick and pinch those taut nipples that are piercing into my chest with her every inhale. I can't stand not touching her, so I fist my hands in her hair and give a little tug. Forcing our lips apart. I want to gaze into her lustful eyes and know she's desperate for my hard cock. Which is thick and heavy between my legs, seeking relief. I absorb all the beauty that is Quinn, and fucking love the way her lips glisten from our shared passion. I crave this girl with every breath I take and I scold myself for not being able to fight this attraction between us.

QUINN

ALL OF MY SENSORY nerves are firing off at once, screaming at me to stop! But I ignore those idiots and get lost in the sensation of his mouth. His hungry and needy kisses turn me into a wanton bitch in heat. Wanting more and he doesn't disappoint when he parts my lips and his tongue tangles with mine.

I'm blinded with lust when I feel his cock press into my quivering belly. Right above my mound, which causes me to tremble. Seeking release. When his hands grip my hair and force us apart, I want to plead. To beg him for more. Oh, he knows exactly what he's doing! Taunting me by the way his penetrating blues search mine. Our attraction is electric! Before I can change my mind, I grab his hand and drag him towards the front door. I know I'll regret this tomorrow, but for tonight, I'm going to get lost in this gorgeous man.

I barely have time to close the door when he spins me around and pins me face-first into the wall. And then his hands are everywhere. "I'm going to enjoy undressing you, one piece of clothing at a time. Kissing and tasting every inch of your exposed flesh. Until you're completely exposed and begging me to come."

Good lord, I thought my panties were drenched from his kisses alone, but when his hands slither across my belly, I'm panting. And when he holds my heavy breasts in his hands before accessing my blouse, I want to beg for his cock, now!

Torturously, he unbuttons my blouse slowly, until it flutters around my feet. Leaving me in my lacy bra with my breasts pressed against the textured wall. As if reading my thoughts, he unsnaps my bra, pulls it away from my breasts, and slides it down my arms until it hits the floor. Now, my nipples are free to glide along the wall with every breath I take.

"Two down and two to go." Ah, he's counting and so am I, but I'm not surprised when his mouth latches onto my neck. Tasting and teasing just like he said he would. This is a slow dance and the anticipation is killing me.

My skirt's the next to join the other abandoned garments on the floor, and when he presses his nose against my panties, I moan. "Mm, you smell so fucking sweet, I can't wait to bury my face in your pussy." When he's had his fill, he hooks his thumbs in the waistband and slowly slides them down my ass, thighs, and knees. I'm still wearing my heels, and like most men he leaves them on and has me step out of the panties. Now I'm as naked as the day I was born and just as vulnerable.

"Spread your legs for me, baby. I'm going to lick your pussy until you come all over my tongue." Fuck yes! I eagerly part my thighs and that's all the invitation he needs.

Wrapping his arms around my waist, he pulls me up against his mouth so my ass is sticking out, then buries his face in my slick folds. Oh dear god, I'm holding onto the wall as he impales me in one swift thrust of his tongue. Over and over again until that sensation deep inside my belly throbs and quakes with an imminent orgasm. "I'm going to come. . ."

As soon as those words leave my lips, he removes his tongue. What? No! "Jet, please. I want to come." A chuckle before his warm breath hits my core, and he swipes that magic tongue over my clit. My legs are trembling as he continues flicking his tongue back and forth, back and forth, and then I'm coming with no warning. "Yes, oh god, Yes!"

Once my head clears and the adrenaline from my very erotic orgasm calms, Jet stands up and holds me close. His cock's as hard as granite against my spine, and his jeans are wet from his leaking pre-cum.

"Mm, you taste so fucking sweet just like I knew you would. Now I'm going to do all kinds of dirty things to you, baby. I hope you're ready to be filled with my hard cock." His dirty mouth is going to be the death of me, but what a way to go. "Where's your bedroom, Quinn?"

"Last door on the right." In one swift motion, he turns me around, grabs my ass, and lifts me off the floor. I wrap my legs around his waist and with every bounce of his hips, I feel his erection throbbing against my clit. I'm about to detonate from the friction alone. And as if that isn't enough, his mouth and chin are glistening with my arousal. It's fucking hot!

Never in a million years could I have predicted for one second that when I got dressed this morning, Jet would be in my bed tonight.

He places me gently on the bed, leaning his elbows to the side of my head. "Just so you know, you're not the boss of me in the bedroom. This is where I take control." Leaning in, he slants his mouth over mine and I willingly open for him. And when his tongue seeks mine, I suck on it just like I'm going to do to his cock.

"Fuck, Quinn. I need to be inside you right now." With one hand, he unzips his jeans while I grab his shirt, tugging it over his head. I'm so desperate to feel his heated skin against mine, I'm pushing his pants down his ass as far as I can reach. Grabbing my wrists, he stands so I can finish what I started. Now he's naked and it's a beautiful sight to see.

Taking my hand, he wraps it around his cock and we stroke it together. I dive in for a taste and he quickly reprimands me. "No! It's been so long I'll come down your throat! I want to be buried inside your sweet pussy when I do." Well, I can't argue that. I know he said he wants to be in control and he is, but I let him go and slide my ass up towards the headboard. I spread my legs and hear him growl. It's the most erotic sound I've ever heard.

I'm consumed with desire when he grabs a condom, rips it open, and slides it down the length of his beautiful cock. And when he crawls on all fours and places himself between my thighs, there's no doubt in my mind that I'm falling in love with him.

"I'm going to spend the whole damn night worshipping your beautiful body, so I hope you didn't plan on sleeping." He doesn't give me time to answer when he impales me in one swift thrust while his teeth latch onto my nipple! Orgasm number two rips through me like a tidal wave and I'm riding it out until the orgasmic end.

17

JET

Quinn and I have spent the last few days in bed and now that we're leaving, it's going to be difficult to focus on the rest of the tour. The long days will surely be grueling, and I know when I step off that stage I'm going to skip all the afterparties with the enthusiastic groupies. Since I'm going to be balls deep inside of Quinn every chance I get. That woman already has me whipped and I'll be the first to admit it. I don't deserve her, but for now I'm going to enjoy this thing we have since I know once the tour's over, she'll be moving onto the next.

I'm spending the day catching up on last-minute tasks since we'll be leaving later tonight. I've already called the post office to hold my mail, set up online banking and secured my apartment building by telling the manager I'd be gone for a long period of time. My sleeping bag is once again tucked in a corner inside of my closet. I'm hoping that someday I won't need the security it brings me.

I just finished packing and ready to head over to Trevor's to meet up with everyone when I hear some mail fall to the floor. Like, what the fuck? What part of holding my mail don't they understand?

Bending over, I pick it up and weed through it. As always, there's so much junk, but the last one catches my attention. The name and address are handwritten, which isn't unusual, but there's something vaguely familiar about this one. My hands are shaking when I tear it open and a picture flutters to the floor. I take a step back when a pair of bright blue eyes gaze up at me.

My mother.

What the ever-loving fuck!

I drop to my knees, and with shaky hands I cautiously pick it up. Afraid to damage the delicate photo. I'd forgotten how young and breathtakingly beautiful she was. It hurts my heart to admit that her image isn't as vivid in my mind as it used to be.

Slowly flipping it over, I check the back for a date or for any info on where it was taken. Nothing. I was hoping there'd be something tangible for me to hold onto. My heart's breaking into tiny little shards all over again. It's been too damn long since I've seen her infectious smile.

I miss her so fucking much!

This picture was the only thing in the envelope. No letter or return address, but I'd bet my right arm that the piece of shit sent it to me. It was inevitable after our last encounter that he has something up his sleeve. My main concern is he has my address, and I guard that with my life. Only a handful of people have it, but now that I'm a celeb, I'm sure someone would sell me out for a few bucks. Hands down. I don't like the fact that I'm leaving for a few months and he knows it. He has to, with all the publicity we're getting. Fuck.

Holding the picture against my heart, I close my eyes. Desperately trying to remember the sound of her laughter, or the way her hair floated on a breeze. How happy she was when she received her favorite perfume on her thirtieth birthday. *Gardenia by Elizabeth Taylor*. It was such a sweet floral scent and perfect for an angel like her.

My chest suddenly feels tight. Too many memories and emotions are crushing me, all because of one lone picture. That asshole knew what kind of emotions this would evoke inside me. Exactly what he intended. This is the only picture I have of her and I'll treasure it until the day I die. But I have no doubt that I'll be getting more of these or something else to remind me of my past.

Picking myself up off the floor, I head into the bathroom. Looking into the mirror is a painful reminder that I look just like her, but the person staring back at me is nothing like her. Esme Penelope Lawless was the epitome of everything genuine. She was an optimist and believed that all people had some good hidden inside of them. For some, you just had to dig a little bit deeper. Hence, the reason she married the asshole. My stepfather was a slimy chameleon, and if she only knew what he was capable of, what he did to her teenage son, she would have killed him with her bare hands.

Splashing cold water on my face, I welcome the frigid temp. I'm in no rush to towel off, since it's lowering my body heat so I won't self-implode. With my head bent, I grip the lip of the sink and steady myself. I need to get my shit together before going to Trevor's, but there's one stop I need to make along the way, and it's going to be the hardest of them all. I need to say goodbye to Mack. I'd never forgive myself if anything happened to him while I was gone. Maybe it's because I lost my mom at such a young age, but I cherish the people who are a constant in my life. I'll stop in, give him a big bear hug, and be on my way.

Grabbing the picture, I place it inside my journal where it won't get damaged and zip my duffle. I hope she doesn't mind, but this time Mom's going on tour with me whether she likes it or not.

I grab my bags and walk out the door, optimistic that the next time I return, my life will be changed for the better. That the event will be a success and lives will be a little bit richer because of it.

* * *

QUINN

I'm ALWAYS ON EDGE whenever I'm ready to go out on the road. This time around it's worse, since Jet thinks we're sharing a room. He hasn't said as much, but after what we just did to each other, it was implied. I'm not opposed to it, but I'm worried how all the others are going to feel about the room changes. Mainly Willow, since she was my bunk mate for so long. Now she'll need to get a room for herself because I don't think she wants to be roomies with Trevor. Especially if they hook up with someone on the tour. Things could get messy. I'll just need to wait and see how it all plays out.

Pulling into Trevor's drive is bittersweet. I'm sure after spending time with his mom for two weeks, the last thing he wants to do is leave her again. I don't blame him—I'd feel the exact same way if it were mine. Thankfully, she has amazing nurses with her around the clock.

Cancer sucks ass!

Everyone's car is in the driveway except Jet's. Should I be worried? Is he having second thoughts about what happened with us? If so, I'd rather it be now and not at the end of the tour. Which, if I'm being honest, scares me when I dwell on it for too long. I'll be touring with another band and Jet will be here working on his next album. For now, I'm just going to enjoy what we have going and not think about the long haul. It's the only thing that's going to keep me sane.

I can't help smiling when I walk in the door. The love and energy in this house is so infectious, it's like a warm hug every time I walk in. "Hey, Quinn," Mrs. C says. "Grab a seat and help yourself before these guys eat everything."

Mrs. C gives me a great big hug before sitting down at the head of the table. She adores having a full house and pampering each and every one of us. My chest aches with the thought that this might be the last time I'm here.

"You okay?" When a warm hand settles on my neck, I instantly know who it is. I didn't hear Jet come in because I was too lost in my own thoughts.

"I'm great, how about you?" He looks so sad, but then again he always does. Unless he's buried deep inside of me. Then and only then does he look reborn.

"Doing as well as can be expected." Ok, what is that supposed to mean? I don't need to wonder for long when his hand settles on my thigh beneath the table. Something happened. I feel his body humming with just a touch.

Now that everyone's here, Trevor stands and clicks his spoon against his glass. Immediately, we all quiet to hear what he has to say. "Today, we celebrate. Not only because we're heading out for the second leg of the tour and the benefit concerts, but because of the most important news of all. Mom, Mrs. C to all of you, is cancer free." He hugs her so fiercely, I'm afraid she's going to break. She's all smiles as everyone gets up to take a turn. This truly is the best news, ever. I've no doubt it sets everyone's mind at ease.

Lucas is yelling, "Speech, speech!" So of course she takes the floor as she wipes her eyes. "All of this wouldn't have been possible if not for all of you. Each and every one of you is my adopted child, and only because of the love I've felt from you am I able to celebrate this wonderful news. So, thank you! Not only for taking care of me, but Trevor too. I love you all to the moon and back a million times ten."

As always, she made a feast for all of us, so while we stuff our faces with fried chicken, ribs, potato salad, and all the side dishes, we laugh and prepare for what's ahead. No one really knows what tomorrow may bring, but today we celebrate being alive.

Several hours later, we're headed to the airport. Jet's been touchy-feely tonight, and if anyone's noticed, they're not mentioning a word. Might be a good thing since Jet's quiet and I can't wait to get him alone so I can ask what's bothering him. Clearly, something is on his mind.

Trevor drove the SUV so we could throw all our luggage in the back. Sometime tomorrow, Carl will pick it up and take it back to his house. The airport would have charged him a bundle to hold it for all those months. I haven't mentioned anything to them yet, but security's beefed up since Jet had a stalker last time around. It's something we should have done from the start. Better to be late than sorry.

The mood's somber since we all know that we have our work cut out for us over the next few months. I'm sure it will be over before we know it. Something I'm not going to dwell on now or later.

"Heads up before we get on the plane," Jet says. "Quinn and I are together and we'll be sharing a room. You guys can toss a coin or do whatever you need to do, but it's non-negotiable. You might want to call ahead to make sure they have extra rooms." Well, I think it's safe to say no one knew because their mouths are hanging open.

"It's about damn time. I was tired of watching the two of you eye fuck each other all fucking day long. Maybe now Jet'll be in a better mood since he's getting laid." Abby smacks Lucas so hard in the arm, I'm worried he won't be able to play the guitar. "What, I only said what everyone is thinking, Jeez."

"Congrats you two! As soon as I can, I'll call ahead and make different arrangements." Abby gives Lucas the stink eye as he rubs his arm. These two are a trip. Seriously!

We board the private jet that Caleb chartered for us and settle in. Our first stop is in Connecticut for a two-night concert, and then we'll do a 360 until the tour's over. Then we have the charity concerts and unfortunately there's no rhyme or reason to them. It's all good, we have access to the jet so we shouldn't have any problems.

Jet's been holding my hand since we sat down and I wait until after takeoff before bringing up his melancholy mood. "You've been awfully quiet. What gives?" At first, he shrugs like he's going to blow it off, but something changes his mind.

"I wasn't going to mention anything and then you told us that you beefed up security. Tell me the reason. I need to know."

I should have known he'd see right through me. "*The*

Sinful Seven is taking the world by storm, especially with the announcement that we're doing the benefit concerts. I want to do everything I can to protect all of us."

"So it has nothing to do with the crazy guy from the crowd the other day?" Crap, I forgot to mention that.

18

JET

I PATIENTLY WAIT FOR her answer, and if I'm correct in my suspicion, I'll give her my truth.

"My gut feeling is you two know each other and it wasn't a happy reunion, so yes. It's one of the reasons I asked Caleb to send more security."

Leaning in, I kiss her pouty lips. It's not a full make-out session considering we have an audience, but I give her a little tongue. Why? Because I love hearing her moan.

Without realizing I'm doing it, my thumb rubs circles over her hand. I'm nervous, but I need to tell her. "Right before I left my apartment today, I received an envelope. It didn't have a return address or a stamp. Which means it didn't go through the post office. Someone dropped it off at my fucking house." I pinch the bridge of my nose, trying to stifle my temper.

"Oh Jet. I wish you had told me this before we left. What was in the envelope?"

Life is funny. Not in a ha-ha kind of way but in a bite-you-in-the-ass kind of way. The only person on earth who knows about my piece of shit stepfather is Lucas. Well, Mack knows of him but not what he's capable of doing. And I'll take that to my fucking grave. So now I need to tread lightly on how much to divulge to Quinn; otherwise, there will be too many questions that I can't answer.

With our heads close together, I whisper, "A picture of my mom." I can see her wheels turning before she even speaks.

"How did he get that picture?" This is where the shit hits the fan.

"That asshole is my stepfather. I haven't seen him in over thirteen years." Her hand quickly covers her mouth to stifle her outcry.

"This changes everything, Jet. He could have paid someone to drop it off or he did it himself. Either way, he knows where you live. Dammit, I wish you had told me right away."

Well, so much for trying to keep this conversation between the two of us.

"What the hell's going on over there? You guys having your first lovers' quarrel?" Trevor's such an idiot.

Quinn glares at me, and no matter how angry she is at me right now, I know she won't out me. She's leaving it up to me whether I want to tell everyone the truth. Ah, fuck it, I should have waited until we landed and we were in our hotel room.

"I confess, I lied to all of you the other day. I do know the asshole in the crowd. He's my stepfather who suddenly decided to show his ugly mug after thirteen years. It's obvious he has a hidden agenda I don't know about."

"Wow, that's messed up. I bet the asshole tries blackmailing you now that you've made it big. Tell him to fuck off and be done with it." I agree with Willow, and I wish it were that easy. I don't know, maybe it is. It's not like he's going to step forward and admit what he's done. Nope, can't see that happening. Jail time isn't on his agenda, but I wish I knew what his game was. Other than playing cat and mouse.

"I don't think you ever mentioned where you lived while growing up. Might be a good time since you're in the confessional." Lucas quirks his brow since he already knows. I bet he's feeling smug right now.

"We're going to be landing there in a matter of minutes." Quinn swears like a truck driver on the side of me. Guess she's kinda mad I left that part out.

"I don't want anyone leaving this plane until I make sure security is in place at the airport, en route to the hotel and at the damn hotel. He could be planning something, and if you had told me sooner, I could have had everything in place!"

I desperately want to tell her that I don't think he's smart enough to pull something off, but I suppose he could have hired someone. To do what? Kidnap me and hold me for ransom? I highly doubt it.

As soon as we land, Quinn bounds out of her seat and is frantically making phone calls. I'm feeling guilty as hell for not letting her know sooner. Especially now that I know her migraines are brought on by stress. It should be me fixing this damn problem and not her, so I unbuckle and saunter over to where she's standing.

The conversation doesn't sound like it's going well.

"I would have mentioned it sooner, but I was just informed of this myself. Do what you need to do. I don't care if we need to stay in this damn plane all night! Just do your damn jobs!" As soon as she ends that call, she begins another. I want to ask her if I can be of any help, but the daggers she's giving me make me take a step back.

The next call pretty much sounds like the last one. I lose count of how many in total before she hangs up for the last time. I hand her a bottle of water as a peace offering and she grabs it without a word.

"Baby, I'm sorry, I wasn't thinking about the consequences in not letting you know earlier." Yep, a pissed-off Quinn is so not a good thing. I'm in big trouble.

* * *

QUINN

His problem is he's so nonchalant about everything. That's why I'm so damn angry. Jet of all people should realize that not only is he putting himself in danger, but everyone else on this tour. Whether he likes it or not, we need to have a very personal conversation when we get back to the hotel. I have no idea how unstable his stepfather is. All I have to go by is what I witnessed the other day, and if I'm being honest, he was chilling. His state of mind was frantic at best and his eyes showed no emotion whatsoever. Dead.

Everyone is getting restless and wanting off the plane. The pilot isn't happy with this extended stopover, either. Apparently he had plans and now that's changed. All thanks to Jet and his lack of information. He's been trying to apologize every chance he gets, and I refuse to give in. I want him to realize how serious this situation is. I'm constantly worrying all the time that an obsessive fan will try to harm one of them. Never in a million years did I think I'd have to worry about someone's stepfather.

Thirty minutes later, security has informed me that everything is clear. I make sure to compensate the pilot for his extra time, and then I follow my friends into the waiting limo. I release a pent-up breath when I notice that not one single screaming fan or mob is scattered about. Security did what they were paid to do. Now, off to the hotel and some much-needed answers.

Check-in is swift and professional. A welcomed change of pace. Fingers crossed the rest of the day goes as smoothly.

I sure could use a break.

Abby made sure to call as many hotels as she could to make the room adjustments. After everything that happened, I was contemplating telling Jet to keep things the way they are, but then I remembered he just received a picture of his mom before getting on the plane. So I relented, because I can only imagine how he's feeling after being punched in the gut. It doesn't mean I'm going to forget what he did. We definitely still need to talk.

The valet closes the door to our room and Jet has his arms wrapped around me from behind. Oh, how I'd love to lean into him and just forget this nightmare, but I can't. Not yet.

"Baby, I'm so fucking sorry for creating all these problems. I wasn't thinking of the domino effect that this would cause. Not only for you but for everyone. I'm worried about you now. How are you feeling?"

I hadn't thought about how I'm feeling because I had too much to do. Now that I'm in the moment, I feel the pinch behind my eyes. Damn, a migraine is the last thing I need right now. "I'm on the edge of a headache. Could you bring me some water?" A curse and a soft kiss to my crown and he walks off to the mini bar to grab my drink. I fish in my purse for my pills so I have them at the ready. Our eyes meet when he unscrews the cap and hands it to me. Oh, those sad and boyish eyes will be the death of me.

After taking a pill, I grab his hand and lead him to the sofa. He sits down next to me and immediately pulls me in close. "With everything going on, I didn't have a chance to ask you how you're feeling. It couldn't have been easy seeing a picture of your mom."

"After everything I put you through, you're worried about me? Why?" Ah, this man is breaking my heart.

"I care about you. It's the reason I was freaking out after you told me. I don't want anything to happen to you or anyone else."

"I'm really sorry, Quinn. And to tell you the truth, I don't think my step is dangerous. Not anymore, since I'm no longer a naïve child where his threats frighten me. If anything, he's probably afraid of me because if my secrets were revealed, he'd be in jail. If I had to take a guess, I'd say Willow hit it head-on. He's thinking dollar signs and I wouldn't be surprised if he tries blackmailing me. With what, I have no idea."

"It's possible, but I still want to take every precaution. Tomorrow's our first concert and we have many more to follow. I don't want any of you to let down your guard. Even if it's the very last set in LA for the benefit concerts. And I want to ask you questions that I'm sure will make you uncomfortable but I need to know." He's nervous, and I understand.

"All I want to do is peel off your clothing and kiss every inch of your body. Let me make you feel good, baby. Let me make all this shit go away for the rest of the day. Q&A can wait until tomorrow."

He wants to buy a little more time. I get it, so I place the cap on my water bottle, stand up, and seductively remove my shirt. "Quinn, if you have a headache—"

"I'm fine, just sit back and enjoy the show." A slow smile spreads across his face so I toss my shirt right at him. He chuckles, swatting it away. Oh, he's hunkering down for a show, with his arms stretched across the back of the sofa. I'm going to give him a striptease he'll not soon forget.

Turning around, I shimmy and shake my ass while unzipping my pants. When they're loose, I slide them down my hips until my hands are around my ankles. I give him more than an eyeful when I lift one foot and then the other since I'm only wearing a G-string. I've no doubt he got a glimpse of my wet pussy.

Grabby hands lunge for me when I have my back turned. "Oh no you don't. Hands on the back of the sofa. Now. That's better."

In my mind, I'm dancing to *Touch It* by *Monifah* as I bump and grind around the room. His eyes follow me wherever I go, so I decide to use it to my advantage. Grabbing the desk chair, I turn it around so the back of it faces him, then I straddle it just like I'm going to do to him in a few minutes. Then I work that chair as if Jet were sitting there and I was giving him a lap dance. Up and down, side to side, and I grind so hard against that chair, I leave a wet spot from my aching pussy. Fuck, I'm going to come.

Reaching behind me, I unhook my bra and let it slide to

the floor. As I continue grinding against the chair, I grab my breasts and begin pinching my nipples.

Oh, my god!

With a roar, he's off the couch, the chair's on its side, and I'm over his shoulder.

19

JET

I'VE NEVER WANTED A woman as desperately as I want Quinn, and after that sexy-as-fuck striptease, I'm desperate to be inside of her. She reaches for me with half-hooded eyes. "I need you inside me, now." Words that I never thought would leave her lips, and they're all mine. She's a sight to behold all sprawled out on the bed. And, as much as I'd love to taste her sweet cunt, I need to feel her more.

Tearing off my clothes, I grab a bunch of condoms out of my bag and toss them on the bed. She picks them up and counts. "There are seven condoms here. Mighty ambitious of you, Mr. Turner." She has no fucking clue.

I slowly crawl up her body, placing tiny kisses in all her most intimate places. She releases a moan and breathy sigh, so eager, and rips open a foil packet. Well, let her finish what she started. "Put it on my cock, Quinn. I want to feel your hands all over me."

It's my turn to moan when she slips it out of the package

and slides it down my hard length. When I feel the heat from her pussy, I plunge deep inside her. Holding it there, until we catch our breath. And then I begin to move and so does Quinn. I could drown in her little gasps and mews as I capture them with my mouth. "You like it when I'm balls deep inside your wet pussy, don't you?"

"Fuck yes. I'm so close."

"That's it, baby. I want to feel you come all over my cock. And when you do, I want you to do it again!" She rides my dick like she needs it to survive, and I match her stroke for stroke. Pleasing this woman has been my mission since our first time together.

I can feel her pussy contract and I know she's so fucking close! Lifting her legs, I push them up against her chest and piston my hips as fast as I can. Grinding against her clit with every thrust.

"Yes, yes, yes, I'm going to come all over your cock!" And she does with my name on her lips while milking my cock until I'm bone dry and have nothing left.

Releasing her legs, she stretches out next to me like a contented cat. No lie, I swear she's purring. "Be right back, baby." I remove the condom, tie it up, and toss it in the trash. Then I crawl back into bed and pull her close.

We're both exhausted, but I'm not ready to go to sleep quite yet. The second I climb back into bed, she throws her leg over me and snuggles in. Feels nice. Her hand glides over my abs and pecs, and then she works her magic around my nipples. I never realized how much that turns me on until now. Then she slowly begins tracing my tattoos. One by one, starting with my left sleeve. Holding my breath, I wait for what comes next.

"Tell me about your tats, I want to know," she purrs.

Here's the thing. All of my tattoos have a story and a special meaning behind them. For others, they just randomly pick something that's on the wall of the tattoo shop because they look cool. Nope, not me.

"Is this one for your mom?" Her hand strokes up and down my right arm. I wonder if she would have asked about this one if I hadn't told her about my mom's death. Linking her fingers with mine, I nod. "I had a sketch artist create a mother holding onto her toddler's chubby little hand. This is what he came up with. He called it, 'Mother and Son.' I had just received my first legit paycheck at sixteen and it was the best money I ever spent. Now she's always with me."

"It's a beautiful tribute for both of you and I'm sure she would have loved it." Yeah, she would. I know it with every fiber of my being.

"How about this one?" Her hand caresses my right flank, where I have a flock of blackbirds that start at my right hip and fly upward towards my neck and then scatter along my chest and out onto my right sleeve.

"A flock of blackbirds is an omen of good things to come. Bringing joy and good news. I added this one after Lucas and I became friends and we started the band. I had just turned nineteen at the time."

"And this one?" I love how she's taken an interest in my history.

Her hand glides over my left arm where I have a full sleeve of a phoenix on fire. "That's my second one, and I got it on my seventeenth birthday. The phoenix symbolizes new beginnings and if it hadn't been for Mack, I might not even be here today." She stops after three, sensing that I've shared more than I intended. I'll be prepared if she asks again on another night.

She's quiet for several minutes. I'm certain she fell asleep until she whispers, "How did you meet Mack?" I knew it was just a matter of time before the Q&A started. Especially after just telling her about my tattoos.

A part of me always wondered if I was brave enough to confide in a woman, that there might be a slight chance I could break my binds and I'd be set free. And you'd think after exposing myself to thousands of screaming fans like I did last night that I'd be able to open up to the woman I love. Since she brought it up, maybe it's best to put on my big-boy pants and get it over with. They say there's no time like the present.

"I was walking down the alley by the diner when three guys jumped me. One of them grabbed my guitar and the other one held me down with his foot. They were mean fuckers, and I knew in a split second that either I do what they wanted or I was dead. Some would have chosen death, me, I'd already been to hell and back. And those fuckers had my guitar!"

"The dude lifted his foot off my chest, while the other two brought me to my knees. Then he dropped his pants. I was seconds away from being forced to give this guy a blowjob when I heard a crack, a scream, and then gunshots. The fuckers ran off while I fell to the ground covering my head. I admit, I was afraid of getting shot more than anything."

"It was the first time I heard Mack's voice. "You okay, boy? Did they hurt you?" I couldn't speak, because truth be told I had no clue if he was friend or foe. Until he picked me up, brushed me off, and handed me my precious guitar. That was the day I became acquainted with the *Hungry Dog*

Diner and befriended Mack Blythe. It changed my life forever."

* * *

QUINN

MY HEART SWELLS WITH every little scar this incredible man rips open for me. He despises pity, and without realizing it, he seeks forgiveness for his stepdad's abusive behavior. When in all actuality, he needs to forgive himself. What happened in the past wasn't his fault. He was just a child! There's no way I could have done what he did and venture out on my own. Regardless of the circumstances, I would have turned around and gone back home. Not Jet. His past made him strong and resilient.

"I'm sorry, that was too much information. I warned you that you might look at me differently if I shared my truth." What?

"I'm in awe of you, Jet Turner." Sitting up, I take his face in my hands. "In fact, I was just thinking how brave and determined you are. You ventured out on your own to get away from your stepdad. That took so much courage! There's no way I would have been brave enough to do what you did."

"You'd be surprised what you're capable of under the circumstances, baby. In my situation, I was safer on my own than I was staying in that house for a minute longer."

"How old were you when you moved in with Mack?"

"Around fourteen and change, but I didn't permanently live at the diner. It was Mack's intention but I had too many friends on the street. I didn't want to leave them vulnerable and all alone. My busking kept us fed on most days and when it didn't, I made sure they had something to eat. We were safer together than alone, so how could I abandon them? It could have been any one of us that Mack saved that day. The way I look at it, better me than any of them. I used the room when I needed it and so did some of the others. As we got older, we drifted apart and moved on."

I can't even right now. Bending down, I kiss his parted lips. I just need to taste his pain and wish I could take it all away.

He's so selfless.

"Quinn, I did what I needed to do. No big deal." He wipes away the tears that I can no longer hide. The thought of all the children still on the streets just makes me so terribly sad. That society allows this to happen makes it that much worse.

"You make it sound so simple when I know it had to be one of the hardest things you've ever done." Shaking his head, he brushes his lips with mine.

"Staying in Connecticut after my mother died was by far the hardest thing I've ever done. And if I had left at that time, I wouldn't be so fucked up today. Let's change the subject. Tell me about your family. Okay?"

"Of course. You already know I have five brothers, so let me see. My parents have been married for almost forty years, and my mom will tell you that out of all of her children I was the most difficult. Don't believe a word she says. I was a saint compared to her boys, but they'll deny it as much as her. Claiming I'm high maintenance and that's so not true. Look at me! I'm a train wreck. You can attest to that since we've been on the road together."

"Baby, you're the furthest thing from a train wreck that

I've ever seen. You're gorgeous, whether you're dressed to the nines or lounging around in sweats and a T-shirt. Your family's just busting on you because they love you. It sounds like you have the perfect family, embrace it." Yeah, now I feel like shit but I know I shouldn't. I know Jet's not jealous. Perhaps a bit envious. He has every right to be, but I'd wager even if he grew up in an amazing family, he'd still be the same wonderful man he is today.

"Well, thank you for the compliment. Much appreciated. You might be biased since you're fucking me and you need to tell me that or else." He swoops in and starts tickling me, and then it's game on!

"Stop, stop, you can't just pounce on me without a warning." I'm laughing so hard that I swear I'm going to pee the bed, but he won't let up. "Jet. . . Oh god!!" No fair since I can't do the same to him.

"I'll stop if you promise me one thing. Quinn, you need to promise me."

At this point I'd promise him a million dollars or the moon if he'd stop. "Yes, anything! Gah, STOP!"

He pins my hands to my side so I can't retaliate, and now I'm crying since I was laughing so hard. I start squirming because I really need to pee, but he's so damn serious that my heart begins pounding.

Leaning his forehead against mine, he begs. "Promise me, no promises. Can you do that for me, baby? No promises."

Dear lord. I'm going to start crying for real this time. I can tell for whatever reason that this is important to him. Swallowing down the lump in my throat, I do what he asks. "I promise, no promises, Jet." I bite the inside of my cheek to stop the floodgates from opening. "Now, I really need to go to the bathroom.

"Thank you, Quinn." A soft kiss to my trembling lips and he releases my hands. I bound out of bed faster than a fifty-yard dash. Once I'm safely inside the bathroom I let my tears free. I get that he's afraid of commitment and he has trust issues after what he's lived through, but the timing just sucked.

No matter how hard I try with Jet, I always feel like I'm taking one step forward and three steps back.

20

JET

TONIGHT, WE PLAY TO another sold out crowd. Adrenaline's running high and I hate that it's difficult to see the crowd with the overhead lights. I can't help wondering if someone out there recognizes me. Or if Joseph is here. It's doubtful, but it's been niggling at me since we landed. My only hope is we're playing miles away from where I lived, so I try to tamp down the anxiety pulsing through me. Tonight I need to be present, not in the past.

We're waiting to go on stage when I steal a last glance at Quinn. She's all business, talking into her headset, and I know she's worried that we're in my home state. She didn't mention it in so many words but she hinted at it. I've no doubt she's talking to security and asking a million and one questions. Never resting until they answer each and every one. I should know, she tries to do the same with me. I used to resent it and get pissed off, now I know she does it because she really wants to know. Who knew I'd fall head-first for an older woman? She'd kill me if I said that out loud since we're only two years apart. "Age is an issue of mind over matter. If you don't mind it doesn't matter." A favorite quote of mine.

Lucas bumps my shoulder since I'm deep in thought. "Hey man, you good?"

"Yeah, I am. It might have something to do with a certain someone, ya know?" The bastard chuckles and I'm waiting for an "I told you so," but it doesn't come. Smart guy.

"Quinn's good people and she has our best interests at heart. Especially yours. Don't fuck it up." Now that's the Lucas I know and love.

"Talking about me when my back is turned?" Quinn asks. I smile, like from ear to ear. This girl just gets me in the feels.

"Damn, you caught us! I thought your ears would be ringing." She stands on her tiptoes and plants a sexy wet one on my mouth. Tease!

"Break a leg, you guys." Yeah, she's including all of us but she only has eyes for me. Not going to lie, it's intense.

I sneak in one more kiss when Jeff begins the countdown. "In, five, four, three, two, and go—"

Taking our marks, we wait for Trevor to tap out a beat. When he does, Lucas screams, the lights come up, and we play *Distraction* just like every other concert. The crowd's singing and dancing, and as always the girls try crowding the stage and breaching security.

In the beginning, I loved the attention. There's something about the fans screaming your name that makes you feel powerful. Now, not so much, and my only explanation is I have Quinn. Someone who believes in me and accepts who I am and where I came from. It's the happiest I've been in a really long time. Something I never thought possible, but like everything else, it has an expiration date. I'm not going to dwell on that, I'm just going to enjoy the time we have together.

One song bleeds into the next, and for hours we pour our hearts and souls into our music. Giving our fans everything they paid for and then some.

When we sing the last song of the night, the crowd goes wild. They're standing, stomping their feet, and singing the lyrics right along with us. It's mind-blowing, intoxicating, and something none of us will ever take for granted as long as we live.

After we sing the last note, Lucas screams, "Thanks for coming out to party with us tonight, you guys fucking rock!" We take our bows and run off-stage, only to run back out for a few encores.

We're exhausted by the time we're backstage, yet our endorphins are kicking in for round two. I'm not sure if everyone else is going to the afterparty, but I know I'll be passing since Quinn and I have a private one of our own.

With several encores, I might add.

QUINN

I FEEL LIKE A CAGED animal as I pace back and forth, waiting for the other shoe to drop. It's stupid, I know, to always think of the worst-case scenario but I want to be prepared. Then I keep asking myself what are the chances that his stepdad would be here tonight? Yes, he might live in Connecticut but Jet wasn't forthcoming with which city. It's so frustrating that he still can't fully open up to me, but my mantra as of late has been to take baby steps. Every day gets a bit easier for him and I'm confident it's because I'm no longer pressuring him for answers. All good things in due time.

Security is tight and I really shouldn't be worried. Maybe I just need to let them do their job so I can do mine. I should be concentrating on everything that I need to get done over the next few months. Easier said than done, but it's time I realize that some things are just out of my control. My time is better spent on the PR side of things.

"Hey, you okay?" Abby always seems to know exactly when I need to be reassured.

"Just a lot on my mind, you know? Kind of worried about the next few months, if I can pull it off."

"Girl, you got this! You've done amazing things with these guys and I know for a fact that Lucas is always singing your praises. They're so lucky to have you."

"Aw, you're so sweet, Abby. I'm going to miss all of you when this is over."

"What's that supposed to mean? Tell me you're not leaving when the tour is over? What about you and Jet?" Oh, crap. I think I just put my foot in my mouth.

"Nothing's written in stone, but I usually move on to another band when it's over. Caleb hasn't mentioned anything different so I just assumed. Maybe I should have inquired before mentioning anything to anyone. Jet and I never talked about being exclusive so I'm not sure about that." Okay, Quinn shut your mouth right the hell now.

"I for one hope to hell you stick with us for good. If

that's what you want, of course. I can't imagine starting over with someone new. Now I'm really freaking bummed."

"We still have four months to go, so no worries. In fact, I'll get it straightened out as soon as possible so we all know going forward. I'd appreciate it if you didn't tell the others. I don't want them to worry about me leaving when they have to concentrate on the rest of the tour."

"Mum's the word. There's no sense in worrying everyone over something that might never happen." She gives me a big hug and walks away. Waiting for Lucas to get off the stage.

One more encore and the guys bound down the steps. Smiling, sweaty, and pumped up on adrenaline. Which is a very alluring combination. I don't need to wait very long before a sexy rockstar saunters over and sweeps me off my feet. I want to protest, but when Jet's mouth finds mine, I surrender and wrap my legs around him. With his long strides, we're in his dressing room and he's kicking the door closed.

"Missed you, baby," he whispers against my lips. "I've been dying to taste you all night long." If he keeps talking like this, I'll never be able to walk away.

My hands are fisted in his slick hair as he nips at my jaw, my neck, and everything in between. My ass hits the hard surface of the dressing room table while his hard cock presses against the fabric of my jeans. Causing an intense friction that sends shivers up my spine. Making me wet and needy, ready to be penetrated.

"Jet, before we get carried away, I need to meet with—"

"The only meeting you're having is with me and my cock. Got it? The rest of them can wait." He groans when there's a knock on the door.

"Go away. I'm busy trying to get laid in here." I smack him really hard on his arm and he chuckles.

"Bro, open the damn door or pull up your pants, we're coming in." Bloody hell, Lucas is going to get a beating.

Jet and I both groan as the door opens, but it still doesn't stop him from ravaging my mouth. "Put me down, we can continue this later."

Jet looks like he's in pain and he might be with the bulge he's sporting in his jeans. He slowly slides me down his body and places me directly in front of him. Hiding his erection. These guys aren't stupid so it's like a flashing neon sign.

Willow walks over to pick up something off the floor. "Here, this fell when you picked up Quinn."

Jet reaches out to take the envelope, then freezes.

"What's wrong? Jet?"

"This has the same damn handwriting as the one that was delivered to my house." Before I have a chance to take it from him, he rips it open. I don't need to see what's inside because the pain is written all over his face. His mom. "I'm going to kill that motherfucker!"

Luckily, I still have my headset around my neck. Turning it back on, I scream. "Send in the head of security. I want to know who the hell had access to Jet's dressing room. Find out, now. Someone was in here while we were backstage. I want answers, like yesterday."

A team rushes in almost immediately and Brett is front and center. "What's wrong? I swear my men were guarding the perimeter and the only ones allowed in here are you and the band."

"Bull-fucking-shit, Brett," Jet fumes. "An envelope was

sitting on top of my table, and I can guarantee you it wasn't there when I left to go onstage."

"Impossible! Is it a threat? A letter? What's inside?" When he reaches over, Jet refuses to give it to him.

"You need to give it to him, Jet. He'll dust it for fingerprints. We need to know who's terrorizing you."

WRATH

*"**Wrath** can't be ignored, so I patiently wait for the time he gets what he truly deserves."*

Jet Turner

21

JET

WHAT AM I SUPPOSED to do? All eyes are on me. If I refuse to give it to him, I'll look like a fool for flying off the handle in the first place. Dread hits the pit of my stomach as I reluctantly hand it over. Now it's just a matter of time before everyone learns my truth and there's no going back. I can feel it in my bones.

Quinn wraps her arms around me as Brett slips on some gloves. "Too little too late since it's already opened and my prints are all over it." He looks furious, but there's nothing I can do about it. When his gaze meets mine, he hesitates. My mind's racing as he gently pulls it free. He won't hand it to me, so he holds it up for everyone to see. Fucker!

It's a picture of me and my mom and I'm holding my guitar.

All of my bandmates are in this room, but you can hear a fucking pin drop. That's how quiet it is, with the exception of my irregular heartbeat.

"Jet, do you know the people in this picture?" I nod, because I can't speak. It feels like I have a hand around my throat, squeezing the fucking life out of me.

"It's a picture of Jet and his mom." Quinn is just guessing, but she hit the nail on the head. I'm sure she would have never known if I hadn't told her about the first picture I received from the asshole.

"That fucking asshole!" Lucas is pissed, and he'd be the only one who would know. Not that he's ever seen any pictures, but he's listened to my stories and he knows my truth. His hand lands on my shoulder and he squeezes it.

Blood brothers for life.

I swear if I keep staring at that picture, I'm going to lose my shit. Quinn senses my mood and change of atmosphere. Thank fuck.

"Guys, I really hate to ask you all to leave, but could we have a minute or two? Please." The only one who knows my mother died is Lucas, so my friends don't truly understand the magnitude of this picture. Or the feeling and emotions that are assaulting me. My mom gave me that guitar when I was ten years old and she died a year later.

After everyone leaves and it's just Brett, Quinn, and me in the room, he asks, "Any idea who could have done this?" Seriously? He's the head of security and he's asking me?

I'm pissed so I do what I do best. I pace. There's no way I can sit still with everything that's running through my mind.

Quinn tries her best to be the middleman. "We suspect his stepfather, but if what you say is true about who has access, then we don't have a clue." She turns to me and I shake my head, because I really don't know who these pictures belong to. I've never seen them before.

"All our staff has been vetted, and I interviewed all of them separately. I can assure you that no one else is allowed in here. No one. Not even the lighting, sound, or the staff can come in this room. They have no need to since their jobs are out there, setting everything up. I'll need to take the envelope and the picture with me so I can do what needs to be done."

"Do what you need to do, but I want it back once you've finished." My voice sounds raspy and rough from singing for over two hours. I'm also dying of thirst. Water won't do, so I walk over to the mini bar and pop open a bottle of Jameson. That will do the trick.

"I'll keep in touch. As soon as I find out anything, I'll let you know. We'll find out who's behind this, it just might take some time." With that, he walks out of the room and I collapse on the sofa.

Bottle in hand.

"Jet—" I hold up my hand because I really don't want to talk. There's nothing to say anyway. My past is colliding with my present and I can't do a damn thing to stop it. I should have known that just when I had the world by the balls, it would split apart.

Quinn sits down, but not close. She's giving me space and I'm forever grateful. Ever since my mother died, I've learned to live without a comforting touch or unconditional love. I wouldn't know how to accept it if it was right in front of me.

The last thing I need right now is her pity, but I feel like I do owe her an explanation of sorts.

"I never met my real father. Same old cliché, since he beat feet when she told him she was pregnant. For years, it was just me and Mom living paycheck to paycheck like so many single mothers. But we were happy! Until Joseph P. Lawless came along and swept her off her feet. He filled her head with happily-ever-after's and false promises. In all actuality he was a devil in sheep's wool. She never knew this about her husband, and she died completely clueless about his true nature."

"Brett will let us know once he has some answers," Quinn breaks in. "Do you want to go to the hotel, or the afterparty?" I hate that she's nervous and tiptoeing around me, but all I really want is to crawl inside my sleeping bag in the corner of my room and forget. Which is impossible since this is the first damn concert of many. "We could pick up where we left off?"

"I'm afraid I wouldn't be very good company, baby. I would like to go to the hotel as long as I can take this bottle with me." Quinn's smile is reassuring. I know she likes me but for how long? Once my past is out in the open, there's no way she'll ever want to be with me again.

"I'd give you the world if it would bring you some peace of mind." There's not a chance in hell that she could give me either, but it's sweet that she'd even try.

Standing up, I reach out for her hand. When she takes it, I can't help wondering if this will be the last time.

QUINN

WE'RE QUIET ON THE way back to the hotel. I'm not sure if it's because our driver forgot to secure the partition or if Jet's once again lost in his thoughts. I'm glad he opened up a bit more about his past, but it's vague at best and I've never been good at solving puzzles. If only I were, then maybe I could start piecing the clues together to make more sense.

Jet's been resting his head against the seat on the ride home. One hand clings to mine while the other tips back the bottle, I stupidly agreed he could take it with him. I'm hoping he'll give it up once we're inside or he'll regret it tomorrow.

I'm relieved that the others didn't insist on coming back with us. I convinced them to go to the afterparty to represent the band. The last thing we want to portray is that something is amiss. If one of the staff members does turn out to be Jet's stepfather, then we want to carry on as if it's no big deal. If we show fear, who knows what could happen.

After we pull into the hotel parking lot, the driver parks under the massive awning. We're flanked by security as one of them speaks into his handheld and then opens our door. No one speaks as Jet and I slide out and walk in. More security is waiting and so is the elevator. The both of us step inside and four security men do the same. I know it's necessary, but we are bringing attention to ourselves also.

"Wait inside until we secure the floor." I'm afraid by the time we do, Jet won't be able to stand up. A few minutes later, we're escorted to our door. And of course they need to follow us through after Jet swipes the keycard.

"Let us sweep all the rooms first. Once it's secured, you can go about your business." So professional, and if this situation wasn't so dire, it would be laughable. It reminds me of the movie *Men in Black*. You need to excuse me. I'm tired and edgy.

Another sweep of his hand, an "all clear" in his headset, and we're finally left alone.

"I'm in desperate need of a shower." I'm disappointed

when he leaves me standing there as he walks into the en suite. Thankfully, he placed his half empty bottle on the table by the door.

I wish with all my heart that I could tell him everything's going to be fine, but I can't. If I only knew the demons he was fighting, perhaps I could. Then again, it might be too much for even me to fix. Now I'm kicking myself in the ass for not insisting he hand over that first picture of his mom. As much as I hate it, I need to let security handle this and pray that Jet cooperates with them when they find out.

When I walk into the bedroom, I'm stunned to see Jet standing there. His fists are tightly clenched by his sides and he looks tormented. The room's thick with condensation and I can hear the shower running, so why is he still in here? "Jet, what's wrong?"

"That old guitar was the last thing my mom ever gave me. And that piece of shit used it to his advantage because he knew how much I cherished it! I sold my soul to the devil but I'd do it again, Quinn. In a heartbeat." Oh wow, another piece of the puzzle but it's not enough. It's too vague.

I slowly approach him. He's angry, wild, and perhaps drunk. Hence the reason he's purging his soul. "Did he threaten you with the guitar, Jet? What happened? Talk to me." I break the spell when I reach out to touch him.

"Forget it. Not important, but can you make sure I get that picture back when this nightmare is over?" He doesn't wait for me to answer, he just walks away.

I can't take my eyes off of him as he undresses, steps inside the shower, and gets lost in the billowing fog of steam. In his own way, he's giving me little snippets of his life. If I'm going to figure this all out and help him through it, I need to do what I do best. Organize everything.

Grabbing one of my notebooks that I keep for personal notes, I scribble down what I know so far. His mother died of a brain tumor when he was eleven. Single mom. Stepdad is POS. Runaway at the age of thirteen. What kind of hell did you live through in those two years, Jet?

I'm going to do some private detective work on my own. Now that I have his stepdad's name, I'm going to call in a few favors and see what I can come up with. It's going to be difficult with the tour just starting again but I'll do what I can. I'm desperate to help him since I have a very small window of time remaining.

While the shower's still running, I undress and get ready to throw on a thick fluffy robe when a hand reaches out and pulls me in. Wet, sexy, and now sober, his mouth dives in and devours me. "I need you so fucking much, Quinn."

"I know, baby. Let me make you feel good." When I drop to my knees, he doesn't stop me this time. He groans when I wrap my hands around his thick cock and shivers when I give him a few good pumps and take him in my mouth.

"Fuck," leaves his lips when I start teasing and swirling my tongue around his tiny little opening. Lapping up every drop of his arousal.

I take him as deep as I can, and then hollow out my cheeks and suck. His hips begin to move and I know he wants to fuck my mouth, so I gladly let him. With his hands tangled in my hair, he pumps in and out. I know he's desperate to face fuck me but he's afraid, so I make it easier for him. "I want you to fuck my mouth hard and come down my throat."

There's something so erotic about the water sluicing down my body while he's fucking my mouth. My body's so aroused that the rivulets of water running down my nipples and clit are setting me on fire. I want him filling my pussy with his thick shaft, but I believe he needs this more, and I'm more than happy to oblige.

"Oh fuck, baby, I can't come in your mouth." Oh, he can and he will.

When he slows his pace, I grab his ass and hum. The vibration has him trembling and he has no place to go but down my throat, and he does. Spurt after spurt and I swallow every last drop. Salty and sweet. My two favorite combinations. When he's spent he pulls me up, wrapping his arms around me, and we stand like this until the water runs cold.

22

JET

LAST NIGHT, I GOT stupid drunk and ran my mouth, but it won't happen again. Nope. If I don't learn to check myself, Quinn will figure all of this out and not only will I lose the girl, but everything I worked for over the years. She's smart, and it won't take her long to piece everything together. I'm not afraid of her revealing anything, but I don't trust anyone else in the industry other than the band to keep my secrets. So, no more drinking and more fucking since it will all be over in the blink of an eye. Not something I want to dwell on right now.

I woke up this morning with a headache and an empty bed. Quinn had a meeting and didn't want to disturb me, so she left me with a thermos of coffee and some pain meds. Coffee's not my thing but the meds and the caffeine were exactly what I needed. My girl knows what's best for me, even if I don't.

Is she my girl? She never said anything of that nature and

truthfully neither did I. Perhaps it was just an understanding the first night and it's continued from there. Yeah, I had my fair share of sex, nothing as drastic as Lucas, but I'd like to think I'm older and wiser. It's an ache I take part in but not an addiction. Sometimes I think of what will happen after the tour is over and it becomes overwhelming. Quinn thinks I don't know, but I've heard the others talking about her moving on. Not sure if it's true and I'm too afraid to ask, so for now I'm going to enjoy the time we have together.

Tonight we play the same venue we did last night. It was a two-night stint at *Grand Stadium* and tomorrow we leave for New Jersey. At least this time around, we have more access to Caleb's private jet so we won't need to use the bus again. Which works great for me since trying to sleep with Quinn in the tiny bus bedroom would be impossible. Bunk sex is a no go since I'm too damn tall. The thought does have me chuckling when I think of us in all kinds of crazy positions. Kinda gets my dick hard just thinking about it when I'm busted and Quinn walks through the door.

"What's so funny?" She's smiling and for a split second my chest hurts. Damn, she's so beautiful. I can't believe she wants to be here with me. Then again, she doesn't know the truth and that's like a punch to my gut.

"Just glad we are using Caleb's jet instead of the bus." I need say no more when she starts laughing. Striding over she hikes up her skirt, kicks off her heels, and straddles my lap.

"You're such a perv. You know that?" A little nip on my jaw, and I'm instantly hard.

"Who, me? Nah, you must have me confused with the front man of *The Sinful Seven*. Now he's the perv! Me, I'm only like that around you." Ah crap. I just admitted that she's got me all tied up in knots. Yep, now she has that starry-eyed gaze.

"That might be the nicest compliment you ever gave me."

"Nope, not true. Did you forget that I'm always telling you how much I love your sweet ass and your tight pussy wrapped around my dick?" She punches me in the arm and I'm relieved she doesn't have her gun.

"I haven't forgotten, but that kind of flattery is frowned upon in a crowded room." I can't argue with that.

"So, would you rather grab something to eat, or go for a swim in the pool? Brett said he'd gladly clear it out if you feel like a swim." Damn, she's biting that bottom lip again. Not good.

"It's very tempting, but since you brought up Brett, do you think we should show him the other picture of your mom? It might be a big help in the investigation."

It crossed my mind more than once as I tossed and turned last night. I just hate the fact that strangers get a glimpse into my life but have no business being there. Sounds stupid, I know, but I like having the picture of my mother. Although she's gone, it seems like a violation of sorts.

"I'll make you a deal. If you go skinny dipping with me in the pool, I'll hand it over to him. Balls in your court, baby." Or in her mouth and hands, but I don't go there or she'll punch me in the other arm.

"That's not fair! You're blackmailing me. It does kinda sound nice, but if we go, I'm wearing my bathing suit. No skinny dipping. Got it?" She has no idea that I'm going to pull her skimpy bikini bottoms aside and ram my hard cock into her wet heat.

"Compromise, baby. We can give him the pic when we

go downstairs. Could you call him to let him know while I make a call of my own?"

"Absolutely, and for what it's worth, you're doing the right thing. Once it's over, you'll get them back." Yeah, and they better be in the same condition or some heads are going to fucking roll.

* * *

QUINN

THE POOL WAS VERY interesting to say the least. No skinny dipping involved, but plenty of hot, carnal sex. I should have known that I didn't need to be naked in order for Jet to play my body like he does so expertly. I should be ashamed of myself, but I enjoyed it way too much to care. There's something so freeing about being in the water. Maybe it's because our bodies are weightless and light, much like our inhibitions. Floating and bottomless.

I'm glad Jet talked me into going. Now I'm lighter and not wound so tight. I know I have a tendency to be too professional on occasion, which might come off as being uptight or a prude. In my defense, I represent Morris Music and I wouldn't want to do anything to jeopardize my position. The pool was on my own time and in no way should reflect on my job. So there's that.

The band had their sound check after lunch and now we should be leaving for the venue in about thirty minutes. Everyone gathered in our room afterwards and we've just been chilling and relaxing ever since. Some bands are so dysfunctional. I'm grateful *The Sinful Seven* are like brothers and sisters. They're so in sync that working with them is incredible. I'm going to miss them all so much when it's over.

Not one of them questioned Jet about what happened last night. They trust him enough to know he handled it the best way he knows how. And, if he wants them to know, he'll tell them. As far as I'm concerned, that's friendship at its finest. They give each other space, but if the time ever comes where they need help, they all come running.

Jet and Lucas are in the middle of a heated discussion when there's a knock on the door, so I get up to answer it. If the look on Brett's face wasn't a tell, the envelope in his gloved hands would be. Jet's by my side before I have a chance to call him.

"From what the front desk clerk told me, this was dropped off a few minutes ago. One of my men are checking the footage as we speak. He'll call if they find something. I'd appreciate it if you could wear these gloves before opening it this time around."

Jet's hands are shaking as he slips on the tight gloves and reaches for the envelope. This is going to continue happening every night if we don't find the person who's responsible for this. Two envelopes in two nights and one before he left is not a coincidence.

He swipes his thumb along the seam and it easily rips open. A ragged breath and he hesitantly pulls out a new picture. Two children with identical blue eyes. Twins? "Do you know the children in this picture?" Brett inquires.

"It's me, but I'm not going to tell you her name." What? Why? He gently runs his thumb over her innocent face before slipping the picture inside the envelope.

"If you want to find out who is behind this investigation, then you need to cooperate. Otherwise, we can't help you."

Brett takes the envelope and slips it back inside his jacket while Jet walks off.

"I'm going on stage in a few hours and I just can't deal with this shit right now. You're the PI, you figure it out!" Okay, so what's going on?

"I'm sorry, Brett. I'll try talking to him." I walk off in the same direction as Jet, but Lucas stops me.

"Quinn, let it go. If and when he's ready to talk, he will. Now is not the time. As he said, we need to focus on the tour. All of this is too much for him to process. Give him some time is all I ask."

"I'd gladly give him some more time if I knew everyone was safe, but I don't. It's my responsibility. If Jet doesn't cooperate in this investigation, then I'm going to be forced to cancel the rest of the tour. It's in the contract, Lucas. We can't jeopardize anyone's safety and if I feel it's unsafe, I can pull the plug now. It would be a shit show, but I'll do it."

"Then let me talk to him. See if I can get through because if I can't, no one can." Abby's eyes meet mine as Lucas knocks on Jet's door and walks in.

I'm grateful that the walls are well insulated, since they're arguing back and forth. I can make out a few words here and there, but nothing tangible. Everyone looks distraught so I suggest they all get ready for the concert. Abby lingers, waiting for Lucas. It's just the two of us waiting for the outcome.

"They're both stubborn jerks sometimes, so this could take all day." If she's trying to make me feel better, it's not working.

"It's just hard for me to understand why Jet's so secretive. I mean, I get that he's a runaway and he doesn't use his real name." Oh no, I just let another one slip.

"What's that supposed to mean, Quinn? And how the hell would you know if it wasn't? Did you have him investigated?"

Damn, damn, damn!

"It's not what you think, Abby. As the band's PR agent, it's my job to make sure no one has outstanding warrants, police records, traffic violations, or anything that could hamper the tour. We need to know all of this before moving forward." She's pissed and I get it. I'm not one of them!

I'm about to plead the fifth when Jet storms out of his room with Lucas close behind. They both look pissed and I'm not sure if their wrath is aimed at me.

"We have a damn concert tonight and we need to leave now. All of this is going to have to wait. Let's rock and roll." I'm holding my breath until he links his fingers through mine and pulls me out the door. Relief fills my lungs and I can breathe again. It might be short-lived so I'll worry about it later.

Apparently, Trevor and Willow grabbed an earlier ride so it's just the four of us. Tension is heavy in the air and I've no doubt it's because of me. Abby's silently killing me with her vibe and I'm going to ignore all of it for now. Jet's right. We have a concert and need to focus all of our attention on that.

They finish with minutes to spare and barely have enough time to change before they need to take the stage. This is the most rushed I've ever felt in all my years. It was a close call, not the end of the world. Some bands are an hour late and the agitated fans calm down once they get going. I feel shunned as Abby stands behind the curtain to watch. Normally, she's glued to my side so we can cheer them on, but it won't happen tonight.

Lucas owns the stage as his voice fills the arena. "Hello

Dallas! Let's get this fucking party started!" The fans go wild as they begin *Distraction.*

My headset is quiet for the first thirty minutes, and when it crackles in my ear, I tense. Until I hear, "What? On stage? Take down now!" Adrenaline has me running towards the stage.

Abby shakes her head, points, and then opens the curtain so I have a better view. Some crazed fan, a girl, is being dragged off the stage by security. I guess she wanted a piece of Lucas and it wasn't happening. I wipe my brow like I'm relieved and she nods. I think we're all a bit on edge with everything going on.

I head back to my post and grab a bottle of water. I'm already exhausted and it's not over by a long shot.

23

JET

I'M ON STAGE PERFORMING just like everyone else, yet I feel detached. Like I'm having an out of body experience. Half of me is playing my bass and singing along, while the other half is sitting on the sidelines, watching from a distance. That's the only way I can explain this feeling coursing through my veins. It's kind of how I feel when I want to crawl inside my sleeping bag and forget. It started the minute I pulled that picture out of the envelope. Too many memories that I desperately tried to suppress.

One song bleeds into the next, and for the first time in my entire life I just want this night to be done. Over. Music isn't soothing the savage beast tonight, and if it weren't for my friends I'd walk off. Say "fuck it" and be done with it. Give myself time to figure out how I'm going to keep my secret any longer. Just when my dream is in my grasp, I can feel it slipping through my fingers. No one will be able to accept my past, and once again I'll be all alone. It's okay. I'll be okay. I've done it before and I sure as hell can do it again.

As soon as our last encore is over, I stumble off the stage and head to the nearest exit. I'm surrounded by security as I slide into the town car and slam my door. The automatic locks click into place and I relax. Complete and utter silence. It's the first time I've felt calm all day and it's a welcome change. I knock on the petition and it slowly descends. "Take me to the hotel."

"Sir, should we wait for the others?" Hell to the fucking no.

"They can take the next one." No questions asked, the petition closes, and the driver pulls away from the curb. I need time to think without everyone hovering over me. Putting in their two cents' worth. If it were that easy, I would have revealed my story a long time ago.

Closing my eyes, I rest my head against the back seat, but all I can see behind my lids is that picture. It's haunting me and might be the reason why I'm drenched in sweat. Yet my teeth are chattering and I'm freezing cold.

The only person who has access to these pictures is Joseph. He has to be the one behind all of this, but what does he have to gain? Five minutes of fame? More likely he wants to inflict pain on me. If that's the case, he's doing a good job. I haven't been able to concentrate on anything since receiving the first picture.

I'm stunned when my door opens and Brett is standing there. I didn't realize the car had come to a stop. Sliding out, I wait for the barrage of flashes, screams, and questions. I'm relieved when it doesn't happen. It's exactly what I needed tonight. Quiet.

"Now that we're all alone, could you tell me who the

young girl is in the picture?" I take it back, I'd rather have the screams and flashes instead of all the questions I'm not ready to answer.

I keep on walking, giving him my back, hoping he takes the hint. Nope, he catches up and hits the button on the elevator. Great. Guess we're riding up together.

"Look, I get you didn't want to come clean with everyone in the room, but it's just you and me at the moment. Whatever you tell me is confidential, so no worries about it getting back to the band."

After stepping inside the elevator, I lean on the wall and fold my arms. He doesn't really know who he's dealing with. I'm a master at keeping my mouth shut. Just ask Joseph. He'll vouch for me… or maybe he won't.

Funny, it's not the band I'm worried about. It's Brett. We all know that money talks and bullshit walks, and if the tabloids or a fancy rag wanted info, he'd sell it to them in a hot minute. I've seen it happen a million times over. Not happening.

I still don't answer or acknowledge him as I step out of the elevator and walk to my room. I swipe my keycard, walk inside, and slam the door in his face. Sorry, you're not invited. Tonight or any other night.

After peeling off my sweaty clothes, I set the shower and step inside. Hoping by some miracle that the water will wash away the numbness that I'm feeling. Placing my palms against the cool tile, I let the water splash over my shoulders and course down my back. Until the tiny rivulets follow the curve of my spine, ass, and legs before disappearing down the drain. Grabbing the body wash, I scrub myself clean and get the hell out. Not lingering any longer than I need to. I just want to close my eyes and forget.

Tonight, the thought of sleeping in a king-size bed is terrifying. Tearing the blankets from the bed, I throw them in the corner and crawl inside. Closing my eyes, I pray for sleep. Without nightmares or black eyes staring back at me.

* * *

QUINN

I'M RELUCTANT TO SLEEP in our room after Jet stomped off the way he did tonight. I thought about grabbing another room but decided against it since all of my clothes are in his room. *Our* room. Then again, after tonight it might not be anymore.

The only good thing to come out of all this is Abby isn't pissed at me anymore. We talked it over and she understands the reason I did what I did. With the exception of Jet, we all went to the afterparty and made excuses for him. "Not feeling well" is the lie we told. It flowed easily off our tongues—honestly, it wasn't far from the truth to begin with. Jet's not well and it's because all of the memories he's suppressed are coming back in full force. There's nothing I can do for him, so for now I'm going to let it go.

It's pitch black when I walk into the bedroom. I love that the scent of his body wash still lingers in the air. I'd love to crawl inside the bed and be the one who takes away all of his pain. Unfortunately, I know he's the only one who can do that by seeking the help he needs. And, if he chooses not to, then he faces a lifetime of torment.

Tiptoeing into the bathroom, I close the door before turning on the lights. His clothes are scattered all over the floor, so I pick them up and toss them into the basket. I'm not going to rifle through his pockets and be accused of snooping again. Hell no. I'm so done with that.

After a quick shower, I dry off and slip into my pajamas. I'm not too worried about looking sexy tonight. That ship has already sailed and who the hell knows when it's going into port again.

Since I don't want to flip on the light, I use the one on my phone to brighten the room. I'm confused when I find the bed empty and the covers are missing.

What the hell?

I'm baffled when I peek in the living room and he's not sleeping on the couch. I do a quick walkthrough and can't find him anywhere in the suite. Should I call security? I get a sinking feeling in my stomach. Did he hook up with someone after he left? The thought makes me sick.

Something in the corner of the bedroom catches my eye when I walk in. All of the blankets are tossed on the floor. Now that's really weird. Why would he do that? I need those damn blankets. I'll text Lucas after and see if he's heard from Jet. First, I'm going to make the damn bed.

Reaching down I grab a corner of the blanket and pull. It doesn't budge. Now I'm getting pissed so I yank it as hard as I can and scream when it moves. I flip on the light and I cover my mouth with my fist when I see Jet lying there. Is he hurt? Dropping to my knees, I reach out and touch him.

"Jet, are you okay?" I can't smell anything on his breath, so I don't think he's drunk. He's sleeping on his back with his arm covering his eyes. My gut's telling me he needs me, so I crawl in beside him and my heart breaks when he moans. Not in ecstasy, but in pain. Sounding like a wounded animal caught in a trap. "I got you. Go to sleep."

A heavy sigh and he rolls over and pulls me in. It's not

the most comfortable position—I really wish he'd go back to bed—but I'll stay here if that's what he needs. I'm dozing off when he mumbles in his sleep.

It's incoherent so I can only make out a few words.

Stop—

Sister—

Breathing—

Oh god, he's sobbing in his dream and I can't for the life of me let him continue. "It's me, Quinn! You're having a bad dream. Wake up, Jet!" I give him a little shake and he slides into the corner.

No, no, no.

"Baby, wake up. It's okay, I'm here." He startles but his eyes open wide and it takes a few minutes for him to focus.

"Quinn—"

"I'm here. Can I get you anything?" He seems a bit skittish. I don't want to scare him. He needs time to get his bearings.

"Water. Please." He sits up, wrapping his arms around his bent knees, and leans his head against one arm. Watching me.

"Coming right up." I stand on shaky legs, rush into the living room, and grab a bottle out of the mini fridge. Taking a few deep breaths, I try calming the beat of my heart because I swear he can hear it from across the room.

"Here ya go." I unscrew the cap and hand him the bottle. When he guzzles the water, I run my fingers through his damp hair. It's so curly when it's like this. "Better?" I ask when he finishes.

"Much, thanks." He's staring straight ahead. Avoiding me. And I do the one thing I promised myself I wouldn't do.

"Do you want to talk about it?" Yep, now he's pissed

again. He quickly stands up and wanders into the other room. I hear the fridge open and then nothing. He's not coming back.

I spend the next fifteen minutes making the bed. Then another twenty minutes waiting for him. Nothing. I can't let it go so I find him sitting on the couch with his head in his hands. Crap.

"There are a lot of things I'm afraid of." His head snaps up in my direction and I hesitate to continue, but something inside tells me he needs to hear this. "Some of them are stupid. Like my fear of spiders and heights. Ninety-nine percent of the population is scared of the same old shit. The fear that keeps me awake at night is the thought of being alone. Not now, but when I get older and I'm sitting in my rocking chair and no one's there. Ya know? Scary feeling." I stop and let him contemplate my words. I'm not sure if this is one of his fears, but I sense it is. He feels he's not good enough, so therefore he chooses to be alone.

"Reverse psychology might work on some people, Quinn. Me? Not so much. I'm going to bed, I'll see you in the morning." I'm guessing he didn't need to hear it after all.

24

JET

I'M SO ANGRY THAT Quinn caught me sleeping on the floor last night. I thought for sure she'd question me, but she let it go. For how long? It's my story to tell and I'll never be ready to share it with anyone. Or with her. So it's time to cut the ties and move on.

I felt the mattress shift when she came to bed early this morning. It was a shitty move, but I faked sleep because I didn't want to talk or have sex with her. I'm not in the right head space for anything and I might never be if those pictures continue coming. Those memories are private and in my past life. They have no room in my present, or in my future for that matter.

Brett texted me earlier this morning, no fingerprints. It's obvious that whoever's doing this wiped them clean. Many people have touched them over the years, so to find nothing is absurd. I know it's Joseph. It has to be. I even went so far as to give them his full name and last known address. I know by doing so I kinda outed myself, but if Brett figured it out, he didn't mention it. Yet. I'm sure that will be coming soon. Even if it does, there's nothing they can do. In fact, I'd sue the agency if anyone revealed that I was Jethro Lawless. The same boy who ran away thirteen years ago.

The only thing I can do is get my shit together. Regardless, of how many pictures continue coming, I need to concentrate on the tour. It's my life's blood and if it all falls apart tomorrow, at least I can say I gave it my all. No one can take that away from me. No one. I won't let them.

Today is an off day since we're traveling. Our flight leaves in a few hours and it's going to be awkward as hell. I haven't spoken to anyone after I stormed off after the concert last night. Well, with the exception of Quinn. And that conversation was minimal at best. What do you say to someone who just about picked you up off the floor? Yeah, not much.

I guess I'm waiting for another picture to pop up. I can't wait forever, so I try to relax and enjoy the ride to the airport. It's quiet because I requested to go alone. It raised a few eyebrows and I can tell Lucas was pissed. Too damn bad. Unlike him, I don't need an audience except when I'm on stage. I've been alone for so long that it makes me uncomfortable when there are too many people around. It's just me and I don't foresee things changing anytime soon. Which kinda blows Quinn's theory to smithereens. Maybe she's afraid of being alone when she's old and gray. Not me. I'll be lucky if I make it that long. If I do, I'd be content in my rocking chair as long as I had an awesome view.

"Have a safe flight, sir. And good luck with the tour." My driver tips his hat as I step out into the fresh air and my mood changes when I spot Lucas waiting for me. Blood brothers or not, he needs to mind his own business.

"Hey, you've been avoiding me. What's up?" Lucas hasn't realized yet that the dynamics between us have changed.

"I'm not avoiding you, asshole. I've got shit to deal with and I'm not bringing anyone down with me. Besides, you're too busy with Abby and I'm not going to interfere." There, I said it.

"Bro, she's much prettier to look at, but I'm always here for you if you need me. You know that, right?" Trouble is I do.

"Yeah, appreciate it. Not necessary, though. I don't need a babysitter." That reference was for Quinn, not him.

"Well, in any case, we all miss hanging out together and if you're up for it, we'd like to chill tonight and shoot the shit. Good food, friends, and alcohol. You in?" My mind is screaming at me to pass, but I've been doing that too much lately.

"Sure, why not. We can't get there from here if we don't get a move on." He slaps me on the back and gestures with his hand for me to go first. And of course when I get on the plane, the only seats available are next to Quinn or Abby. I opt for Quinn, since I don't want to die today.

I've avoided her all day and she's given me my space. This makes me wonder how the sleeping arrangements are going to be moving forward. Makes me wish I hadn't been too hasty in wanting to share a room. Well, nothing says we can't go back to the way it was before. I throw my bag in the overhead and take my seat, making a mental note to mention something to Quinn before we get there.

She's too busy writing in her planner and avoiding me,

so I put on the headset and watch the movie. I've seen the damn thing a few times before but never finished it. I just couldn't get into a hot shot fighter pilot taking out all the bad buys. Boring, but it beats having to make conversation with Quinn. Hey, maybe today's the day I finally finish the damn movie.

Didn't happen. I fell asleep and now I'm chastising myself for not finishing the movie and having that talk with Quinn. Either I mention it on the ride to the hotel or I wait until we get there. Might be best to wait since I don't want to have that talk in front of everyone. Especially since I'm the one who went all caveman and insisted we were switching things up. Feels like years ago when it was just a few days ago. I should have known that I couldn't live a normal life like everyone else. It's just not in the cards for me.

I grab both my bags and Quinn's bags in the overhead. I'm an asshole but I'm still a gentleman. To some degree. "I got the bags, let's go."

"Thanks," she says. "Did you sleep well?" I bristle because it's just a slap in the face of what happened last night.

"I guess. I blame it on the boring movie they were playing." She laughs and my chest tightens. I love her laugh. Fuck!

"Well, I promise I'll let you sleep tonight since we have a rough week ahead of us." Great, the window of opportunity just slammed shut. Now what do I do?

All of us pile into the limo and Lucas says, "Party tonight in our room, so make sure to be there. All of you. It's our last night off for a week. We all need to unwind and drink. Within moderation, of course."

* * *

QUINN

I GET THE FEELING that Jet would be happy if I passed on the party. He didn't look too happy when I mentioned I'd let him sleep. Dammit, I put my foot in my mouth, again! After last night, I promised myself I wouldn't discuss what I'd seen, or anything that pertained to sleeping, and there I went. I'm an outsider. The boss, and I get that I don't fit in. I never will. I'm supposed to be in control, keep them in check, and make sure everything runs smoothly. I'm just like a parent who is trying to be best friends with their kids—it doesn't work. From now on I need to be the Quinn I was when I first met them. In charge, guiding them to make the best decisions, and keeping it professional rather than personal. So tell me, how the hell I can do that when I'm sleeping with the sexy bassist for *The Sinful Seven*? Impossible!

We all agree to get together in Lucas's suite at seven tonight after checking in at the desk. Then we go our separate ways. Normally, we'd all be on the same floor, but since Abby had to switch things up at the last minute because Jet insisted, we're not. He doesn't look too happy about it. Too bad since it's all his fault.

After walking into the room, he throws everything on the bed and stalks into the bathroom. Slamming the door. He hasn't been the same ever since he saw that picture. If I had to take a guess, the girl in the pic is his sister. Just a hunch, since the first one was his mom, then the both of them together. Would make sense that the last would be of a sibling, and the blue eyes just solidified that fact. I haven't figured out the reason why he had such an adverse reaction, though. With Jet, I might never know.

I'm hanging up all of my clothes when he comes strutting out of the bathroom with a towel wrapped around his waist. He's glistening and has his hair slicked back. Without a care in the world, he rips off the towel and hunts for a pair of boxers in his duffel bag. Something's wrong. On inspection, I think I'm witnessing for the first time that he's not hard. In our short time together, I don't think I've ever seen him flaccid. Other than being sated and exhausted after a night of carnal, deviant sex.

He takes a minute to towel off before slipping into his boxers. It's a shame, really. And it's all the proof I need that he's troubled and in desperate need of an intervention. But I won't be the mediator. Not this time. The evidence is clear. I've done enough damage and he doesn't want anything to do with me. Period.

It's too hurtful to wait, so I grab my clean clothes and stride into the bathroom. My turn, and then I'll go to Lucas's room with everyone else. If I can get Willow alone, I'll ask if I can bunk with her again. I should have run for the hills the night he came to my house. Nothing good ever comes out of falling for a rockstar. I know that first-hand and yet I did it again. Thank Christ this time around I had enough common sense to end it before it truly began. Or worse, tie the knot along with my heart.

After showering, I spend some time blow drying my hair. Lately, I've just been too busy to fuss, so I throw it up in a bun or a quick French braid. I don't remember the last time I've worn it down. I even take the time to put on a touch of makeup to hide the dark lines and creases in my forehead. Mom calls them worry lines, and she might be right. I don't remember having them before Jet Turner came along.

The steam follows me as I open the door and step into the room. I half expected Jet to be gone, but he's sitting in a chair, texting. Must be intrigued since he doesn't even look my way. It's all good. I'm rocking it tonight and I must admit I'm feeling pretty damn good about myself and my decision.

Before I head out the door, I grab my phone and keycard. It's not quite seven so I think I'll stop at the bar and grab myself a drink first. I deserve it for all the hard work I've been doing. It just sucks that I need to walk by Jet before leaving. When I do, he reaches out and grabs my wrist.

"You're gorgeous, Quinn. Not just tonight but always. I'm sorry that I'm so fucked up that I've screwed things up between us. I really wanted this to work out, but I think we both know it won't." His thumb's sliding back and forth over my wrist and I'm desperately trying to hold it together. There's so much I want to say to him.

Here goes. "The only one who doesn't think it will work out is you. Look, I can't force you to be with me if you don't want to, but I can't do this again. I won't. I made myself a promise a long time ago that I'd never get involved with another musician again, and then you came along and, well, you know what happened. We started off as enemies and then we became lovers. Maybe it's better if you just go on hating me. It was easier that way."

"I never hated you, baby. Just the opposite. I wanted you from the very first day I laid eyes on you. Then I realized it wouldn't be fair if I dragged you into my world, and I was right. My past is coming back to haunt me and it's just a matter of time before the truth comes out. After that you won't want anything to do with me, so it's best if we end it now before it's too late." At this time, I wish I was a literary genius so I knew what to say. Instead I'm going to speak from my heart. Something I haven't done since my divorce. It's hard tearing down walls that you've spent years trying to build.

Sitting down next to him, I grab his hand and link our fingers together. My heart is thrumming in my chest, but I'm determined to get this out. It's now or never.

"Whatever happened in your past doesn't determine the man you are today. That's why it's called the past. It no longer exists, it's how you live your life today that matters. And, from what I've observed over the last few months, is you are caring, loyal, and compassionate. You're a survivor. I'm in awe of you because you had a dream, and with your determination it came true. It's happening right now. If you don't want us to work out, it's your choice. But I think you're worth fighting for." I gently kiss his cheek and stand up. I was hoping he wouldn't let me go, but he does. Once again my words had no meaning. I just need to get it through my head that when someone is so broken, maybe I can't fix them.

25

JET

I WATCHED HER WALK out the door and there wasn't a damn thing I could do about it! Letting her go was the right thing to do. At least that's what I keep telling myself as I watch her laughing and having a good time. Our music is playing in the background and she's dancing with Willow and Abby. They're acting like a bunch of college girls and my heart squeezes at the thought that I didn't get to do that. Every now and again I get angry that I missed out on so damn much in my life. Quinn's words come back to bite me when she said the past is in the past. True, and I should be concentrating on the future. Hard to do when I'm waiting for the other shoe to drop.

Joseph has something up his sleeve, I can feel it.

At eleven, I make up some lame excuse to leave. I'm just bringing the band down by sulking in the corner, and now they can party till the sun comes up if that's what they want.

There's something that Quinn mentioned earlier that's

been bothering me. "*I made myself a promise a long time ago that I'd never get involved with another musician again, and then you came along—*" I'm assuming by that remark that she dated someone else in the Biz.

Swiping my phone, I punch in her name and scroll through until something catches my eye. "*Rebel Riot takes on a pro in the PR department, Quinn Taylor. Zander Stone and Ms. Taylor were seen out and about and it looked more personal than professional. Tons of PDA as they were caught kissing and holding hands.*"

Fuck me! I don't read the tabloids for my own nefarious reasons, so I had no idea those two dated. I continue reading several articles and the gossip cools down after a messy break up is mentioned a year later. Well, I'm a saint compared to that asshole. Doesn't mean I want to pick up things again. She's had her share of idiots. Quinn deserves someone who's going to treat her right and be open and honest with her. And that sure as hell isn't me.

I'm not sure if I'm trying to stay awake until Quinn gets back or if I'm afraid to close my eyes. It really doesn't matter because the next time I open them, the sun's shining through the balcony doors and Quinn's nowhere to be found. She never came back last night. Isn't that what I wanted? Maybe, but it still sucks because, once again, I'm alone. I'm beginning to think she was on to something when she brought that up yesterday. Doesn't matter, she's still better off without me.

After I call room service, I hop into the shower and take a quick one. I want to be dressed and ready when they come to deliver my breakfast. I'm slipping on my shirt when there's a knock on the door. Right on time.

I'm assaulted by the aroma of eggs, bacon, and coffee

when I open the door. "You can leave the cart if you don't mind. I'll take it from here."

"Of course. Just leave it out in the hall when you're done and someone will grab it." I mumble a "Will do" as I shut the door and wheel the whole damn thing out on the balcony. It's a beautiful day and I want to enjoy it.

I curse Quinn as I take a sip of the strong coffee. It's all her fault that I look forward to a cup in the morning. It gives me that little kick and much better for me than an energy drink.

I'm just finishing up when something distracts me. A creepy-crawly feeling sends chills down my spine. I slowly slide the napkin to the side and an envelope falls to the floor. Hitting the deck with a thud and this time around, it's not addressed to anyone. What the hell?

Clearly there's more than one picture in this one since it's bulging at the seams. In fact, I'm surprised it didn't split wide open when it fell. This time around, I'm calling Brett. He'll need to question the wait-staff before the next shift change.

I'm walking into the room when Quinn walks through the door. Grabbing my phone on the nightstand, I hit his number and he answers instantly. "You'd only call if you received another envelope. Am I right?"

"This time it was on my fucking breakfast cart from room service! It was hidden underneath the napkin. I haven't touched it. I'm waiting for you."

"I'm in the elevator right now. You did the right thing." He hangs up and when I turn around, Quinn's standing there. Glad she decided to come back.

"Sorry, I couldn't help but overhear. You did the right thing." She sounds like a broken record.

"Yeah, that seems to be the consensus of the day." I don't bother asking where she's been because it's none of my damn business. Quinn walks off when there's a knock on the door. Brett rushes in and looks around for the cart. "Out on the balcony. I was all alone so I thought it would be a great time to enjoy the day." Yeah, it was a dig. Ask me if I care.

"Jet, I—" Quinn begins.

"No need for an explanation, Quinn. In case you didn't notice, we have more important things to worry about than whether or not we're fucking." Yep, it stung.

Suddenly, I need air. Best to be outside and face the music than stifling in this room with someone I hurt time and time again.

With gloved hands, Brett rips open the envelope and pulls out several pics. I stumble back when all of them are of Quinn. Brett meets my troubled gaze and shakes his head. It's not just about me anymore. Now, it involves the both of us. "Are you thinking what I'm thinking?" I ask him. "Like now you have two investigations, because this isn't connected to mine?"

"Yeah, it could be but we won't rule it out. It's throwing me off since the first pictures that were sent are of your family. Now it's just Quinn. I need to go question the kitchen staff. Both of you stay put until I have some answers. No leaving." He scoops up the pictures and leaves.

She's sitting on the bed with her overnight bag by her side. Okay, was it something I said? If it were any other time, I'd let her walk out the door. She's better off without me. But now, she needs to stay and I don't know how the hell I'm supposed to convince her after I've treated her so badly.

* * *

QUINN

I STAYED WITH WILLOW last night. I had to because I knew if I came back, I'd regret it. I probably would have told Jet how I really feel about him, and that would ruin not only our working relationship but our friendship as well. Willow was sympathetic, but she also scolded me for being so stubborn. Everyone in the band knows how much I care about Jet... except Jet! And if he does, he ignores it by pushing me away. I know what he's doing. He's pushing my buttons and being nasty so I'll hate him, which will never happen. Am I angry? Yeah, I don't like being his doormat, but I understand why he's doing it. Doesn't make it hurt any less.

"You're not leaving, baby. You're stuck with me so you might as well unpack." Who the hell does he think he is?

"I'm sick and tired of you running hot and cold! One minute you want me gone and the next I can't leave. Well, this time around, I'll make the decision, not you." With one hand wrapped around my bag, I stand to get the hell out. Of course, he stands between me and the door.

"Quinn, stop! Did Brett mention anything to you about the pictures before he left?" Seriously, why would he?

"No, as you so eloquently put it, it's none of my business." He tucks his chin against his chest and pinches the bridge of his nose. Yeah, I'm right there with you, buddy, because you're giving me a headache.

"All the pictures we got today are of you." Come again?

"Are you serious? Why me?" Shivers capture my arms, making the hair on the nape of my neck stand out.

"I know, it doesn't make sense. I'm thinking this isn't

related to the pictures that I received. Brett's going to question the kitchen staff, check the cameras. All that shit. He doesn't want us leaving until he does. Sorry you're stuck with me a while longer."

"Could it be a copycat? I mean, there's only a handful of people who know about what's going on with you, but there could be a leak. Right?" I fluff up the pillows and prop myself up against the headboard. Getting comfortable for the long haul, but I'm not going to lie. I'm scared.

"It's possible, I suppose. I guess we just need to wait and see. Hey, can I ask where you were heading? You don't need to answer if you—"

"Nah, it's all good. I was going to bunk with Willow again. Have some girl time, no big deal. Give you some space since you're no good for me." Now that got his attention. So much so that he climbs on the bed next to me.

"You'll thank me later, Quinn. Years down the road when your grandchildren come to visit and your rocking them in that damn chair, you'll thank me." My word, he breaks my heart.

"You deserve to be happy, too, Jet. Contrary to what you might think, you do. And I don't want to sound like a broken record, but nothing you could ever tell me would make me hate you." I reach out to grab his hand, and I'm stunned when he lets me. "Even if you were to tell me that you killed someone I wouldn't hate you, because I'd know it would have been in self-defense."

"Good to know, 'cause I killed a hundred of them." He nudges my shoulder with his when I gasp. "Only in my nightmares, baby. No worries."

He gets quiet and pensive in that moment. He's a million miles away and I wish with all my heart that he'd open up to me. "Don't hate on me but I did some detective work on my own after something you said. About never wanting to date a rockstar again. Found some interesting pictures on the net. You and some hotshot lead man locking lips."

I can't believe he spied on me! Well, I suppose I can. It's only fair since I did the same to him and the rest of the band. So, do I rip off the damn Band-Aid and tell him the truth? And, if I do, will he reciprocate? Might be worth a try. I know if I told him something in confidence he'd never repeat it.

"It was the first time I got involved with one of my clients, and it was disastrous. The biggest mistake of my life. I thought I was in love and I couldn't have been more wrong in my life. We went at it hot and heavy and it fizzled out almost as fast as it began. Zander is larger than life and didn't have any room left for me. We parted ways and I haven't seen him again." I don't realize I'm crying until he wipes my tears away.

"I'm so sorry, baby. I promise when we meet up with *Rebel Riot* I'll keep the asshole far away from you. You deserve so much better than Zander Stone and Jet Turner. From here on out, stay far away from rockstars because they'll only suck the life right out of you."

He's so serious, but I know with all of my heart he'd keep me safe. His lips are so close to mine that all I need to do is sit taller and I would taste what I've been missing. So I do. When he moans, I take it to the next level by straddling his lap. Never breaking contact. Love the feel of his cock straining between my thighs. If I wasn't devouring him, I'd make sure to tell him the only rockstar I want is him.

"Quinn, fuck, baby. I'm gonna come in my pants if you

keep grinding on me like that." Well, I guess I need to fix that real quick.

My lips never leave his, but my hands do some roaming of their own. A snap, a zip, and he seizes my wrists in his hands, stopping me from going any further. He searches my face when we break apart. I'm sure I look like a woman possessed, but I don't care. My feet are constantly telling me to run, but my heart is what's keeping me here. I've never felt like this with anyone before. Not even Zander.

"You can continue pushing me away, but I'm like a boomerang—I'll keep coming back. I want you, Jet." I wait with bated breath and for the life of me I have no idea how this is going to play out. Until he flips me over and pins me with his solid body.

With his hands cupping my face, he leans in and whispers, "I can't promise you tomorrow, but I can promise you today."

GREED

*"**Greed**, like the love of comfort, is a kind of fear."*

Cyril Connolly

26

JET

WHAT I TOLD QUINN YESTERDAY, I meant every word. I don't want her thinking long-term about us. I'm not capable of that kind of commitment, and truth be told I'm saving us both a lot of hurt and heartache. It's just the way things need to be from here on out. I'll give her anything I can, within reason. I can be her knight in shining armor, but I can't safeguard her heart. She needs to do that on her own. For now, Quinn left all of her clothes in my room. We're just going to take things one day at a time, and if we need our space, she'll bunk with Willow or I can bunk with Trevor.

We still don't have any news from Brett. No news is good news so they say. Not sure it is in this case, but for now we need to keep plugging away. It's all we can do.

Now we're driving to the venue so we can do a sound check. And I swear we have more security now than ever. All of us kind of feel like we're some hotshot politician with all the amped-up surveillance. Might be the reason everyone's so quiet. The tension is high, and for the first time it has nothing to do with Quinn and I going at each other.

We pull into the lot and the doors open almost immediately. All I can hear is the chanting of the crowd as I exit the limo. You'd think I'd get used to this by now, but I don't think I ever will. Adrenaline pumps through my veins as we push through surrounded by security. I have my arm around Quinn until she disappears inside, and I'm just about to step in when a hand snatches out and grabs my wrist.

"Jethro, oh thank god it is you! He's my son! Let me go, please. Jethro, please tell them who I am." I'm blinded as a million cameras go off in my face. Until I focus on the man who has his hand wrapped around my wrist.

Joseph Lawless—

Seconds later, I'm being escorted into the building while the asshole is being placed inside the nearest cruiser. I'm confused as Brett grabs my elbow and guides me into an empty room. I'm not the fucking criminal here!

"What the fuck! Let me go, I didn't do anything wrong." I'm rubbing my wrists when I notice there's blood on my hands? I'm relieved when Lucas and Quinn crash through the door.

"Let him go, Brett. He's coming with us now," Lucas says. When I stand up to leave, Brett pushes me down.

"If you fucking put your hands on me one more time, I'm going to fucking lay you out right here."

"I have every right to hold you in here, Jet. You just pummeled the man who grabbed you." I what? Oh fuck, I don't remember a thing after the flashes.

Lucas steps up, chest-to-chest with Brett, and he's a big guy. "That asshole grabbed him first! If you guys had been doing your fucking job, he wouldn't have had to defend himself. You," he sticks his finger in Brett's chest, "are getting paid so shit like this doesn't happen. Got it? Now, go fix this."

I'm shaking with rage when Quinn separates the both of them and reaches for my hand. "Come with me so the doctor can check those hands." The last thing I want to do is taint her with the blood, so I stand up on my own. Like I've always had to do.

"You best call your lawyer. Got a feeling that asshole will press charges. Unless you know him and can talk it out."

Gripping the edge of the doorframe, I look over my shoulder. "I have nothing to say to him."

First stop, bathroom. Quinn's fussing over me as she gently washes my hands. I watch the blood drip down the drain while Lucas paces back and forth. He looks worried. Fuck, this isn't going to be good.

"Lucas, stand still. My head's about to explode and your pacing isn't helping." He grabs his phone and I sigh because I think he's calling our lawyer, Mr. Miller. Wishful thinking.

"I'll be right back. I'm going to grab Abby." Seriously?

"I don't need an audience, for fuck's sake. Just get out." Quinn dries my hands and turns them over.

Lucas is fuming. "I don't want her in here, I want her to put out the social media fires." Quinn stares at my reflection through the bathroom mirror and I feel like I'm on display.

"It's not good, Jet. We need to take care of it as soon as possible. Abby will know what to do." With that, he walks out. What a shit show.

"I swear if you ask me if what he said was true, baby, I'm going to lose my fucking mind!" She does something so unexpected, I stumble. She wraps her arms around me and presses her face to my chest. Holding me.

"I didn't hear a word he said, Jet. I was already in the building, remember? When I heard everyone screaming your name, I thought something happened to you. I've never been so scared in all of my life." She's so selfless and sweet. The very reason she shouldn't be here with me.

"I'm fine. You should see the other guy." I couldn't resist a little humor. I think she's laughing until I lift up her chin and see tears streaming down her face.

"Aw, don't cry. I swear I'm fine and I'll prove it to you. Let's go do the sound check before it's too late. C'mon, baby." She doesn't budge, so I just hold her as tight as she's holding me. We're so close, her heart beats in rhythm to mine.

* * *

QUINN

JET DOESN'T HAVE A clue how terrified I was. Of course I care about his hands, but I care about the man so much more. I'm already invested and I can easily admit that I'm falling in love with this closed off, stubborn man. All of his warnings are in vain because I'm too far gone already.

A sudden knock on the door has us pulling apart. Not that I want to, but we need to figure out what's happening next. "Come in."

Trevor sticks his head inside. "Hey guys, hate to bother you. If you're feeling up for it, they're calling us for our sound check."

I really wanted the doc to check Jet's hands, but he

kinda read my mind. "I'm fine, really. Let's do sound check, and if it makes you feel better I'll let him check me afterward. Okay?" I nod because I don't trust myself to speak. I'm still trembling from the thought of him being hurt.

Abby pulls me aside as soon as the band begins testing their equipment. "Quinn, I know you are preoccupied with everything going on, but I need to show you something. My heart plummets the minute I read the first Instagram post with the hashtag #jetturnerisaposer.

Scrolling through all the posts has me feeling sick to my stomach. Most are in favor of Jet, but some are being so condescending it's offensive. And the pictures underneath the hashtags portray Jet as being the aggressor when in all actuality he was the victim. He'll be devastated if he sees any of this. It's his worst nightmare.

"Can you fix this, Abby? Make a few posts about Jet acting out in self-defense? That guy put his hands on Jet first and he defended himself." No, no, no. I can feel the throbbing behind my eyes, so I quickly reach inside my pocketbook for my meds. This can't happen now.

"I'll do the best I can, but it's on every social media site and I'm only one person. I'll see if Sarah will help me, too. You going to be okay, Quinn?" Am I? I can't answer that. Abby doesn't need to fix me, just Jet.

"I'll be fine. Do what you can. I'm calling his lawyer now. Maybe he can write something up and post it, too."

Forty minutes later, the sound check is over and so is my phone call with Mr. Miller. He assured me he'll do everything within his power to take care of this fiasco. Even if he has to pay off Joseph Lawless. Jet's stepfather. I know this since he told me that fateful day, but it's just a matter of time before the truth comes out. I fear I'll lose him forever when it does.

I put on my happy face when he strolls over. "You sounded great even with a busted-up hand." I stand on my tiptoes to kiss his flawless lips and he lets me. "It looks swollen so let's go check it out." He snickers at what else that could mean. Is it wrong that I love the fact he's hard from just my kiss? And that he just experienced something very traumatic and he's still thinking of sex?

The doctor doesn't seem surprised to see us walk in, so I'm sure Lucas or someone gave him a heads up. "Did you have any trouble playing your guitar?"

"It's a little swollen, but other than that, it's fine." The whole time he's talking to the doc, his smoldering stare is locked on mine. Yep, must be because of that word again.

"Step over here. I want to take a few X-rays just to be on the safe side." Jet doesn't argue but I can tell he thinks it's a waste of time. Once he's done, he checks the screen to review them. "You're very lucky, young man. Nothing's broken but you should ice it. I'll give you some pain meds before leaving."

"Thanks, but I don't need anything for the pain. Everyone's making a big fuss about nothing. Thanks, we're out of here."

While Jet was having his hand checked, I received a text to meet everyone out the back entrance. After what happened earlier, we need to lay low until we figure this out. I'm hoping tonight's concert goes without a hitch.

As far as I know, Jet's oblivious to what's happening on social media, but that's not why he's uncomfortable when he slides in. I'd say he's afraid of facing his friends and the questions that will follow. I'm relieved when they just ask how he's doing and if he'll be all right for tonight's concert.

He's relaxed, but he's always one step ahead of them. "I haven't bothered to check, but I'm sure social media is a shit show, am I right?" All heads turn towards Jet since they didn't think he'd be the one to bring it up. Since Abby's our go-to girl for everything social, she takes the plunge.

"It's nothing we can't handle, Jet. You concentrate on healing and we'll take care of everything else. Miller's doing everything on his end, and if we all stick together, it will blow over before you know it."

He looks nervous when he leans forward and places a fist underneath his chin. "I know without a doubt that all of you have my back. It's how we roll. With that said, that jackass was telling the truth."

Oh my, Jet's going to finally tell them his truth.

"You already know that the asshole in the crowd is my stepfather. What I've never mentioned, is that my real name's Jethro Lawless, the thirteen-year-old-kid who ran away all those years ago. I'm not sure if he's the one who's been sending all the pictures, but I think it's safe to say he's been planning to out me for quite some time."

"Dude, you don't owe us any explanations," Trevor says. "We knew you'd tell us when you were damn good and ready."

"I appreciate the vote of confidence, Trevor. Unfortunately, I don't think our lawyers or our fans are going to forget about it anytime soon. And, in case they don't, I just needed to give you a heads up so we can all get our facts straight."

I have no idea how much he's willing to reveal, so this time around I'm going to intervene. "I think our best approach with the press or your fans is to say 'No comment'. No matter what they ask, it's for the best."

Everyone agrees and Jet doesn't continue. It's just as well since I want them at their best for tonight's concert. I've no doubt it's going to be distracting enough without the added burden of Jet's personal life. Once this tour is over, maybe he'll come clean.

When we pull into the hotel, I need to put in my two cents. "Rest up for tonight and be prepared for some retaliation. Security's going to be tighter than ever, but be aware of what's going on around you. We'll see you in a few hours."

Jet grabs me by my hips as soon as we walk through the door. "Did I ever mention how much it turns me on when you get all bossy?"

I can't help chuckling. "You could have fooled me. Maybe it turns you on in the bedroom but not anywhere else."

"It's possible. Or maybe I like older women. Now there's a thought." He can't fool me. He's in pain and he's trying to cover it up with his dry humor. It has nothing to do with his hand but everything to do with his heart.

Jet's hurting and I wish I knew how to help him.

27

JET

I'D BE A DAMN liar if I said going on stage tonight doesn't concern me. It does because I'm not sure how the fans are going to react after everything that happened today with my stepfather. Unfortunately, he holds all the cards and I don't know which way to turn. One thing is for certain, I won't, under any circumstances, meet with him in private or in front of the press. Either way, I would kill him. I know this as well as I take my next breath.

Quinn thought it best if we went to the venue in unmarked cars. No limos since they'll stick out like a sore thumb. So the four of us hop in one, and Willow and Trevor get in the second. I bust on Quinn all the time but she's so fucking smart it hurts. I'm going to try like hell not to push her away and just enjoy our time together. It'll all be over in the blink of an eye.

"You good?" Lucas thumps me on the back before we sit

in the chair for makeup. This by far is the worst part of the job.

"Yeah, but I feel like shit that I dragged all of you into this mess. Maybe if I had come clean the first time we had a confrontation, it would be all over by now. It sucks that I don't know what's going to happen next."

"I just want you to know that whatever happens, I got your back. If this asshat is smart, he'll crawl back inside his hidey-hole and never come back out. Otherwise, he's in for a world of hurt if he gets too close. Hear what I'm saying?"

"Loud and clear, and I appreciate it." We don't speak as Chloe and Gina start our makeup. It's good because I'm lost in my thoughts again. I'm back at the hell hole in Connecticut with Joseph standing over me.

After makeup, we get changed and normally head backstage to listen to *Laid Bare*, our opening act. Unfortunately, after everything that's happened, security requested we sit tight in here and wait. It sucks big time since listening to them pumps us up before we go on stage. So, we just hang out and make small talk. Until the heavy shit is brought up.

"Whatever happens tonight, just keep on playing," Brett pipes in. "All of us will be there to keep you safe, and if you show the audience that you're vulnerable, they might strike."

Willow contemplates this. "That's bullshit, Brett. Our fans aren't going to 'strike'. They wouldn't do that. They come to see *The Sinful Seven* perform. I highly doubt some crazy lunatic is going to change their minds." She has a point.

"Did you forget that Jet punched the asshole? He claimed he found his long-lost son and instead of a happy reunion he gets clocked. Sometimes that's all it takes for some people to switch sides."

"Okay, stop. We understand you're trying to give us the worst-case scenario but there's no need to go into detail. We were there, remember?" Lucas looks like he wants to kill him and I just might let him.

A knock and Bruce pops his head inside. "Ready in fifteen. Hustle, hustle, and break a leg." We chuckle because he tells us that at every concert.

When Lucas stands, I know our other tradition is soon to follow. We've been doing this since the very first concert.

"Time to gather around in a circle." Once everyone is in position, Lucas wraps his arm around Abby's shoulder and then Quinn's. Now, we are one circle, symbolizing infinity. We all bow our heads and wait for our lead man to continue. "I want all of you to know, there's no one else I want to do this with but you. You're my backbone, my heart, and my fucking team. Whether or not you believe in a higher power, we didn't get here today on our own. Someone's watching out for us. Now, let's have the best night ever!" Lucas starts singing *Distraction,* and one-by-one we follow.

> *" 'Cause you're a distraction*
> *A fatal attraction*
> *Seeping into my bones*
> *Running through my veins…*

Once the song ends, we head backstage and wait for our cue. The crowd's chanting our names as the stage crew finish up so they can get our set ready. With five minutes left, Quinn puts on her headset and gives me a kiss. "Knock 'em dead, babe." With a wink, she's gone and my nerves overtake me.

They call our names and we take our marks on stage. Ready, waiting, and anticipating as adrenaline rushes through my veins. The spotlight flips on, Lucas screams, "Hello, Boston! It's great to be here with all of you tonight! Let's bring down the fucking house!" And it begins.

I get lost in the thumping beats as the music blasts and the crowd cheers. Lucas and I send the audience wild with our kickass duets. Trevor's drum solo brings the crowd to their feet, and as always Willow hits the melodic components like a pro.

With our backs pressed together, Lucas and I start playing *Don't Look Back* by Boston, which we thought was only fitting since we're in the city. This song has one of the best duo guitar riffs of all time.

We're on a high after we finish that song when someone in the front screams, "Jethro, hey Jethro! Which one of us are you going to take a cheap shot at today?" I ignore them and dive into the next song.

I'm halfway through the next song when a guy lifts up a girl and she runs across the stage, coming right for me. Security beats her to it and carries her screaming off the stage. I try telling myself that shit happens.

Our next song is one of our ballads, so it's soft and melodic. That's when the whole front row starts screaming, "Jet Turner is a poser!" as they hold their phones up and take a ton of pictures. By the time security reaches them, the song is over and so am I, but the show must go on.

To say I'm relieved after the last encore would be an understatement. Until I'm the last one to walk backstage and I'm pushed from behind and fall to my knees, scraping my hands in the process. I'm dazed and confused as I turn around and see a few guys with raised fists.

A few kicks and punches to the side of my head and everything goes black.

* * *

QUINN

HE'S BROKEN AND I don't know how to fix him. His pain's not only evident by the bruises on his body, but etched in his soul as well. I can feel it in the way he's curled in on himself, hiding and withdrawn. I hate seeing him like this, but I'm terrified to talk about what happened. If I do, he'll shut down and I don't know if I'll get him back. I'm afraid there are too many shattered pieces and I'm not sure if he can be put back together.

Lucas was desperate to talk to him and I refused. It's the first time I ever separated the two friends but I felt it necessary tonight. As painful as this is for Jet, he needs to process everything that happened. It's the only way he's going to come to terms with it.

Right now, he's sitting on the floor with his head in his hands. Refusing to acknowledge that I'm even in the room. He was adamant about me staying with Willow tonight, but I flat-out refused. No fucking way I was leaving him alone. No can do.

Kneeling down in front of him, I sit back on my heels. I want to touch him but I don't think that's what he needs right now. So, I'm going to reach down deep inside of me and hope I can reach him with my words.

"All of us think you did an amazing job in the way you

handled everything tonight, but it's not good to keep it all inside. You need to let it all out. Tell me everything you're feeling. Throw things, punch the walls, do whatever you need to do. Material things aren't important but you are."

Jet starts rocking back and forth, trying to relieve the tension bottled up inside. My heart aches at the thought of him being alone when he was younger. I tried, I really did, but I want to comfort him. It's embedded in my soul to reach out and hold him.

He freezes instantly. No more rocking, just breathing in short shallow gasps.

"Sometimes we need to confide in someone. To get it off our chest. You'd be surprised how better you'd feel if you did. I felt tons lighter when I told you about Zander. I've told you time and time again, no matter what you tell me, I'll still love you. Yes, Jet, I'm irrevocably in love with you." His hands fall limply by his sides and he peers up at me through his messy hair.

Very quietly, almost inaudibly, he says, "No one's told me they loved me except my mom." Oh my god! This man is twenty-six years old, and he's only ever heard those words from the woman who gave birth to him.

"Some people can't voice how they're feeling, but we both know that Lucas, Abby, Willow and Trevor love you so very much. And I'm sure Mack does, too. Now you can include me in the mix because I told you before that you're worth fighting for. You're an extraordinary man, Jet Turner."

"I'm nothing and no one, Quinn. You deserve a man who can give you all of him. I'll never be that man for you. I'm sorry—"

My fingers press against his lips because I don't want

him to finish that sentence. Nothing he will say can convince me otherwise. He kisses them before speaking. "I need to tell you something before I lose my nerve. Please don't hate me." I crawl inside his lap and he stiffens, but I refuse to let him go. No matter what he has to say, "Quinn, I can't when you're this close."

"I'm holding you and loving you so all of my strength will transfer over to you. I'm not leaving, so get used to it." He sighs but gives in when his arms wrap around me and whispers in my ear, "You're too damn stubborn for your own good."

Maybe, but if I don't hold him I'm afraid he'll run.

"Tonight, when the crowd started chanting *Jethro*, I wanted the stage to open up and swallow me whole. I've been Jet Turner for the better half of my life and I can't relate to that name anymore. It's not who I am and never want to be. Ever again. It was the happiest and darkest times of my life. Joseph is being portrayed as my long-lost stepdad when in all actuality he's the devil in disguise. Adults are supposed to protect their children, not abuse them. Quinn, I can't—"

"Yes, you can. Together we can conquer the beast once and for all. I'm not going anywhere. I promise." If he can feel my tears drenching his shirt, he doesn't acknowledge or complain. And if this conversation is heading in the direction I think it is, I'm not going to be well.

A ragged sigh, and he continues. "My guitar, the one my mom gave me, was the most important possession I owned, and he used it to his advantage. That, and the fact that I needed my hands and my fingers to play. Not only did he threaten to smash my guitar into smithereens, he told me he'd break each and every one of my fingers if I told anyone. I, oh god—" Sobs wrack his tall frame as he relives the memories from his past. I'm desperate to take away his pain. He doesn't need to finish, I already know where this story is headed and I feel nauseous that a small boy had to endure the fate he was so cruelly dealt.

"You're so damn brave, Jet. Then and now, and I love you even more for trusting me with your secrets. I love you so damn much, baby. Together we'll get through this and I promise you that I'll be standing beside you no matter what."

The evil fucker is a pedophile! He should rot in jail for what he's done to Jet. The thought of him continuing with his sick and twisted ways is enough to make me lose my shit, but I won't. I'm going to be strong for this vulnerable man who has had to relive all of this on a stage where he's supposed to feel free and alive. Damn those idiotic fans for taking that all away from him.

"I don't deserve you, Quinn. I'm broken and I don't think I'll ever be whole again. You need to let me go and be with someone who deserves you."

"That's never going to happen. You're stuck with me so you better get used to it. All there is to it. Now's your chance to get it all out. I've told you before I'm a good listener."

"I know and thank you, but I'm exhausted and my confession is over for the night. I've told you more than I intended." He places a soft kiss to my crown and I continue holding him tight. "How about pouring us a few shots while I go take a quick shower?" It's not lost on me that he didn't give me an invitation and I get it after everything he's been through. Tonight and in life.

I don't take my eyes off of him for a second as he strides

into the bathroom and shuts the door. The click of the lock is like a knife to my heart, but when his screams turn into sobs, I slide down the bathroom door, clutching my chest, and join him in his anguish.

28

JET

AFTER WHAT HAPPENED at the concert last night, our lawyers called an impromptu meeting. I'm not surprised, I knew it was inevitable. I'm pressing charges against my assailants and although physically I'll heal, my psyche took a beating. As much as I love my fucking music, I'm not sure I'd be able to endure that night after night. I have no idea how we can stop the hecklers and the haters, but they assured us they have a plan.

As far as Quinn goes, she's the real deal. If it weren't for her calming demeanor and gentle touch, I don't know what would have happened. I owe her everything. She listened and let me talk. When I couldn't go on, she read between the lines. Which made all the difference in the world. Sometimes saying it out loud makes it too real. There's so much more that I could tell her but I can't. Not now.

Maybe someday.

Quinn's making a few calls before we leave so I thought

I'd jot down some lyrics to a song that's been playing out in my head. Some would spend time writing in their journal, for me I write lyrics. I'm sure if I made some sense out of them, I could turn it into a song. Who knows, maybe it will be something for our new album. I like the thought of all of us coming up with our own songs, collecting them into a new album. If I could give this album a name, I'd call it *Rebirth*.

Quinn pokes her head in. "You ready to go?" I'd like to tell her no, but it's something that needs to be done.

"Yep, let's get this show on the road. When we get back, I'm all yours." She looks stressed and I feel like it's all my fault.

"Promise?" she asks as she slips her thumbs in my belt loops and pulls me close.

"Absolutely. There's no place else I'd rather be." I mean every word.

Lucas pulls me aside before we jump into the car. "You hanging in there, bro?"

"Yeah, I'm ready to take the fucker down."

"Good, he deserves all the pain that you've had to deal with all these years. I tried to talk to you last night but the boss refused. Just wanted to remind you that I'm always here for you. We all are."

"I know and that's what's gotten me through some tough times. Quinn was amazing last night. I even told her about what Joseph did to me. I'm still a long way away from telling her everything."

"It's the first step in the right direction. I'm proud of you, bro, really! I know how hard it is for you to get close to someone." The conversation ends as we're ushered into the car and speeding off to the lawyer's office.

I've no idea what awaits but I'm glad that everyone is here and on the same page. I lucked out when I was introduced to all of them. My lifeline.

Quinn threads her fingers through mine when we step inside the elevator. Once again, giving me all her strength like she did last night. I care so much about her and I'm hoping that someday I'll be able to tell her that I love her, too.

Sarah is at the receptionist desk when we enter. "Good morning, everyone. Blake would like to speak to Jet privately. He'll call all of you in once he's ready. Jet, right this way."

There's a lot of sputtering going on behind my back and I get that they're angry for having to wait. All but one, because Quinn hasn't let go of my hand the whole time. I've no doubt she'll insist on being with me. She's def a keeper.

"Jet, come on in. Ms. Taylor?"

"As *The Sinful Seven's* PR agent, I must insist on being in here with him. And, as his girlfriend, I'm also here for moral support." She squeezes my hand and then glances over and winks. Such a sassy girl.

"Since this is a personal matter for my client, I need his permission for you to be present. Jet, do you authorize Ms. Taylor to be present during these negotiations?"

"I do, and if there's something that's too personal, I wouldn't tell either of you." Lawyer or no lawyer, I draw the line.

"Fair enough, but you do realize in order for us to get to the bottom of all of this, you're honesty is of the utmost importance." I nod in understanding and then he pulls out a thick file.

Holy shit, my life isn't that long!

"I took the liberty of searching for everything I could possibly find on Jethro Lawless. A missing persons report was filed on March 8, 2011 by Joseph Lawless. A BOLO, Be On The Lookout, was issued by law enforcement and then the FBI was called in since the first forty-eight hours is critical. Your room was secured and searched for any evidence as to your whereabouts. Joseph was questioned by both, asked to write a detailed description of you along with any pictures he could find. The point I'm trying to make here is Mr. Lawless did everything a concerned parent could possibly do to find their missing child. And all the evidence proves he continued this search up until the day he found you going into the photoshoot."

"Just because he did what was necessary doesn't make him the good guy! Maybe, just maybe, he was afraid the kid would talk and reveal all of his dirty secrets. Maybe he wanted to find his kid to shut him up!" I didn't realize I had gotten out of my chair and now I'm standing in front of his desk with my hands fisted against the slick wood.

The lawyer sits back in his chair with his arms folded across his chest, studying me. I'm fucking angry and he knows it.

"Perhaps, but the question is, how can we prove he was the bad guy?" Point taken. We can't, since it would be his word against mine. "Also, how would a thirteen-year-old runaway go about getting a new identity?"

"So what? Do we pay him off and hope he doesn't keep coming back for more?" At this point, I'm defeated so I go back and sit down. Quinn's there to hold my hand. This time, I don't feel her strength, only weakness.

* * *

QUINN

MR. MILLER WAS GRUELING, but I get that he needed to be a bit of an asshole in order to smooth over what Jet destroyed when he punched his stepfather. And it wasn't lost on me when Jet avoided the question about how he could obtain a new identity at such a young age. I have a theory and, if I'm correct, I'd say it has to do with a certain selfless man who helps feed the homeless. Mack is my first and only guess. They have a bond that can never be broken. I also know that Jet would never, ever tell his lawyer if it was under any circumstances. He'd go down with assault charges first if it ever came down to it.

All of the other band members were called in individually after Jet gave his statement. Of course, each and every one took Jet's side.

I wanted to cancel the next few shows but Jet flat-out refused. I'm scared since Brett fired the guys who were supposed to be guarding the band. Yeah, they fucked up big time and Jet could have been seriously hurt if not killed. This tour has turned into a shit show thanks to Joseph Lawless and I'm sure that was his intention all along. Stir up the pot and fade into the sunset. Well, not going to happen since I will personally take him down if I have to.

After the incident, Caleb stepped up to the plate and hired his own security team. Brett and his team now work for them and he's not too happy. If I had my way, I would have fired them all! Being that the tour's in full swing, it would have been difficult to get so many on board at the last minute. In this business, we learn to adapt, but at what cost?

I shudder to think.

Tonight is our last night in Boston and I know after what

236

happened, everyone's on edge. We were all reassured that there will not be a repeat of last night. Hecklers, angry crowds, there is now a zero-tolerance policy on that kind of shit. They will be thrown out, no questions asked. We can't control what they say but we can end it before it escalates out of control. I'm confident that after what happened last night, it won't ever happen again.

My brave man has been hiding in his room all day. Not sulking or licking his wounds like he has every right to. He's writing in his notebook, where Lucas told me he jots down lyrics for his songs. Abby and Willow tease him that it's a diary, but Jet insists on it being his song pad. I've been tempted to sneak a peek ever since I found out what's inside but I'd never betray his trust. Girl here, with five brothers who have read my diary on more than one occasion. Embarrassing.

My heart skips a beat when he stalks out of the bedroom and is tuned into me. I fight the tears that threaten to fall when I'm reminded about what happened when I see his handsome face. The bruises are purple and turning yellow after just one day. Thankfully, he covered his face when he realized what was happening. If his eyes had been swollen shut it would have been the end of the tour. "Baby, what time are we leaving?" He captures my lips before I can answer. It can wait.

"In an hour. We decided to stay there after sound check and just relax after we've eaten. Just make sure to bring everything you need."

"I only need to grab some clean clothes and I'm good. Should I bring some boxing gloves with me tonight?" He's joking, I think, but it still breaks my heart.

"No one is going to touch you tonight or any other night,

or I will kick their fucking ass." I wrap my arms around his waist and press my ear to his chest so I can hear his heartbeat. I know he's nervous but he'll never verbalize it. Instead he'll crack jokes.

"I was kidding, baby. Don't get all teary eyed on me or I'll be forced to throw you on the bed and have my way with you."

I tilt my head and get lost in his baby blues. "Promise?"

"Without a doubt, and I'll prove it when we come home tonight. Tomorrow's a travel day, remember?" He looks so damn sexy when he waggles his brows trying to seduce me. Hands down, it works every time.

"I do, and that means we can sleep in a bit longer since our flight isn't until two." Oh, the look on his face is priceless.

"Sleeping is so overrated. I'm sure something else will come up in the meantime." Oh, he's good, this guy. And yes, I'm crazy about him.

His lips collide with mine. I swallow down his groans as he tries to destroy my mouth with his tongue. His five o'clock shadow scratches my tender cheeks as he grips my head firmly in place. I'm panting with a pulsating ache between my thighs when the door flies open and I hear, "Get a fucking room for fuck's sake." Lucas!

"We have one, asshole, and the door's closed for a reason. Knock next time!"

"True that. Sorry, I was hoping we could leave soon so we can practice that new song for tonight." New song? Jet didn't mention anything about changing up the set.

And, apparently, I'm not supposed to know since he's looking at Lucas like he's going to die. "When did you plan on filling me in on this little change? Or maybe you were going to surprise me, hmm?"

"Okay, don't be pissed. In light of what happened last night, the band and I thought it would be great to kick off the night with something different. To set the record straight, so to speak. I'm opening the show." He's fucking joking, right?

"Bad idea because of what happened yesterday. Whatever you have up your sleeve could backfire in all of your faces, and if that happens, it could ruin the rest of the tour. Did you all think about that?" I'm angry and this time it has nothing to do with them not checking with me first.

"That's all we've been thinking about, Quinn. I was there, remember? I won't need makeup tonight since my face is the color of an ugly rainbow. I'm sorry, baby. Nothing you do or say is going to change our minds, but I'd love for you to listen to us practice."

Well crap, if it's something that means so much to him, who am I to stand in his way!

29

JET

TONIGHT I'M OPENING the show. It's something I've never done before. If all goes well and the fans accept what I'm putting down, it will be an addition to the tour. It's way out of my comfort zone, but sometimes we need to push our boundaries. If the audience's reaction is the same as Quinn's, well, let's just say it will be a success.

The plan is for everyone to take their marks as usual, but Lucas will open with a small intro. The spotlight will be on me as I pour my heart and soul into the lyrics of this amazing song and hope that the audience will read between the lines just like Quinn did a few nights ago. Realizing once and for all who the true villain is in my situation.

I'm not going to lie, I'm nervous as fuck. When the audience notices the bruises all over my body, maybe then they'll understand the severity of what happened after the concert.

We all line up to grab some food before cleaning up and

getting ready for the concert. Quinn hasn't let me out of her sight since we finished practicing and doing our sound check. There's something bothering her and I need to find out what it is.

"Baby, do you have a migraine? Want me to grab your medicine?" When she snuggles into my arms, I calm. Immediately.

"I'm fine, really. I just wanted to get you alone so I could tell you how proud I am of what you're doing tonight. Especially after what you went through yesterday. I know how hard it is for you to be in the spotlight, but I understand how important it is for you to convey this message. Personally, I think it's going to be incredible. I bet your fans do, too."

"Thanks, but I haven't pulled it off yet. If all goes well, you can remind me once the show's over. Remember, we have a date." We're next in line, and for the life of me I have no appetite. I grab a few things just to pacify the chef and move on.

The next few hours fly by. In a few minutes *Laid Bare* will take their final bow, the crew will do a set change, and then we're next. Lucas memorized the message he wants to deliver to the crowd and I'm hoping I don't forget the lyrics. That would be fucked up. I'm pacing back and forth when Trevor slaps me on the back.

"You're going to wear out a path in the concrete. It's a great idea and I'm sure it's going to knock them dead. No one will ever question who the villain is again. It's like this song was written just for you. It's uncanny." I totally agree, but the only two who understand the full meaning are Quinn and Lucas. The rest of the gang doesn't know what kind of abuse I endured at the hands of Joseph. But there are a million other kids and adults just like me who can relate to this song. I'm not only singing it for me, but for all of them as well.

"Well, I'm thankful that all of you were on board, because if you didn't want to switch things up, I couldn't have pulled it off. Appreciate it."

"It's going to be epic," Willow chimes in.

"Well, you guys are the best and I can't think of anyone else I'd want to be doing this with." We were so wrapped up in doing our thing we didn't take the time to catch *Laid Bare*'s show. Now that their set is over, we're on in ten.

We do our traditional warm up and then we all take our marks. The only difference is after Lucas gives his speech, I'll be in the spotlight.

I can feel the restlessness of the crowd. I'm not sure if they sense something is different or if they're planning another rebellion. Take the bad boy out and watch him bleed. Hopefully after tonight I'll never have to worry about that again. I just need to get through the next five minutes or so and I got it made.

Jeff begins the countdown. "In, five, four, three, two, and go—"

During an ordinary night, Trevor would tap out a beat and then we'd all join in before Lucas would thank the audience for being here. Tonight there's silence. Then the spotlight shines down on Lucas, without his guitar. The crowd goes wild until they realize he's not playing or singing. Then, all goes quiet. Cameras are flashing in the silence, the anticipation thick. When Lucas begins his speech, my nerves take hold.

"Something happened after the show last night. Something that's so deplorable that our PR agent wanted to cancel the rest of the tour." When the crowd becomes heated, Lucas holds up his hands in surrender. "Of course, we vetoed that idea out of the gate. Why? Because we're musicians. Performers, but we're also human. We bleed, we hurt, and we cry just like each and every one of you. We get knocked down and we pick ourselves up and we do it again. And for that reason, we're all here tonight ready to rock and roll thanks to Jet Turner. You can thank him because he's the reason we're standing here with all of you tonight. Like me, he has a message, but he chose to sing it for all of you. Put your hands together for Jet Turner, my brother from another mother!"

The spotlight flips on, I'm front and center, and all eyes are on me. Waiting. Willow begins playing the keys, and then I'm up.

I open my mouth and feel every word I sing down to the marrow of my bones. "I was born in a thunderstorm, I grew up overnight—" The words to *Sia's* heartbreakingly beautiful song *Alive* bleed through my pores. We're jamming to the newest rendition by Daughtry's edgy, tormented version.

"I'm still breathing, I'm still breathing—"

"I'm Alive—"

Every emotion that I've held back all these years seems to overflow in this moment. Throwing my head back with my mic pointed to the sky, I scream, "You took it all, but I'm still breathing—"

When I'm about to sing the next verse, I fall to my knees and implore the audience to absorb all of my pain. "I took and I took and I took what you gave. But you never noticed I was in pain—"

The song is almost over and to finalize my statement, I throw my beanie in the crowd so my hair tumbles down.

Then I reach over my shoulder, tug on my shirt, and throw it into the audience. With my last breath, I stand so they can witness my battered body and broken heart. Without thinking, I scream, "I'm Alive!"

* * *

QUINN

I DON'T THINK THERE'S a dry eye in the arena when Jet stands tall, bare from the waist up. His chest heaves with emotion as the glistening sweat trickles down his torso from his gut-wrenching performance. I'm in awe of this complex man who was brave enough to execute this very emotional moment for thousands of his fans. Cutting himself wide open and exposing his pain.

When the lights flick off, the crowd cheers, chanting his name. Over and over again—*Jet, Jet, Jet, Jet*—to the point where it's almost deafening. I watch his retreating back before the lights go out. Clapping hands and stomping feet resonate around the arena. The stadium is alive! Even more so when Trevor taps out the beat and the spotlight is back on Lucas as he begins *Distraction*. The original opening number for the show.

I only have eyes for Jet as I watch him slip on a new shirt the crew hands to him. He insisted on this T-shirt and I knew better than to argue. "Karmas is like 69, you get what you give." Care to take a guess on who it's aimed at?

The Sinful Seven is on fire tonight, and if I'm being honest it's their best concert to date. I'm sure Jet's opening song will be added for the rest of the tour. Social media is already erupting with pictures, videos, and comments. He's won them over by sharing his reality and I'm so damn proud of him.

All of a sudden, my headset is going crazy. "Quinn, someone here is insisting on talking to Jet after the concert tonight. He's a big dude, but he swears you know him. Name is Mack Blythe from the *Hungry Dog Diner*." Mack's here!

"Yes, yes! He's welcome anytime. Jet will be thrilled to see him. Send him out. He can stay backstage with Abby and me." I'm all smiles as Abby raises her brows in question. I mouth Mack but she shakes her head like she doesn't understand. Then the man himself is strutting in like he owns the place.

"Quinn. Abby. What the hell's going on with my boy? Who hurt him? 'Cause I swear when I find out, they're dead." I love this uncensored man. To death.

Abby gets the first bear hug and I get it since he's known her the longest. I'm next and I can feel his body vibrating with anger.

"It happened after the show last night. The security team has been fired and there's a new one in place. He was shaken but he's back on track. Did you see his performance?"

"I sure did and it was spectacular. I'm so proud of my boy. But when he took off his shirt, well, let's just say I was livid. There was no way I could head back to New York without seeing him with my own two eyes first."

"Well, he's going to be happy to know you're here." I hope. Fingers crossed that I'm doing the right thing.

"Amelia, you remember her from the diner. Right?" When I nod, he continues. "She had tickets to tonight's show and something came up so she couldn't go. When she found out I had a business meeting in the city, she gave one to me. Reason I'm here, and I'm glad I took her up on the offer."

We all chat for a few more minutes and then Mack relaxes and we enjoy the show. I've no doubt when Jet bounds off the stage, Mack will beat me and join him first. He's Jet's family so he has every right to.

Three encores and the audience is screaming for more, but the guys are exhausted. As they head backstage, one of the stagehands gives them each a bottle of water and a clean towel to wipe down their sweaty faces. Jet's the last one through the door and his gaze finds mine instantly. Almost immediately, he sees who's standing beside me.

"Mack, what the fuck are you doing here?" He scoops up the man like he weighs a feather and gives him the biggest bear hug ever.

"I can't take my eyes off of you for a second, can I? Let me look at what those fuckers did to you, boy."

Jet's self-conscious now that his time in the limelight's over, but he takes off his shirt so Mack can inspect him. Yep, the big guy's none too happy.

"All I can say is it's a good chance that security team is gone because they'd have to answer to me!" His voice booms through the large room and everyone turns to look.

And, right on cue, Brett ambles over to see who the stranger is. Jet bristles, instantly.

"I don't believe we've ever met. I'm Brett, and I'm in charge of security for the tour."

"The name is Mack, and I hope you weren't responsible for what happened to my boy here." Crap! I couldn't help noticing the light bulb that went off in Brett's pea brain when Mack mentioned "boy".

"I wasn't responsible, and you can rest assured that the men who were no longer work for me. Did I hear you correctly? You called Jet your boy. Is that right?"

Mack's a smart man and he can smell a rat a mile away. He's quick to cover up since he doesn't trust the asshole any more than we do. "It's a figure of speech, is all. He ain't no relative of mine or anything like that. He worked for me way back in the day." I'd say we're all pretty sure we need to break up the party. Brett's not a friend, and he doesn't need to know anything personal about Jet or anyone else.

"Let's go grab a drink, old man," Jet says. "We have a lot to catch up on since we haven't seen each other in forever."

30

JET

I've been on a high ever since last night. Singing that song in front of thousands of screaming fans was cathartic. Now I feel like I can finally move forward and leave my past behind. Quinn was absolutely right when she said that Joseph Lawless doesn't define who I am. I do!

It was great catching up with Mack, too. The drinks flowed like water and we all chatted for hours until our driver whisked him away to the airport. I'm glad he was able to witness me purging my heart and soul through my music. And everyone agreed, I'll be opening for the remainder of the tour. For once, I'm good with that.

Thankfully, today's a travel day with a day off in between. Works great for me since I want to spend my day off buried inside my sexy PR agent. I kinda like the sound of that. A month ago, not so much, but now more than ever. Just goes to show how things can change in such a short period of time. Sometimes for the good! Speaking of good, she's taking her sweet-ass time in that bathroom.

When the door opens, she's all business as usual. Oh, that won't last long.

"Have you checked your feed this morning? Social media is blowing up with clips from last night! Here, check out this post." When she hands me her phone, I want to throw the phone and grab the girl, but I don't dare. Quinn's scary when she's in business mode.

"Baby, I'd much rather check you out. You're far more interesting." She giggles when I sit up and bury my face between her luscious breasts. No place else I'd rather be. Scratch that, between her thighs is pretty amazing, too. I love it when she tugs on my hair and rides my face. Fuck, now my dick's hard again! And of course she can feel it rubbing along her thighs.

"You're insatiable! The sun's barely risen but you have twice already. I'm a little sore, can we snuggle so I can catch my second breath?" Well, I can't deny her anything.

"Woman, you're killing my ego. Come here." I pull her against me and tuck her safely in my arms. I love it when I can feel her breathing against my neck. It calms me.

"Sorry, I'm exhausted since I only slept for an hour or so. Although, it was worth it since we had a chance to hang out with Mack and the gang. He's so proud of you."

"Yeah, I'm glad he decided to come but I wish he had told me first. We could have given him a heads up about what was happening. I can't imagine how he felt when he noticed all my bruises. Kinda like déjà vu, I bet."

She sighs and snuggles in closer. "It's obvious the two of you have a very special relationship. Maybe someday you'll feel comfortable enough to share a few Mack and Jet stories. I'd love to hear them."

I'm angry at myself for not wanting to share everything with her. She's proven time and time again that she's trustworthy. And now Mack is her friend as well as mine.

It's time to give her another truth. "One of the reasons it's so hard to confide in you is because for years I was told to shut up. Be quiet. Don't tell. "That whatever happens in this house, stays in this house." I realize now that these words were threats. The only way Joseph could control me. Then you come along and want to know all of my secrets. All of my truths, without judgment. If you can be patient with me just a little bit longer, I promise you'll be the first to know."

"Thank you for sharing that with me. Now I have a better understanding of why you hold back and find it difficult to open up to people. I know when you're ready, you'll trust me with all of your truths."

"There's something that's been heavy on my heart that I'd like to share with you now. It's time—" Her fingers press against my lips.

"Only if you're ready, Jet. I don't ever want to feel like you owe me anything. Just remember, there's nothing you could possibly tell me that would change how I feel about you. Ever."

"The little girl in the photograph was my older sister, Jolie. She was a year older. She drowned when she was only six years old. It was the worst day of my life."

Quinn's holding me so tight that I swear nothing could fit between us. And I'm good with that. I don't feel smothered, or claustrophobic. I actually feel like there's been a weight lifted off my shoulders. It's one of the most euphoric sensations I've experienced in a long, long time.

Quinn doesn't ask any questions and for that I'm grateful. Since that's all I could give. "Thank you for gifting me with another piece of the puzzle. I love you even more today than yesterday and I can't wait for tomorrow, Jet."

I quickly change the subject. "Now, if we can only figure out what Brett has up his sleeve, we can stay one step ahead. Why are we letting him stick around?"

"Steve, the new head of security, is certain he has an ulterior motive. So he wants him to stick around to find out what happens. He assured me that he's not a threat, just kind of stupid. Which I must totally agree on."

I really don't want to talk about Brett or Steve, so I decide to change the subject.

"Are you still sore or can we fuck like rabbits again?' A swat to my chest is the only answer I get. Doesn't she realize that I'm twenty-six years old and I'm at my peak? Not my fault she knows her way around the bedroom.

"I heard every word you said, Jet Turner. Oh, and don't blame my poor vag, she hasn't seen so much action in years nor has she ever had to accommodate someone of your girth and size."

QUINN

MEN, ALL YOU NEED to do is mention the size of their package and their egos inflate a thousand times. In Jet's case, it's well deserved since he is the whole package! And as much as I'd love to participate in some extracurricular activities, I am really sore. Not complaining. Just need a breather in between is all.

There are still so many questions running through my mind about Jet and his childhood. But I keep telling myself, in due time. I can't push him any further since he was open about his sister in the picture. I'm devastated for his mom and him. I can't imagine what it's like to lose a child and then have to go on since you have someone else who loves you and depends on you. Jet's life is one devastating tragedy after another. I'm going to cherish everything he's willing to share and not push anymore. I'm positive it will all come out when the time is right.

While he's busy packing, I take this time to answer a few emails. That's one thing about my job, it never ends. It doesn't matter whether I'm on the road or in the office, it's something I need to constantly stay on top of.

I'm just about finished when my phone pings with an incoming message. Usually I'd ignore it, but just in case it's Abby or Willow, I reach for my phone. Apprehension flows through my body when I notice it's a number I haven't seen in a long time.

Zander Stone. Question is, do I open the message or ignore it completely? Sadly, it's never been in my nature to avoid something that makes me feel uncomfortable. On the contrary, I usually go in with both barrels. I blame that on my five brothers.

Swiping my phone, I open it up and hold my breath.

Zander: Can't wait to see you in a few weeks. It's going to be just like old times.

Is he fucking serious? The ink is barely dry on the divorce papers and he can't wait to see me! What a joke. Well, maybe it's best if we get the awkwardness out of the way so when the time comes, pleasantries will be in order.

> **Me:** Sorry, I can't say the same about you. Let's keep it professional, Zander. This time it isn't about you.
> **Zander:** Oh, I beg to differ, baby. It's always about me.

I can't do this. Nope, I shut off my phone and close my laptop. I'm so done with him. I actually feel bad for *Rebel Riot*. Those guys are amazing and why they put up with Zander is beyond me. Well, I guess they do because he draws in the fans. Lead men always do.

I startle when warm lips caress my neck. Just below my ear. The place that's connected to all of my pulsating girlie parts. "You look angry, Quinn. Something I said?"

"No, just trying to catch up on my never-ending emails. You all packed?"

"Yep, did you finish or did you get sidetracked?"

"I finished while you were in the shower. Limo will be here in twenty. Are you ready for Philly?"

"I'm ready for anything as long as you're there with me. Kinda cheesy but so true. Don't get me wrong, I like my band, but you're so much sexier than they are." I love this funny side of Jet.

"Thanks for your vote of confidence." Now, if only my ex would leave me alone, maybe I'd be able to relax.

"I'll grab all our stuff and leave it by the door so the bellboy can do a grab-and-go when it's time to leave."

"Sounds good, I'll be out soon. I'm going to pack up my

laptop and grab my purse." I throw everything together and meet Jet in the living room.

He strides over and grabs my hips, pulling me in. "You'd tell me if something was wrong, right? Like a migraine, or if you're getting tired of me hanging out with you?" Insecurity comes off of him in waves and I feel awful that I'm the one who made him feel that way.

"Of course I would. I swear it's nothing. I'm just trying to dot my I's and cross my T's. Just because I'm screwing around with the sexy bassist for *The Sinful Seven* doesn't mean I can slack off ya know."

He dives in for a kiss and parts my lips with his tongue. A sigh and a moan later and there's a knock on the door. It's for the best since we don't have time to spare.

"Your limo's waiting, Mr. Turner. Everyone's already downstairs." Jet slips him a tip and we walk hand-in-hand to the elevator.

The gang's already popped a bottle of bubbly for the ride to the airport and I gladly accept a glass. That message is weighing heavily on my mind. Zander's up to something and I'll be damned if I know what it is. Can't be good. I pray he doesn't do anything to sabotage the concert. He'd be a fool if he did.

"I call dibs in the bedroom, Quinn, and I need to be a part of the mile-high club before this tour is over." As much as I'd love to have him inside of me as we fly five hundred miles per hour, it wouldn't happen with all of my friends on board.

"Down boy. You'll need to wait until we get to the hotel. I don't think your friends want to hear us going at it like a bunch of animals."

That gets a chuckle from the crowd. The next thing we

hear is the pilot telling us to buckle up, ready for takeoff. It'll be great spending the night all alone with Jet. It's been a rough couple of days but he pulled it off beautifully. Closing my eyes, I rest my head against his shoulder. It's the last thing I remember until the wheels come crashing down as we land in our next destination.

PRIDE

*"If you believe in yourself, have dedication and **Pride** and never quit, you'll be a winner."*

Paul Bryant

31

JET

Tonight is bittersweet, since it's our last concert for the *Distraction* tour. Caleb's throwing us a huge afterparty with thousands of guests, and my anxiety is off the charts. We begged him to keep it small and simple but he didn't listen. He wants to shout it from the rooftops since our album has been number one on the Billboard charts for over six months. *The Sinful Seven* went from zero to sixty in two seconds and it's all because we won the battle of the bands that Morris Music hosted last year. Now, Caleb wants to cash in on the publicity, and Quinn agrees it's a win for both parties. She's the boss, so we just go with the flow.

Our opening act, *Laid Bare*, is taking some much-needed time off before going on tour with *Wicked Immortal* next year. I'm sure the time will come, when the record companies will be competing for them to sign on the dotted line. These guys are the real deal and there's no doubt in my mind that, Decker, Finn, Levi, and Miles will have a bright future. It's only up from here.

The production people have been busy behind the scenes, filming us throughout the tour. So now we have several live music videos up on all our social media platforms as well as our YouTube channel. As well as some fan-made videos that were filmed during our concerts. I must admit, they're really cool and now everyone can get a free clip of us live in concert. Quinn mentioned earlier they'd be doing a few more during the benefit concerts, too. I know it's all part of the PR and marketing process but it's never-ending. I'm thankful that she's in charge of the whole thing and not me.

At this time, we still have no clue who sent us those pictures. The prints they lifted off the pics were not found in any of the criminal databases, so they were of no use. Therefore, we have no proof whatsoever that my stepfather was behind it. And Mr. Miller told me in private that it's not a criminal offense for someone to send pictures of your family members. The envelopes didn't contain any threats, letters, or anything of that nature. As far as I'm concerned, there are no other suspects, case closed.

Miller assured me that Joseph wouldn't bother me again. In person or in the media. I didn't ask for specifics and he didn't tell since I'm paying him to do a job. I'm sure it was a hefty lump sum and I informed him to take it out of my cut and not the band's. This isn't their fight, it's mine. He agreed. I need to trust whatever agreement they came to and if Joseph shows his face again, this time he'll be thrown in jail for breaking a restraining order and a contract. If it doesn't stick, I have something up my sleeve. Whether I'm brave enough to pull it all off is another question. Time will tell.

We thought it was appropriate to end our tour where it all began, so we're in New York, playing to our home crowd. It will be nice to see some familiar faces, and Mack promised to bring Amelia and a few of her friends. It was my way of saying thank you for giving Mack her ticket that night he watched me bleed on stage. It was a pivotal moment in my life and I was glad to share it with him.

The tension backstage is off the charts and tonight there's a heaviness in the air. Being that it's our last night together since the start, it's very emotional. We all knew this time would come, but it doesn't make it any easier. When you work this closely with the same people day in and day out, we become a close-knit family. The camaraderie is unlike anything I've ever felt in my lifetime. It feels like hope and contentment all rolled into one.

Out of everyone on this tour, hands down, I'm the one who's changed the most from this experience. In the beginning, I acted like a prick. Keeping everyone at arm's length. If they hated me they couldn't hurt me is what I thought. Being on the street made me realize that I wasn't the only kid who had been sexually abused. Some talked openly about it, others like me let it fester for years and years. Not good, because then your mind tricks you into believing it was all your fault.

The shame and self-isolation are debilitating.

* * *

QUINN

I'VE BEEN RECEIVING text messages from Zander for a month now. I haven't responded to any of them, with the exception of that first one. I keep telling myself I'm not going to read them, and then I do. Only because I'm afraid that if I don't open them, he'll know and make my life a living hell when we get to California. Is it wrong of me to hope he falls off the face of the earth or gets an STD so his dick falls off before we do?

I haven't mentioned anything to Jet about the messages because if I do, he'll be furious. I'm desperately trying to avoid confrontation between the both of them, and I might be going about it all wrong. Out of sight out of mind might not work this time around but I'm hoping if I ignore Zander's messages, he'll move on. Could be wishful thinking on my part, but I know all too well that when he doesn't get a rise out of someone he gets easily bored.

I'm standing backstage and there's a buzz that's never been here before. I think it has a lot to do with the fact it's our last night together. Some will follow us to the benefit concerts and some will go home to their families. It's always tough and I usually get sentimental because we are like one big happy family. Hopefully, it won't take too long for the guys to cut a new album and they can all be together again.

Fingers crossed.

A pair of leather-clad arms wrap around me and I just lean against Jet for support. It should be the other way around but I'm having a very sentimental moment. "Hey baby, are you ready?" I turn around in his arms and breathe in his scent. Spicy with a hint of leather and citrus. It's seductive, irresistible, and downright panty melting. Yeah, I got it bad and he knows it since my nipples always salute his arrival. It's embarrassing as hell. But, in all fairness, picture a six-foot-two Jet in leather from head to toe. Now that's what I'm talking about.

"So ready. How about you?" I've seen that look on his face many times. Only this time around, he's conflicted. On the one hand, he's sad that the *Distraction* tour is over but happy that the benefit concerts are coming up next. I've told him several times in the past that when one door closes, another opens.

I can't help reaching out to smooth over his frown. His voice is husky when he replies, "I'm good, really. We're all excited about *Coins for Change* and meeting up with all of the bands, but it sucks that it's going to be a long time before we're all together again."

"Yep, but that's part of the process. Think of how exciting it will be when you start planning the next tour. It will be like coming home when everyone's together again." The words "except me" are on the tip of my tongue. Nope, not going there tonight. I'm on the verge of tears as it is.

"Sure will and I've no doubt that we'll be so damn busy that time will fly right by." Both of us can read between the lines. In a little over a month from now, I'll be working with another band and they will hire a permanent PR agent. If his stare is any indication, he's reading my thoughts. It's that elephant in the room that we've been evading at all costs. Unfortunately, it's creeping up on us and with everything else I have going on right now, I can't deal with the thought of not being with Jet every day.

Leaning in, he kisses one cheek, then the other. So soft and gentle it brings tears to my eyes. When one falls, he crushes his mouth against mine. Greedy and demanding. Making me lose all train of thought which I bet was his intention from the start.

We're interrupted when Bruce pops his head in and

shouts, "You guys are on in ten, let's make it the best one yet!"

"Break a leg, baby," I say as I reluctantly slip away from him. That gorgeous smile and those baby blues will haunt me for the rest of my life.

Before walking away, he gives me an embrace that I'll not soon forget and then whispers, "I love you so much, Quinn, and I'm going to spend the rest of my life showing you just how much."

What? I'm sobbing so much that I can't find my voice, so I mouth, "I love you more." With a smile and a wink, he walks onstage to thousands of adoring fans screaming his name. I want to yell "Back off, he's my man!" and the thought has me hiccupping because I'm both crying and laughing simultaneously.

"Sweetie, are you all right?" Abby asks. She's been my sidekick through thick and thin in this crazy thing called *The Sinful Seven*.

"These are happy tears for a change. He loves me, Abby! Jet finally told me he loves me." Okay, so I don't usually kiss and tell but I'm euphoric right now and I need to share my good news with someone. She gives me a big hug and then we squeal like a bunch of adolescent girls. It feels wonderful!

"I knew it. I told you. I'm so happy for the both of you. Now you can stay with us. I'm so excited." We chat for a bit longer and then I focus on my headset and what's happening on stage. But you couldn't wipe the smile off my face for all the greasy burgers in the world.

Four encores later, and they bound off the stage with so much adrenaline that they're higher than a kite. It's well deserved after all the blood, sweat, and tears they put in night after night. *Laid Bare* is right there to congratulate them and the next thing I know, champagne is being popped and sprayed all over them. My heart's near to bursting when Jet crosses his arms over his stomach, trying to catch his breath. It's a beautiful sight to see.

"C'mon, Quinn. They want us to join them." Abby grabs my arm and we rush over to join the craziness that's happening all around us.

Jet pulls me in, holding me close. Funny how I'm not bothered by the stickiness of the champagne or the noise of the crowd since I'm just focused on the man holding me. He's all that matters. My beautiful broken man. "I love you, Jet Turner. So much."

He leans in, captures my lips and whispers, "I love you more, Quinn Taylor. Thank you for loving me."

32

JET

ONE MONTH LATER . . .

We're on the last leg of the benefit concerts and I couldn't be happier with the outcome. With only two more concerts to go, we've already raised twenty-three million dollars, which equals a little over one million per concert. Twenty cities will now have the funding they desperately need to help house and feed the homeless. We all know it's just a drop in the bucket and we're already in negotiations to do more concerts in more cities within the next few years. I'm amazed at the outpouring of love and support that so many have shown for this necessary cause. This might be my proudest accomplishment by far.

Tonight, we're playing at *Clark Stadium* with *Rebel Riot.* Not looking forward to meeting Quinn's ex but I'm confident in knowing she's chosen me over him. She's told me time and time again. So, I've already talked to the band to see if we can afford to hire her on moving forward. Of course they agreed wholeheartedly. Once the last set has been broken down and the last truck is packed and loaded, *The Sinful Seven* will approach her with a deal she can't refuse. And I'll be the first one to admit after sharing my space, truths, and love for over six months, I can't let her go. Unless it's what she wants. I'd never hold her back but I'm hoping she chooses me.

Lucas, Trevor, and I are just hanging out in the private pool area while the girls have a much-needed spa day. We had a few hours to kill and we felt restless and just needed some down time. I can't think of anything better than a few good friends and a couple of cold beers for a little R&R.

"So what's our game plan when we get back home? Any thoughts?" I lean my elbows against the wall and take a long pull on my beer.

"We need to get working on the new album as soon as possible," Lucas says. "I really like the idea of all of us coming up with two or three songs on our own and blending them all together to create a different kind of album. It's risky but I think our fans would love it." Lucas feels the way I do about the collaboration. Trevor, not so much.

"I'd have to disagree. Maybe a third or fourth album but not our second. We need to solidify our brand first. If there's too much inconsistency with the music, we'll lose them all."

"I'd have to agree."

The three of us whip our heads up to catch Zander Stone approaching us. Here to crash the party. Oh fuck to the no.

"*The Sinful Seven* isn't established after only one tour. You'd lose the majority of your fans if you put out a collaborative second album. That's my advice, you can take it or leave it since I don't know what the fuck I'm talking about."

Lucas glares in my direction before he slowly steps out of the pool. "Thanks for the tip, Zander. We'll def take it into consideration." I want to gag as he reaches out to shake his hand.

"This is a private party and we were just tossing a few things around is all." Trevor quips as his lips quirk before tipping his bottle back to polish it off.

"No worries. I have a habit of putting in my two cents where it's not needed. It's one of the things that used to piss off Quinn big time." Yep, he had to go there and now I'm the one bounding out of the pool.

"In case you didn't get the hint, this is a private party and you weren't invited. As much as we appreciate *Rebel Riot* giving their time for this event, it's best if we keep this professional and not make it personal." Lucas stands between us because he knows I'm street smart and I'll take this fucker out if he so much as looks at Quinn.

Zander holds up his hands, palms out. "I agree and I didn't come here to pick a fight with my ex's new boy toy. I just wanted to talk to Quinn. Now that I know she's not here, I'll make my leave. We can chat later."

Now I'm flanked by Trevor and Lucas after that idiotic remark. "I'd be more than glad to pass on a message since you won't get within one hundred feet from where she's standing. Understood? Concert or not, I'll take you the fuck out right here and now." Lucas groans and I laugh because this is exactly how I knew our first encounter was going to go down.

And wouldn't you know the girls choose this exact moment to walk in. Quinn's face pales when she notices we have an unexpected guest. My heart swells when she ignores the enemy in the room and strolls in my direction. Very protectively, she laces her fingers through mine and gently kisses my lips.

"This is a private party, Zander, and you're not a welcomed guest. Please leave." She stands tall with her head held high, but I can feel a slight tremble in her touch. She loathes him and that makes two of us.

"That's a shame, really, since we have so much catching up to do. You never answered my texts." His what??? I want to look down at my girl but it's exactly what the asshole wants. Two can play at this game.

"Clearly she didn't want to talk, otherwise she would have answered them. Besides, she was too busy with her new boy toy so there's that, too." Yeah, I just peed on his leg and it was a dick move, but I'm already tired of this conversation. Quinn tugs on my hand, so we start walking away. She's had enough and so have I. The rest of the guys follow.

"It's all good, baby. I just wanted to know if you liked the pictures I sent you. It was right before our wedding. Good times." I stop dead in my tracks and let go of her hand. Wedding? What wedding? I have my answer when she slowly turns around and I notice she's biting her bottom lip. They were married? She never told me! He sent her the pictures, so why were they on my cart? Why did she insist on me sharing my truth when she hid hers from me?

I need to get the fuck out of here. I can feel the darkness pulling me under and I don't want to be here when it happens.

Someone's screaming but I don't wait around to find out who it is. I keep on walking. Then I'm running and I keep going until I have no more air in my lungs and I can't fucking breathe.

* * *

QUINN

ALL I REMEMBER IS SCREAMING his name over and over again as I tried catching up to him. I fell to my knees and swore to the gods above that I screwed up by not telling him about being married to the asshole before today.

Two strong arms pick me up off the ground. I wish it were Jet, but it's Lucas. He's shushing me as I wail against his chest, but he doesn't tell me it's going to be okay because we both know it won't be. It never will. He trusted me with all of his truths and I gave him nothing in return.

"Willow, I'm bringing Quinn to your room. I think it might be a good idea if she bunks with you tonight." That makes me cry even harder because Jet and I haven't been apart in so long.

"Quinn can stay in my room, give her to me. She's better off without him." Is that Zander or am I losing my mind?

"Over my fucking dead body, now get the fuck out of my way. If you were smart, you'd show up for the concert and then pack your shit and move the fuck on. After what just happened, I'd wager a guess that the only reason you signed up for this event is because you were hoping to split them up. It's just a bump in the road. Once they have a chance to talk, they'll be back together because they love each other. Trevor, get this fucktard out of my face, NOW!"

What time is it? I'm not sure if I passed out or if I'm in shock. I try opening my eyes but I'm blinded with a migraine. Oh no, I need my meds. Where are they?

I hear whispering and I can feel a cool cloth pressed against my forehead. I'm either floating on a cloud or cocooned in a soft, fluffy bed. I want to move but the pain is excruciating. I need my meds.

Silence.

Drifting.

Pain.

"I have your pills. Can you sit up?" Jet, is that you? I'm so sorry for not telling you my truth. Something touches my tongue before a cold liquid slides down my throat. My pill! Thank you. I swallow several times and then I'm propped up against a warm body. Jet, is that you?

"Why didn't someone call me? Fuck, I can't believe she's been suffering all this time." Oh, he's angry and I want to tell him to shush but nothing comes out.

Sleep, I need to sleep.

I'm going to be late for the concert!

I wake up in a start and quickly close my eyes. It's too bright and that alone sends waves of nausea running through me. I'm so screwed. I won't be able to stand backstage. With or without my headset.

Rolling to my side, I cover my face with my hand and try peeking through my fingers. Ouch. Better, but still hurts. What am I going to do?

"Here, drink some water and I'll give you another pill." Jet's still here? I try propping myself up against the headboard and I'm glad when he assists me. I betrayed him and when I think it was just a month ago he had the courage to tell me he loved me, I want to cry. He trusted me with his heart and I let him down because of my insecurity.

The bottle of water is placed in my hand and I take a much-needed drink. Then his fingers nudge against my lips and I open them. Chills race along my spine as he places the pill on my tongue and I wash it down with the rest of the water. He doesn't speak, he just goes through the motions.

I don't bother testing my voice, I just open my mouth and wing it. "I'm sorry," squeaks out. Barely audible. I want to cry when I open my eyes and the room is empty.

He left.

I'm alone.

When I was a little girl, I would stare at my bedroom door and will it to open. I'd fantasize about all of my celebrity crushes and all of my favorite boy bands walking through that door, and now all I want is for just one man to walk through that damn door. But the longer I stare at the door, the more my heart breaks because he's not coming back. I know it.

Several hours later, I force myself out of bed and walk into the bathroom. My heart skips a beat when I take a minute to really focus and realize I'm in my own room. Well, the one I shared with Jet. I start opening all of the cabinets and drawers to see if his stuff is still here. It's gone. Everything.

I'm left with two choices. I can get my shit together and do my fucking job, or I can wallow in self-pity that I brought on myself. I opt for the first choice.

Turning on the shower as hot as I can stand it, I climb in and let the water soothe my aching heart. When I'm finished, I'll grab something to eat and get ready for the last concert. I've done it before and I can do it again.

Saying goodbye to everyone is going to be one of the hardest things I've ever had to do. So much harder than my divorce from the asshole who ruined everything. No, I take that back, he lit the match and I couldn't put out the fire. If I had been honest from the beginning, no matter how much he fanned the flames, nothing would have happened.

I only have myself to blame. I should have practiced what I preached and then I wouldn't be in this mess.

Jet, please forgive me.

33

JET

LAST NIGHT I WENT on stage and performed to the best of my ability, but my heart wasn't in it. That's because I left it at Quinn's feet after she stomped all over it. And she had the audacity to be a no-show. George filled in for her because she couldn't face me after what she'd done.

Married!

She was fucking married to Zander Stone, which is so much more than just being in a relationship, but she failed to mention that in any of our conversations. Why? Is she ashamed or embarrassed that she took the plunge and it didn't work out? I have no idea and no matter how hard I try, I just can't wrap my head around it!

Thank fuck Lucas was there to stop me from killing the cocky bastard when *Rebel Riot* came backstage to say goodbye to thank us for hosting the event. They were all oblivious when Zander walked right by me without shaking hands. It's all good because that fucker would have tasted my fist. I wouldn't have given two fucks about rearranging his face. That asshole didn't even question why Quinn wasn't there. His ego is so inflated he might have thought she didn't go because she was still pining over him. I wanted to yell, "Hey asshole, it's not all about you anymore."

Rebel Riot left right after their set, and all I can say is good riddance. I'm only grateful for the money our concert cashed in on for the homeless and that's it. Now he can rot in hell for doing what he did.

Earlier in the day, I cleared out my room so I could bunk with Trevor. When I found out Lucas took it upon himself to move Quinn into Willow's room, I flipped my shit. Whether she was right or wrong in what she did, I wanted her to be comfortable. And when I found out the reason she missed the concert was because she had a migraine, I was livid.

A fucking migraine!

I immediately brought Quinn back to our room and gave her the meds. I even stayed there with her so I could take care of her. As soon as she was coherent, I closed the door and walked away. Happily-ever-afters only come true in romance novels and fairy tales. Not for men like me.

Now I need to concentrate on the last performance and then I'm going to take the red eye home. Alone. I should have known that a loner like me has no room in their life for someone else. Things just never work out. I'm just waiting on the guys to get here so I can let them know.

Opening the balcony doors, I step outside to gather my thoughts. They're a jumbled mess right about now, and if one more person tries telling me things will work out, I'll scream. I don't bother turning around when I hear a knock. I guess it's time to get this party started and get ready for the fallout.

One by one my bandmates file in, but when Quinn steps through the door, I'm pissed. Yeah, I get she's PR and all but can we have a fucking conversation without her for a change? Is that asking too much?

"Thanks for inviting me to the meeting, but I can't stay," she says. "I just wanted to thank all of you for such an amazing experience and congratulate *The Sinful Seven* on a successful tour. After everything we've been through, I consider all of you my close friends. If you ever need me, I'm a call away. I'm going to miss you." Her voice breaks and I know she's on the verge of crying, but I don't give two fucks. "Sorry, I'm already packed and George is taking over for me again tonight. My flight's in three hours and I need to leave for the airport soon."

Lucas is pacing like a caged animal and I know he's waiting for me to ask her to stay, but I don't. And I won't. Too much has changed since we agreed to put her on our payroll, and maybe it's selfish of me and I should put the band's needs ahead of my own, but I can't be around her every day.

I just can't.

All three girls are bawling and hugging it out, and I'm not blind so I can see how upset everyone is. Still don't care. When Lucas grabs Quinn's shoulders and asks her to stay on as our PR agent, I fucking growl like a wild animal. This is the second time he's betrayed me. When will it ever end?

Quinn clings to him like he's her lifeline and that pisses me off! Why? I'm not sure, but when she glances over in my direction, she says, "Thank you for the generous offer, but it's best if I move on." I want to shout "Hell yeah!" but I refrain.

Quinn gives everyone, with the exception of me, a kiss

and hug goodbye and walks out the door. I press my hand to the center of my chest because it fucking hurts. Why does it hurt because she's walking away and not me?

"Jet, don't just stand there. Go after her!" Willow screams at the top of her lungs.

Lucas strides over and gets right in my space. "Haven't you figured out a fucking thing yet? Zander sent you those pictures, not her, because he wanted to plant the seed of doubt in your mind and it fucking worked!" He presses his finger into my chest. "Zander crashed our party so he could rub it in your face that they were married. Google it, dude. There is no evidence anywhere of their marriage. Either he was lying and you fell hook, line, and sinker, or it was the best kept secret."

"You love each other, Jet," Abby breaks in. "Please don't make the same mistakes that Lucas and I made. Go after her before it's too late."

Are they right? Did I just take Zander's word for it? I did, and I never gave her a chance to explain. What if I'm letting the best thing that's ever happened to me walk out the door? I'll regret it for the rest of my life. Can I grab my girl and make it back in time for the concert? When my answer is "Who the fuck cares", I know down to my core that Quinn means more to me than my music. I run out the damn door as everyone cheers behind me.

QUINN

LEAVING BEFORE THE LAST concert was the hardest thing I've ever done. I pride myself on finishing a job to the best of my ability. But after Lucas asked me to stay on and Jet clearly wasn't happy, I thought it best to leave and let them embrace their last concert. I was just excess baggage and I didn't need to stick around. I'd be lying if I didn't say I'm heartbroken, but I'm resilient and I'll get through it. I always do.

I decided to leave for the airport. I'll be early, but I just couldn't stick around that empty hotel room. And after such an emotional goodbye, I had to leave. Jet made it very clear he doesn't want anything to do with me. It's all my fault and I only have myself to blame. I wasn't open and honest about my marriage to Zander, but I signed an NDA that neither of us would discuss it. Ever. I suppose I could sue the asshole, but the damage is done and I don't care about the money. Besides, if it means I need to see him again, no amount of money is worth it.

I'm surprised when the limo comes to a complete stop. Are we already at the airport? When the door opens and I get ready to slide out, I'm met with piercing blue eyes. Jet.

"What are you doing here?" It's not the question I really wanted to ask him, it just popped out.

"Come with me." He holds out his hand and I'm hesitant to take it. I've no idea why but when I realize he doesn't look angry, I accept.

Tears threaten to fall when I realize we're going on a helicopter ride. We talked about going on one of their tours before going back home and he remembered. When his hand lands on the curve of my spine, I lose it. Either he's going to push me out of the damn helicopter or he's going to tell me he forgives me. I'm praying it's the latter. An hour ago, I never thought I'd recover from losing Jet, but by him bringing me here, I know it's not over.

It's just begun.

Neither one of us speaks, as the pilot settles us in with our headsets for the real tour experience! I'm in the front with him and Jet is sprawled out in the back because of his long legs. I'm both nervous and excited that we're actually doing this. My tears keep on flowing but this time they are happy ones.

We fly over Universal Studios, the Hollywood sign, the California coastline, just to name a few sights, and then we land on freaking Malibu Mountain! It's way more than I could have ever dreamed of. I'm still pinching myself that I'm here with Jet.

"There's some amazing views out over the bluff, why don't you and Quinn go see for yourself?" Tony, our pilot, is so informative and funny. The best tour guide, ever.

"Thanks. Come on, baby, let's go check it out." My heart's pounding out of my chest as we walk down the pathway that overlooks Malibu Beach. It's a breathtaking view.

"You're going to be late for the concert." Yep, open mouth insert foot. He chuckles and takes me in his arms. Pressing my back to his chest. Where I never thought I'd be ever again.

"I really don't care, Quinn. That's how I knew I could never, ever let you walk out of my life—because I'd choose you over music. Once I realized that, I was booking this tour and on my way to meet you. I admit, it wasn't too hard since I knew Barry was driving you to the airport, but I intercepted you instead."

"Jet, I'm so sorry—"

"We both made a mistake. You didn't tell me you were married and I didn't let you explain. I was so busy being angry because I told you my darkest secrets and you didn't tell me yours. Then Lucas mentioned something that made sense. Zander sent me the pics, crashed our private party, and insisted on taking you back to his room when you passed out because of your migraine. It was a setup from the beginning and we made it too easy for him by doing the benefit concerts. It was the perfect opportunity for him to sabotage our relationship."

"But why, though? He doesn't love me so it shouldn't matter whether I'm with him or you." A soft kiss to my neck and I'm putty in his arms.

"All of the pictures he sent me were taken during our tour. Not before your wedding like he suggested. I didn't notice it the first time around, but when I got them back I looked at them more closely. The love shining in your eyes was for me, not for him, and that pushed him over the fucking edge."

"Why didn't I notice someone taking pictures of me? That's kind of scary."

"It is, and it had to be someone we never would have suspected. Someone who had access to all areas. Care to take a wild guess?"

Turning around in his arms I ask, "Brett?"

"Bingo! My guess is he worked security for *Rebel Riot* at some point. One call from Zander and he defected. Proving that money talks and bullshit walks. He's been fired and charges have been filed. Enough about them, let's talk about you."

Oh, I do love the sound of that.

"Lucas mentioned that we want you on payroll, and we do. I do. I can't imagine what my life would be like if we went our separate ways. Truthfully, I don't ever want to find out. If you decide not to take it, I'm going to be working on my frequent flyer miles since I'll be jetting out as often as I can."

Is this really happening? Just a few hours ago, I was devastated and heading to the airport, now I'm here with Jet. This is surreal and so unexpected. "If it's okay with everyone in the band then my answer is yes. I'd be thrilled and honored to work exclusively for *The Sinful Seven*. On one condition—you promise I can sleep with the sexiest bassist on earth."

"It's more than okay. I swear. Now I have another surprise for you." We walk back to the helicopter hand-in-hand and I'm excited when I notice the checkered blanket that's spread out over the ground. There's a nice wicker picnic basket sitting on top. We drop to our knees and open it up to find a bottle of champagne with cheesecake and a few other goodies. So cool!

We spend the next thirty minutes, talking, laughing, kissing, and enjoying one another. When Tony announces it's time to leave, he graciously packs up, settles us in, and we fly back to LA. I'm content when we land on the rooftop of our elegant hotel and still have twenty minutes to spare to catch the concert.

Thanks to Jet, I made the last concert after all!

EPILOGUE

JET

IT'S BEEN FOUR MONTHS since we performed our last encore for the benefit concerts. Since then, *Coins for Change* has raised forty-five million dollars. I feel this by far is my greatest accomplishment to date. Yes, my music is very important to me, but my roots are who I am and always will be. I'm not the best bassist in the music industry and I might never be. I'm okay with that because at the end of the day, when I take my last breath on this earth, I want everyone to remember me for being a philanthropist and helping as many of the homeless as I could. That's the legacy I want to leave behind.

In other news, our second album is a wrap and our next tour is scheduled for November of this year. It's not the individual songs we were hoping for, but the album's kickass like the first one. We all agreed that we have plenty of time to do one of those collaborations once we have several albums under our belt. We don't need to rush since we plan on being around for a hell of a lot longer. Maybe as long as The Stones!

Now for the big news: Lucas and Abby set a date and the wedding's in October. And guess who the best man is? Yep, you got it. That would be me. It's going to be epic since Willow was kind enough to decline so Quinn could be the Maid of Honor. I'll always have a soft spot in my heart for Willow, and Quinn's all right by that. She should be since she holds my heart in her hands.

Forever.

Speaking of which—Quinn and I did get the chance to take a sunset flight with *Orbit Tours* and that's when I got down on one knee and proposed to the woman of my dreams. Quinn's my one true love, the one I never knew I was looking for and never thought I deserved. Just knowing that she embraces my darkness as well as the light makes getting out of bed—instead of the corner of the room—so much easier to endure.

The End

If you enjoyed Jet, you'll love Willow, Book 3 in The Sinful Seven series. Here's a sneak peek…

Willow

A WISE PHILOSOPHER ONCE said, *"What doesn't kill you, makes you stronger."* Well I beg to differ, since it's been over five years, and not a day goes by where I don't ache for what could have been. Wishing I could hold you in my arms one last time, before you were so brutally taken away from me.

Not only did I lose the love of my life that day, I lost a piece of my soul that I'll never get back. And the person who was responsible for it all, was no longer my hero but a monster who destroyed so many lives.

There's not a person on this earth who can convince me that loving someone is a curse, it's a blessing. The heart can't distinguish a person's age, it just recognizes the euphoria it feels when they're near.

If it hadn't been for my bandmates, Lucas, Jet and Trevor, to hold me up, I wouldn't be here with all of you today. They're the glue that put all of my jagged pieces back together. Not once, but twice and if I'm being honest, it's been more times than I care to count. . .

Pre-Order Willow Today

PLAYLIST

Imperfect by Stone Sour
Can You Hold Me by NF
Medicine by James Arthur
Sanctuary by Welshly Arms
Anywhere From Here by Rag'n'Bone Man and Pink
Heavy Is The Crown by Daughtry
Run To You by Lucey Sturm
Outta My Head by Daughtry
Hymn For The Missing by Red
Alive by Daughtry

Jet Playlist

https://www.youtube.com/playlist?list=
PLwsEDrpYaIWs5RpnETj6ZLiO-RspKFfTG

AUTHOR'S NOTE

Hey guys and gals! If you started off with *Lucas*, the first book in *The Sinful Seven Series*, you must be scratching your head. Yeah, I get it because Jet was by far the hardest book I've written to date. This beautiful broken man's voice was so loud that I knew I needed to be HIS voice so his story could be told.

I'm not a therapist or an expert on abuse of any kind, and I'm not pretending to be. I would never give advice to someone who's lived through it. With that said, please keep in mind that this is a work of fiction. Yes, I did a lot of research and spoke to several people who were abused, and there are little snippets throughout of their experiences. The only reason I wanted to add an author's note (which I've never done in any of my previous books) was to add several hotline numbers. If only one person is courageous enough to dial a number, then it will not have been in vain.

A big shout out to all of my amazing readers for taking the time to read my books. I strive to make each as personal and one-of-a-kind as possible. We all know that no two people are alike and that's what makes all of us so unique. Same goes with books!

Am I right?

Love you guys to the moon and back a trillion times ten! Until next time,

Connie XO

If you suspect or know a child is being (or has been) abused, please call the National child abuse hotline at 1-800-4-A-CHILD. (1-800-422-4453).

The National Coalition For The Homeless
https://nationalhomeless.org/

Housing Assistance https://www.hudexchange.info/housing-and-homeless-assistance/

Printed in Great Britain
by Amazon